BATMAN BEGINS

DENNIS O'NEIL
Screenplay by Christopher Nolan
and David S. Goyer
Story by David S. Goyer

Batman created by Bob Kane

BALLANTINE BOOKS • NEW YORK

Batman Begins is a work of fiction. Names, places, and incidents either are products of the author's imagination or are used fictitiously.

A Del Rey Books Mass Market Original

Published in the United States by Del Rey Books, an imprint of The Random House Publishing Group, a division of Random House, Inc., New York.

ISBN 0-345-47946-7

Printed in the United States of America

Del Rey Books website address: www.delreybooks.com
www.dccomics.com
Keyword: DC Comics on AOL

First edition

OPM 9 8 7 6 5 4 3 2 1

To Marifran and Larry . . . oh, and the Universe. I'm always happy to acknowledge the Universe.

ACKNOWLEDGMENTS

By now, the Batman saga is huge. Bruce Wayne and his crime-fighting alter ego have been appearing continuously for sixty-five years, in every medium. But we should remember that it all began with "The Case of the Chemical Syndicate" in *Detective Comics* #27, written by Bill Finger and with art by Bob Kane. I thank them both.

I've never met Christopher Nolan and David Goyer, who wrote the film script that became *Batman Begins,* and probably never will, but I'd like to state for the record that they did a nifty job and it was a pleasure collaborating with them.

Chris Cerasi is that increasingly rare kind of editor whose concern is only that the work be good. I appreciate his courtesy, astuteness, and encouragement.

It was nice, and surprising, to be again involved in a project with a fellow yeoman from the old Marvel days, Steve Saffel.

When I was writing Batman stories for comics, my primary editors were Julius Schwartz and Archie Goodwin. They were, each in his way, superb colleagues and wonderful friends. I miss them and will always be grateful to them.

DENNIS O'NEIL
Upper Nyack, New York
January 2005

BATMAN BEGINS

PART I
BRUCE WAYNE

FROM THE JOURNALS OF RĀ'S AL GHŪL

I remain committed to my goal of saving humanity from itself, but my latest efforts are meeting with mixed results.

The Austrian madman is intoxicated with his successes in North Africa and thus he agreed with our suggestion that he invade Russia. It will be folly, and he will fail as the Frenchman before him failed. The war will end soon. Not this year, certainly, nor the next, but soon, and when it does, Hitler will suffer defeat.

Once, I thought he would be a useful tool. I was mistaken. His hatred is too narrow and narcissistic to accommodate a large vision.

In the meantime, we have managed to divert the energies of his munitions scientists into fruitless efforts. They will not succeed in making a nuclear bomb in the foreseeable future. In America, by way of contrast, our men in New Mexico report that progress on the Americans' atomic weaponry goes well. I will be interested to see against which enemy the Allies will deploy it.

After the end of hostilities I will initiate a new kind of attack. I will use economics as a weapon and attempt to debilitate the despoilers with their own favorite instrument.

That is in the future. For the next several years we will remain in Switzerland. The Austrian is not likely to violate this nation's neutrality, which means my retinue and I will remain in these mountains for the duration. We are undisturbed here and the place pleases me. It is clean and pure and when I breathe the chill, bracing air I am reminded of what a paradise the earth once was and will be again, and I am prompted to redouble my efforts.

Last night, the woman who is my current consort gave birth to a female. I am a methodical man and I keep records. Thus, I know that I have now sired four hundred and fourteen children, all of them except two female. The two who were male, Hector and Claudius, both died before their first birthdays.

It is a source of the greatest vexation to me that I have been unable to produce a healthy male child. I am a man of rationality and science. I do not believe in curses. But at times I think I am cursed.

I must have a son.

Later, Bruce would come to understand the power of myth: how those ancient stories could deepen and amplify—and distort and falsify—human experience.

It was to be one of many lessons he learned from Rā's al Ghūl. But that was later. At the moment, though, he slouched in a desk chair in a midwestern class-room, staring out the window and wondering if the bald stick of a professor, who was wearing a tweed jacket even though it was July and this hundred-year-old university could not afford to air-condition its buildings, would ever finish his drone. On and on went the professor, about Jungian archetypes and mono-myths and other stuff that Bruce considered absolutely nonessential to any conceivable life he might want to lead, if not plain stupid. Today's topic, the prof had announced in a voice that even he had to know was somniferous, was loss of innocence as exemplified by the biblical Adam and Eve tale and the Buddhist leg-end of Siddhartha's first exit from his father's estate.

Ho hum, Bruce thought. He had read the material the prof had assigned and several other books on the subject, too; all of which presented the material more cogently than the prof, and none of which interested him.

He vowed to himself that he would never, never waste his time in a liberal arts course again. He had signed up for this one as an experiment and the ex-periment was a colossal bust. He dropped his gaze to the gold Rolex on his wrist. Would this purgatory ever end?

Twenty minutes later, it had, and Bruce was walk-ing across a quadrangle toward the clock tower in the center of the campus where he had promised to meet the cute girl from his advanced calculus class. He would lend her his notes and she would buy him coffee—that was their deal. To his surprise, he found that his mind kept returning to the class he had just finished enduring and specifically to the Siddhartha story. There were several versions: the simplest of them related how a prince, scion of a wealthy Nepalese family, had been sheltered from the harshness of reality until one day he had left his father's grounds and encountered a sick man, an old man, and a corpse. These encounters so upset the young prince that he vowed to live a life of denial until he could make sense of them.

Suddenly Bruce stopped in midstride as he realized, astonished, that he *identified* with Siddhartha.

And then he remembered the garden behind his parents' mansion. Of course, he did not *know* it was a "mansion," not until years later, after his parents had died. It was just "indoors" as the garden was "outdoors," and they were all he had ever known, apart from Mother, Father, and funny old Alfred. During his fourth birthday party, Mother, Father, and Alfred brought other children into the house, a lot of other children, who yelled and ran around and gave him presents. He knew he was supposed to like them, but he couldn't. Except for one. She was a little taller than Bruce and she wore a yellow dress and white shoes and in her hair, a yellow ribbon. She didn't yell and run like the others. Her name was Rachel and she was nice.

Rachel, his mother explained, lived in the staff housing near the manor, wherever that was, and Rachel's mother was the Waynes' housekeeper. Mother said that if Bruce wanted to play with her, she could come and visit him often. That was okay with Bruce.

Over the next three years, Bruce had what his mother called "play dates" with other kids, including some he secretly wished would stay away, but Rachel was the friend he saw the most. Sometimes, they would go to where she lived, which seemed very strange to Bruce, full of different smells and old furniture, but mostly they played at Bruce's. Together, they explored every room and then ventured outside. Once, they asked if they could play in the guesthouse, near the front gate, where Mother and Father sometimes entertained friends over weekends, but Mother thought that was not such a good idea. But they could pretty much go anywhere else on the grounds, as long as they stayed within the high fences.

The garden, which Bruce had once thought stretched to the ends of the earth, now seemed quite negotiable, and when he and Rachel dared to venture beyond the gate, they discovered that the big, silvery thing they had seen from afar was actually a small building made of glass. Alfred said it was a "greenhouse," where his mother and father grew plants. Usually, the greenhouse door was locked but today, this bright warm, breezy day in mid-June, Alfred had left it ajar. Cautiously, hand in hand, Bruce and Rachel entered. Bruce stopped just inside the door, released Rachel's hand, and looked around at rows of tables covered with potted plants and tools he had never seen before. There were more plants hanging from the sloping ceiling and lumpy bags on the floor. Bruce was hot and sweaty and a thick, heavy odor clogged his nostrils. He didn't like this "greenhouse" at all.

Rachel had gone ahead of him and was crawling under one of the long tables. She crawled back out and peered up at Bruce, her small hand held over her head and closed around something. Bruce knew that she had found something, some kind of treasure, maybe.

"Can I see?" he asked.

"Finder's keepers," Rachel said, smiling. "I found it."

"In *my* greenhouse."

Rachel's smile changed to a frown and for a second or two she seemed to be thinking. She smiled again and opened her hand. A stone arrowhead lay on her palm. Bruce wondered how it had gotten there, under the table, but not for long. He grabbed it, stuffed it into a pocket, and ran out the nearest door to hide.

Bruce ran onto a small patch of ground enclosed by a low fence. In the center was a low, round well.

Knowing that Rachel was following him and wanting to impress her—he didn't know why—Bruce climbed up onto the top of the well. The hole inside was covered with green-painted boards that had splinters of yellow showing: *old* boards. Slowly, Bruce climbed on top of the wood.

Then he heard a creaking sound and the world seemed to tilt and the stone wall of the well was rushing past his eyes.

He just had time to realize he was falling before he

stopped so suddenly that his teeth clicked and for a moment he could not breathe. Then he gasped and filled his lungs with air. From somewhere above him, he heard Rachel screaming: *"Mister Alfred!"*

He looked up and saw the opening of the well, a circle of light far, far above. Glancing back down, he saw that he had landed on a pile of dirt and rubble. He put his palms on the cold stone wall and slowly, wondering if he had broken anything, he stood. He was trembling and aware of a nasty scrape on one knee, but his body felt basically all right.

I can really *show Rachel how brave I am,* he thought. *I can find a way out of here and—*

He heard a sound like a door with very rusty hinges being opened. It seemed to be coming from a gap in the stones. He put his face to the black opening, hoping to see the source of the sound—

Something stiff and scratchy rasped across his forehead and in an instant he realized—he did not know how—that the thing was alive.

The thing, the dark, horrible thing, flew from the gap and spiraled upward and was followed by other things, a swarm of them, hundreds of them, flapping and screeching, tearing at Bruce's clothing and hair. *Bats,* he realized, and Bruce felt himself, his personality, his very *being,* shrink and vanish and only a voice that shrieked and shrieked remained . . .

Then the bats were gone. The shrieking stopped. Bruce lay atop the dirt, gasping and sobbing.

He heard someone call his name, and when he

looked up, he saw his father, wearing a long black coat, climbing down a rope.

Strong arms enveloped him and he felt himself being lifted, and raised, and then his father was carrying him past the greenhouse, toward the mansion, with Alfred trotting alongside. Rachel walked next to them, crying. Her mother put her arms around Rachel to comfort her.

"Will you be needing an ambulance, Master Wayne?" Alfred asked.

"We have everything we need," Bruce's father replied. "I'll take X-rays later."

"Very good, sir."

Smiling, Bruce held his hand out to Rachel. When she moved next to him, he gently placed the arrowhead in her open palm. Looking up at Bruce, a small smile appeared on Rachel's tearstained face.

A few minutes later Bruce was in the room his father called "the office," being cradled in Mother's soft arms while Father, his sleeves rolled up and his tie loosened, examined Bruce's scrapes and bruises. Bruce was still crying, but only a little.

"There, there," Mother cooed. "Everything is all right, Bruce. Everything is fine. Nothing like that will ever happen to you again, I promise."

Father finished his ministrations and Mother led Bruce up to his room.

The next morning he awoke to see his father standing over him.

"You were getting kind of noisy in your sleep," Father said. "Bad dream?"

Bruce nodded.

"The bats?" Father sat on the side of the bed. "You know why they attacked you? They were afraid of you."

"Afraid of *me*?"

"You're a lot bigger than a bat, aren't you? All creatures feel fear."

"Even the scary ones?"

"*Especially* the scary ones."

Standing under the clock tower on the midwestern campus, waiting for the cute girl from advanced calculus, Bruce understood his identification with Siddhartha. Falling down the well, Bruce had, like Siddhartha, passed through a gate, albeit a metaphorical one. Before his tumble, he had heard the word "fear" and similar words like "scared" and "afraid" and "dread" . . . but they were only words. Afterward, despite his mother's comforting and his father's deft attentions, Bruce knew, to the marrow of his being, what "fear" was. Within a week, he was to add "hate" and "grief" to his lexicon.

FROM THE JOURNALS OF RÃ'S AL GHŪL

My daughter, who is uncommonly mature for her age, last night told me that I am a "self-appointed messiah." She meant it as an affront. I startled her by choosing to accept it as a compliment. Actually, it is neither affront nor compliment, but something far greater. It is the simple truth.

We have prosecuted our newest experiment for two and three-quarters years using Gotham City in the United States as our place of experimentation. Our results are inconclusive. We have destabilized the business life of the city but have not destroyed it. A savior, in the form of a wealthy doctor, has come to the rescue. Would similar saviors appear elsewhere? I cannot discount the possibility.

I have begun to conclude that economics is not the weapon I hoped it would be and that I must seek another. I do not know where to search.

They were "going to the opera" and Bruce knew from the way his parents were acting that "going to the opera" was special—the kind of event Father called "a big deal." Bruce had only a dim notion of what an "opera" was, and what little he did know he had learned from Miss Daisy, the blond, motherly woman who came to the house five days a week to teach him. Bruce knew that his parents disagreed about Miss Daisy because he had overheard them arguing. Father wanted Bruce to attend a regular public school. He used words Bruce was unfamiliar with, words like "pampered" and "overprotected." Mother replied that there was no public school anywhere near Wayne Manor and to drive Bruce into the city would be a hardship on whoever had to do it. Finally, they compromised: Bruce would be "home schooled" until he was a teenager, at which time he would go to Mark Twain High School in Ossaville, a town that was, apparently, closer than Gotham.

Meanwhile, Mother taught Bruce geography and arithmetic every morning until lunch, and from one to three Miss Daisy taught him history and English. It was during one of their English hours that Miss Daisy had explained opera.

"It's a story, but with music. People sing instead of speak. They use music to make what they're saying more emotional."

That sounded kind of interesting to Bruce. Not exciting, but kind of interesting, so he was looking forward, sort of, to attending the opera with his parents.

Father wore a black suit and black bow tie and a snowy white shirt—what he called his "tux"—and Mother had on an elegant short black dress. Bruce stood in the doorway of his parents' bedroom, watching Mother dab rouge on her cheeks.

"Help me a second, Tom?" she called and Father joined her and circled her neck with a string of pearls. He snapped a catch into place, took his wife by the shoulders, spun her around, and said, "Gorgeous!"

Mother smiled and kissed him on the cheek.

Bruce smiled, too. He liked it when his parents were nice to each other.

The three of them descended the wide, curving staircase to where Alfred was waiting in the foyer.

"We won't need you tonight," Father told him.

"Ah, that's right," Alfred said. "You're riding the monorail. But might I take you to the station, Master Wayne?"

"No thanks. I feel like driving."

They went in the "smaller car"—a Lincoln, Bruce had heard his father say—down the winding driveway, out onto the main road, past several small clusters of stores and houses to a lot which was lit by tall,

bluish lamps on curved stands. There were already
several cars in the lot, neatly parked between white
lines. Father stopped the Lincoln near a row of steps
that led to a platform.

The Waynes went up the steps, Mother holding
Bruce's left hand and Father holding his right hand.
Several other people were already on the platform,
which was alongside a metal rail, gleaming in the blue
light. Father glanced at his watch. "The train should
arrive in about a minute," he said.

Bruce saw a round light coming down the rail and
as it approached, he could see that it was on the front
of a vehicle of some kind. There was a rumble and the
train stopped in front of them. Doors slid open with
a soft hiss and the Waynes entered the train car and
found seats. Another hiss, another muted rumble, and
Bruce was watching the sights of Gotham City speed
past the window. He had been to Gotham City before, of course, with his parents and Alfred and once
with Miss Daisy. But he had never seen it as he was
seeing it now. On those earlier visits, Gotham had
seemed to be nothing but walls and cars and lights
and confusion. He had never thought to look up, at
the tops of the buildings, and so he had never realized
how tall they were—tall and, in a way Bruce could
not quite understand, *impressive.* Looking out the
train window, Bruce began to get an idea of what the
city actually *was,* and it both fascinated and frightened him.

"Your father built this train," Mother told Bruce.

"Not exactly," Father said. "I didn't actually *build* it—"

"Well, you *paid* for it," Mother said.

"*That* I'm guilty of," Father said to Bruce. "Kind of a family tradition. Your great-grandfather built the first trains in Gotham. The city's been good to our family, but now the city's suffering. People less fortunate than us are enduring very hard times. So we built a new, cheap public transportation system to unite all of Gotham."

"And at the center of it," Mother added, "is Wayne Tower."

"Is that where you work?" Bruce asked.

"No," Father said. "I work at the hospital. I leave the running of the company to better men."

"*Better?*"

"Well . . . more *interested* men."

The train slowed. Mother pointed out the window to a gigantic building that seemed to stretch to the sky. "Wayne Tower," she said.

The train slid beneath a roof, hissed, stopped. "Here we are," Father said.

The Waynes left the train and walked among a crowd of commuters, beneath a vaulted ceiling, and went through a wide door to a covered walkway that spanned the area between the station and the tower. Bruce saw a sign in the form of an arrow that read: TO OPERA HOUSE.

The Waynes walked toward where the arrow pointed, Bruce's hands again folded into his parents'. They went up an escalator, through a hallway with red fabric on the walls and thick red carpet on the floor, and passed through a door. Father handed three tickets to a pretty young woman who glanced at them, smiled, and led the Waynes down an aisle to a row of seats only a short distance from a stage that was partially covered by a red velvet curtain. They sat in cushioned chairs and Bruce looked up at a gigantic chandelier, even bigger than the one they had at home, and to the left and right and behind himself, at row upon row of men and women dressed like Mother and Father. Bruce saw no children; apparently, he was the only one in the place, which made him feel a bit funny. There was a funny smell in the air that reminded Bruce of Mother's closet and the backseat of the family limousine. The operagoers were rustling as they shifted in their seats, getting comfortable, and murmuring in the voices that people used in libraries.

Father leaned over to Mother and whispered, "I forgot to ask. What are we seeing, anyway?"

"*Mefistofele,*" Mother said, "by Boito."

"French?"

Mother nodded.

"Any good?"

"Excellent."

"Okay," Father said, and leaned back in his chair.

Bruce saw a bunch of men file into an area below the stage and pick up musical instruments: *musicians,* he realized.

A minute later the musicians began to play music that sounded much like what Mother listened to in the sunroom, and the red curtain rose, and Bruce was looking at women dressed like Halloween witches—wearing *costumes,* as Miss Daisy predicted—singing and cavorting around the stage. Bruce knew they were only performers, people like himself who happened to be able to sing and whose faces were covered with some kind of paint. But to him, they seemed real, more real than the unpainted audience members around him. Then bats dropped from above, hung from wires, their black wings flapping, and began to circle over the witches' heads . . .

Bruce stared at the bats.

And he was again at the bottom of the well and the screeching bats were exploding from the crevice and tearing at him . . .

He was being silly, he told himself. He was not in the well, he was in a *theater,* watching a—what had Miss Daisy said?—a *story,* an *opera,* and there was nothing to be afraid of . . .

But he could not control his terror.

"Sweetheart, what's wrong?" Mother said, her face inches from Bruce's.

Bruce was gasping, unable to catch his breath, and he could not answer his mother . . .

Finally, he was able to ask, "Can we go?"

Mother looked over Bruce's head at Father, giving him a questioning look, and Father said, "I guess we'd better."

Father stood and held Bruce's hand and said, "Take it easy, champ." Then the three of them were moving across the carpet and down the stairs and out onto the street.

"We'll just take a few minutes to get some fresh air," Father said and, squeezing Bruce's hand, added, "A bit of opera goes a long way, right, Bruce?"

Bruce looked up at Father and Father winked. "What say we take a little walk?"

Bruce nodded yes.

"Come on," Father said.

Then, in the shadow cast by Wayne Tower, Bruce saw something move and a moment later a man stepped from the darkness and approached them. He was tall and young, dressed in dirty clothes. His face was thin and scared, and he was pointing something at them that gleamed in the light of a nearby streetlamp.

"Wallet, jewelry—fast!" the man said.

"That's fine, just take it easy," Father said, stepping between the man and his family. He shrugged out of his overcoat and handed it to Bruce.

"Hurry up," the man said.

Father took his wallet from beneath his jacket and extended it. "Here you go," he said.

The man grabbed at the wallet with a shaking hand and missed, and the wallet fell.

"It's fine, it's fine," Father said, in the same tone of voice he had used when he pulled Bruce from the well.

The man knelt on the pavement and groped for the wallet. Bruce recognized the object he was pointing up at Father from pictures he had seen in the news-paper: *a gun.*

The gun was shaking.

The man retrieved the wallet and shoved it into a pocket. "Just take it and go," Father said.

The man stood and shifted his gaze to Mother. "I said jewelry, too."

Mother began to pull off her diamond engagement ring. Father took a step toward the man. "Hey, just—"

Bruce saw the gun twitch and in the same instant he heard a sound like two boards being slapped together. Puzzled, he turned to his father for an explanation. Father was staring down at a red splotch on his snowy white shirt that spread outward from a small, black hole.

Father crumpled, as though all his bones had dissolved at once.

Mother screamed. The man reached for the strand of pearls around her neck. Mother pulled back from him and the man said, "Give me the damn—"

The gun twitched and there was the slapping board sound again. The man curled his fingers around the pearl necklace and yanked and the necklace broke. Pearls spilled past Bruce's face and clattered lightly on the pavement.

Bruce stared up at the man's eyes. The man jerked, as though he had been stung, and he spun and ran into the shadows.

For a long time, Bruce stared at his father's face. He heard a groan and bent down so that his face was close to Father's.

"Don't be afraid," Father whispered. He smiled at Bruce, then closed his eyes. Bruce sat among the bloodstained pearls. Something began to swell within him. He had no idea what it was, just that it was somehow connected to his parents and that he had to keep it in check ... . *had* to.

A while later a policeman came, and then more policemen, and some of them put Mother and Father into bags and loaded them into the rear of an ambulance. Someone, Bruce did not know who, took him in a car to a big building. There was a crowd on the sidewalk in front of the building, and some of them snapped pictures as Bruce passed by. Bruce, still clutching his father's overcoat, went inside and was led to a chair. He sat, and waited, and felt himself becoming numb all over, inside and outside, except for the swelling thing in his chest. He wondered if everyone had forgotten about him and decided he didn't care if they had. After a while, he seemed to leave his body and watch it from somewhere else—not any particular place, just somewhere else.

A hand on his shoulder jerked him back inside his body.

"You okay, son?"

Bruce saw that the hand belonged to a tall, ruddy man whose hair and mustache were thick and black and whose blue eyes were warm and kind.

"I'm Jim Gordon," the man said. "You need anything? A sandwich? Soda?" He gestured to the overcoat in Bruce's hands. "Is that your father's?"

Bruce nodded. Gordon gently took the coat and draped it over Bruce's shoulders.

Another man, wearing an officer's uniform, approached and said loudly, "Gordon! You gotta stick your nose into everything!"

Jim Gordon turned to the man in the uniform and stared, not saying a thing.

"Get outta my sight," the uniformed officer commanded. Gordon touched Bruce's shoulder again, then spun on his heel and stalked away.

The man knelt in front of Bruce and said, "My name's Captain Loeb, kid, and I got some good news for you. We got him."

"Got . . . who?" Bruce murmured.

"Who do you think? Joe Chill. The skel that iced your folks."

The man's words were English, yet it was as though he were speaking a foreign language. Bruce *understood* the words, but he could not grasp their meaning. So he just sat and felt the thing inside him continue swelling until it filled him, and his own skin was just a thin covering over it, a garment he was wearing like the opera singers' costumes, and after a while it *became* him. *It* was the real Bruce. Everything else was false.

Detective Jim Gordon got home late that night, but Barbara had put his meal in the oven to keep it warm. He kissed her soundly and ate the pork chops and mashed potatoes she had prepared. In the six months they had been married, Babs had not once neglected to make a hot dinner for her Jimmy.

Afterward, they watched the late news on television. As they were preparing for bed, Barbara said, "Something's wrong."

"It's nothing."

"Yes it is. Tell me."

He told her about the killing of the Waynes and the frightened little boy who had been orphaned by it. He told her about Loeb and how Loeb had treated young Bruce.

"Loeb is the whole damn department," he concluded. "He's not the exception, he's the rule."

"You're thinking about Chicago?"

"The offer's still in place, but it won't be forever. So yeah, I'm thinking about it. I know it'd be a pain, moving away from your family and friends . . ."

Barbara was sitting on the edge of the mattress, her slender body tense. "Yes. Yes, it would."

"Well, we don't have to decide tonight."

Barbara rolled onto her back and pulled the blanket up to her chin.

Two days later, at a plot of unused land behind the greenhouse, Bruce watched as coffins containing Mother and Father were lowered into two oblong holes. Some of the mourners were crying softly and a few of them looked at Bruce, as though trying to gauge his feelings. He wanted to cry, he really did, because he realized that tears were expected and, more important, appropriate. So he bowed his head, but no tears would come. The thing inside him, the thing that filled his body, would not allow crying.

A crowd of people, all of whom had spoken condolences to Bruce, began to walk slowly away from the gravesite. Bruce stood beside Alfred until the coffins were out of sight and then turned toward the mansion. It started to rain, and the wind was cold.

"There's someone who would like a word with you, Master Bruce," Alfred said, and escorted Bruce to the driveway in front of the mansion. A tall man in what Bruce recognized as a cashmere overcoat stood next to a black car—a Rolls-Royce, Bruce knew.

"This is Mr. Earle," Alfred said to Bruce, and Mr. Earle smiled and reached down to shake Bruce's hand.

"Pleased to meet you," Bruce said.

"I want you to know that you're in excellent hands," Mr. Earle said, nodding at Alfred, "and we're minding the empire. When you're all grown up, it'll be waiting for you."

Bruce understood none of what Mr. Earle had told him, but thanked him anyway.

Mr. Earle ducked into the Rolls-Royce and Alfred led Bruce into the mansion.

Bruce took off his coat and went to his favorite window, the big one that looked out on the drive. He peered at the rain, now heavy and beating against the windowpanes, and at the mourners, hunched in the rain and wind, folding umbrellas as they got into their cars.

Rachel walked past, glanced up, and waved to Bruce. Bruce hesitated, then returned the wave.

From the doorway behind Bruce, Alfred said, "I thought I'd prepare a little supper."

Bruce continued to stare out of the window.

"Very well," Alfred said. "I'll leave you to your thoughts."

Suddenly Bruce felt the urge to speak swelling within him and without knowing what he was going to say, he blurted, "It was my fault, Alfred. They're dead and it was my fault."

Alfred hurried across the room and knelt in front of Bruce. "Master Bruce . . ."

"I made them leave the theater."

Alfred put his arms around Bruce. "Oh, no, no, no . . ."

"If I hadn't gotten scared—"

"No, no, Master Bruce. Nothing you did—nothing *anyone* ever did—can excuse that man. It's his fault and his alone. Do you understand?"

Bruce pressed his face into Alfred's chest and for the first time he sobbed. "I miss them, Alfred. I miss them so much."

"So do I, Master Bruce. So do I."

3

It was the day after Bruce's twentieth birthday, a year and a half after he'd stood beneath a clock and waited for a cute girl who never arrived, and six months after he had completed an advanced race-driving course in western Missouri, which he had really enjoyed. He stood at the front of the first car of the monorail train, swaying, enjoying the spectacle of Gotham City rushing past—the many-colored roofs, the tiny side streets and wide avenues, the millions of windows gleaming in the morning sunshine. The train slowed, stopped. Bruce picked up his duffel bag, swung it over his shoulder, and stepped onto the platform. He saw Alfred at the far end of the platform and waved.

"You didn't have to pick me up," he said as Alfred approached. "I could have transferred to the red line—"

"I'm afraid not, Master Bruce. The red line . . . well, it's closed. Apparently Mr. Earle thought it wasn't making enough money."

Bruce followed Alfred through a station he barely recognized. His father's splendid achievement had become shabby: cracked glass, chipped marble, men and women huddled against the walls, some of them next to fires built in trash cans, others huddled by shopping carts filled with rags and bottles.

"How *is* Mr. Earle?" Bruce asked.

"Oh . . . successful."

They left the station and Bruce looked up at Wayne Tower, gleaming in the sun, magnificent as ever.

A few minutes later, driving through start-and-stop rush-hour traffic, Alfred guided the Rolls-Royce up the Walnut Street ramp and onto the freeway.

"Will you be heading back to the university tomorrow?" Alfred asked. "Or could I persuade you to spend an extra night or two?"

"I'm not heading back at all," Bruce replied.

"You don't like it there?"

"I like it fine. They just don't feel the same way."

Bruce smiled and settled back in his seat. They had left the city and were proceeding along a country lane, past tall elms and oaks, their foliage glorious this fine November morning, and, every half mile or so, past a cluster of buildings that included a big house.

Alfred slowed the car and pressed a button on the dashboard. The gates that fronted the Wayne property swung open and Alfred drove past the guesthouse and up a curved driveway to the mansion.

Bruce got out of the car and stood staring at the huge old home. After a minute, he followed Alfred inside. Wayne Manor was not as he remembered it. The place was clean and stark and, although Alfred had kept everything preserved, there was a musty smell in the air. White dust cloths covered the furniture, and all the paintings and pictures were covered with white paper.

"I've prepared the master bedroom," Alfred said.

"My old room will be fine," Bruce said.

"With all due respect, sir, your father is dead. Wayne Manor is *your* house."

Bruce allowed irritation into his voice. "No, Alfred, this *isn't* my house. It's a mausoleum. A reminder of everything I lost. And when I have my way, I'll pull the damn thing down, brick by brick."

"This house, *Master Wayne,* has housed six generations of the Wayne family."

"Why do you give a damn? It's not your family, Alfred."

"I give a damn, sir, because a good man once made me responsible for what was most precious to him in the whole world."

Bruce stared at Alfred, and nodded.

"Miss Dawes has offered to drive you to the hearing, by the way."

Bruce raised an eyebrow. "Rachel? Why?"

"She probably wants to talk you out of going."

Bruce gestured to the window and the grounds behind the greenhouse. "Should I just bury the past out there with my parents, Alfred?"

"I don't presume to tell you what to do with your past, sir. Just know that there are those of us who care what you do with your future."

"Still haven't given up on me yet?"

"Never." Alfred said the word as though it were a vow.

Bruce climbed the staircase and entered his room. It hadn't changed much. The childhood toys were gone as were the bedspread and pillows festooned with cartoon characters. But his high school pennant and the picture of his graduating class were still on the wall. He dropped his bag onto the bed. Breathing deeply, he looked at a photograph on the mantelpiece: young Bruce, on his dad's shoulders, arms raised in triumph. His father's stethoscope lay beneath the photograph. It was the same stethoscope Father had held to Bruce's chest after the incident with the bats. Bruce smiled. He returned to the bed and opened his bag. Reaching inside, past a wad of T-shirts, he removed an automatic pistol and a cardboard box full of nine-millimeter cartridges. He dumped the magazine from the gun and, with steady hands, began inserting bullets into it.

He heard a car engine on the drive outside and footsteps on the walk. He finished loading the gun, stuffed it into his belt, and put on a cashmere overcoat he had never before worn, a Christmas gift from Wayne Enterprises.

He left his room and descended the rear staircase to the kitchen. A young woman in her early twenties, with a face that mixed *cute* with *beautiful* and was enormously attractive because of it, stood just inside the pantry, running her fingers over shelves of cans and boxes. This was Rachel and she was not what Bruce was expecting. All these years, he had carried the image of Rachel as a scabby-kneed, freckly child—

Rachel as he had last seen her. *This* Rachel, this grave young woman, was definitely not that child. She wore a camel overcoat over an aquamarine top and black skirt, and just a hint of makeup. She was devastatingly attractive.

"Hello," Bruce said. "By the way, Alfred still keeps the condensed milk on the top shelf."

"Hasn't he noticed that you're tall enough to reach, now?"

"Old habits die hard, I guess."

Rachel grinned. "Never used to stop us, anyway."

"No, no it didn't."

"You still trying to get kicked out of the entire Ivy League?"

Bruce shook his head. "Turns out you don't actually need a degree to do the international playboy thing. But you . . . head of your class at law school, editor of the law review, and now assistant at the D.A.'s office . . . quite the overachiever."

Rachel shrugged. After a while she said, "I miss this place."

"It's nothing without the people who made it what it was. Now there's only Alfred."

Rachel stepped close to Bruce and looked up into his eyes. "And you?"

"I'm not staying, Rachel."

"Oh. I thought maybe this time . . . but you're just back for the hearing? Bruce, I don't suppose there's any way I can convince you not to come."

Bruce stopped smiling and turned away from her.

"Someone at this *proceeding* should stand for my parents."

"Bruce, we all loved your parents. What Chill did was unforgivable—"

"Then why is your boss letting him go?"

"Because in prison he shared a cell with Carmine Falcone. He learned things and he'll testify in exchange for early parole."

"Not good enough, Rachel."

Rachel looked away.

"Are you still good for a ride to the courthouse?" Bruce asked.

"Of course."

Bruce passed the ride into Gotham City staring out at a metallic blue sky that spread above the city's spires. He and Rachel were both silent, which was fine with Bruce.

Rachel left the freeway and, a minute later, turned in to a blacktopped lot and parked the Honda in a slot with her name stenciled on it.

Bruce touched her shoulder and said, "Rachel, this man killed my parents. I cannot let that pass."

Rachel opened her mouth to say something, then apparently changed her mind and merely shrugged.

Bruce spoke more urgently now: "Rachel, I *need* you to understand."

Rachel studied Bruce's face as though seeking answers there. Finally, she nodded and silently opened the car door. Bruce, too, got out of the car, knelt quickly, slipped the gun out from under his overcoat, and slid it behind the front wheel of the car.

Bruce stood and looked over at Rachel, who was giving him a questioning look. "Shoelace," he said.

Bruce followed Rachel through a side entrance into Gotham's Central Courthouse, a rambling old pseudo-Roman building erected just after the Civil War by one of Bruce's ancestors and refurbished by his father twenty-two years ago. They ascended a flight of marble steps to a small chamber on the second floor. A five-person panel sat at a long table at the front of the room—four men and, sitting in the middle, Judge Faden, a heavyset man with red hair. Four other men sat at a table facing them. Bruce took a chair near the rear wall as Rachel continued to the group of four and, smiling a greeting, joined them.

Bruce waited while others, men and women in business attire, filtered in and sat. Ten minutes passed. Finally, from a rear door, a red-haired cop entered with a tall man whom Bruce recognized instantly, although he had seen the man only once before, fourteen years earlier, on a cold November night in the shadow of Wayne Tower. Joe Chill's face was even more pained and his hair had thinned slightly, but in all other ways, he had not changed.

"We all know why we're here," said Judge Faden. "Mr. Finch, would you like to begin?"

A handsome man in a dark suit who was sitting next to Rachel stood and addressed the panel. "The depression hit working people like Mr. Chill hardest of all. His crime was appalling, but it was motivated not by greed but by desperation. Given the exemplary prison record of Mr. Chill, the fourteen years already served, and his extraordinary level of cooperation with one of this office's most important investigations . . . we strongly endorse Mr. Chill's petition for an early release."

The judge looked at Chill. "Mr. Chill?"

Chill rose, cleared his throat, and glanced around nervously. "Your Honor, not a day's gone by when I didn't wish I could take back what I did. Sure, I was desperate, like a lot of people back then. But that doesn't change what I did."

Chill sat.

The five people he had spoken to all nodded, as though on cue, then glanced down at papers on the tabletop. One of them, a florid man wearing tortoise-shell glasses, cleared his throat and said, "I gather a member of the family is here today. Does he have anything to say?"

Joe Chill turned his head and scanned the onlookers who sat behind him. For a moment, his gaze locked with Bruce's. Then he lowered his eyes and turned back to the front.

Bruce stood and walked from the room, aware that everyone, including Rachel, was watching him. Moving briskly, he went down the steps and out into the parking lot. He knelt by the front of Rachel's car, picked up his gun, and crammed it into the left sleeve of his coat.

He leaned against the car, facing the courthouse, and waited.

The side door opened and the red-haired cop came

out followed by an officer in another kind of uniform—
a security man, or a prison guard, Bruce guessed.

There was a shout from the street and dozens of
reporters and television cameramen rushed around
from the front of the building, where they had been
waiting for Chill's appearance.

"They're taking him out the side," someone shouted.

Chill, surrounded by uniformed cops and men in
overcoats—obviously detectives—followed the red-
haired cop and the security guard out into the parking lot as the reporters and cameramen stampeded
toward them.

"Mr. Chill," someone in the mob called, "any
words for the Wayne family?"

Joe Chill bowed his head and ignored the question.

Bruce straightened and gulped down cold air. Hands
in his coat pockets, he began walking toward Chill.

"It's Bruce Wayne," another reporter yelled and the
mob parted, making a path for Bruce.

A bright light mounted on a camera momentarily
blinded Bruce and when he could again see clearly, a
tall, blond woman holding a tape recorder was approaching Chill. Bruce took his hands from his pockets. He slid his right fingers into his left sleeve and
walked faster.

"Joe, hey, Joe Chill," the blond woman said. She
was only inches from Chill now. "Falcone says hi."

She pulled a revolver from her shoulder bag, aimed
it at Chill's chest, and fired: *a sound like two boards
being slapped together.* Bruce saw Chill's eyes widen,
and the corners of his lips curl upward, as though he

had just experienced a wonderful surprise. Then, as he started to sag against the red-haired cop, his expression changed to one of disbelief, and he slipped from the cop's grasp and crumpled to the blacktop. For a moment there was a confused milling around and then people began yelling.

The other cops in Chill's escort had wrested the woman's gun away and shoved her down before she was dragged off. Bruce was fifteen feet away, his right fingers curled around the gun in his sleeve, staring.

Eventually he realized that someone was shaking his arm and speaking his name. From the corner of his eye, he saw it was a young woman and realized it was Rachel.

"Come on, Bruce. We don't need to see this."

Bruce yanked his arm away. "*I* do."

He watched it all: the arrival of the ambulance, the putting of Joe Chill into a bag and the closing of that bag, the ambulance leaving, belching blue smoke, and the ebb and flow of reporters, cops, medics—watched until everyone was gone except for himself and Rachel.

They got into Rachel's car. A few blocks away, Rachel turned onto the freeway and headed for the suburbs.

"The D.A. couldn't understand why Judge Faden insisted on making the hearing public," Rachel said. "Obviously, Falcone paid him off to get Chill out into the open."

"Maybe I should be thanking them," Bruce said, his lips barely moving.

"You don't mean that."

"What if I do, Rachel? My parents deserved justice."

"You're not talking about justice, Bruce. You're talking about revenge."

"Sometimes they're the same."

"They're *never* the same, Bruce. Justice is about harmony. Revenge is about *you* making yourself *feel* better. That's why we have an impartial system."

"Well, your system of justice is broken," Bruce said.

Rachel's eyes narrowed and her voice was low and edgy. "Don't tell me the system's broken, Bruce. I'm out there every day trying to fix it while you mope around using your grief as an excuse to do nothing."

She spun the steering wheel and, tires screeching, cut across two traffic lanes to an exit ramp. "I want to show you something."

They went down an off ramp and glided into an area Bruce had never visited. His parents and Alfred had always taken him to Gotham's glories: wide, tree-lined streets and lavish homes and museums and theaters and parks—places full of smiling people and bright lights. Here, the streets were narrow, cramped, and dark because most of the streetlamps had been broken. They passed blocks of storefronts with sheets of plywood nailed over their windows. Trash littered the gutters and sidewalks, and despite the car's window being closed, Bruce smelled something fetid and decaying. There was occasional movement in the shadowed alleyways—furtive people engaged in furtive transactions.

Rachel gestured to the filthy streets. "Look beyond your own pain, Bruce. The city is *rotting*. Chill being dead doesn't help that—it makes it *worse* because Falcone walks. He carries on flooding our city with crime and drugs, creating new Joe Chills . . . Falcone may not have killed your parents, Bruce, but he's destroying everything they stood for."

Rachel steered the Honda to the curb and turned off the engine. They were parked in front of a nondescript, two-story building. Above a doorway there was a neon sign—CLUB—and a neon arrow pointing to a flight of stairs.

"You want to thank him for that," Rachel said. "Here you go. This is Falcone's main hangout. It's no secret—everyone knows where to find him. But no one will touch him because he keeps the bad people rich and the good people scared."

Rachel poked a forefinger into Bruce's chest, hard, and asked, "What chance does Gotham have when the good people do nothing?"

"I'm not one of your 'good people,' Rachel. Chill took that from me."

"What do you mean?"

Bruce pulled up his left sleeve and removed the gun. "All these years I wanted to kill him. Now I can't."

Rachel looked at the weapon lying on Bruce's palm, gleaming in the glow from the neon sign, and then up into his eyes. "You were going to kill him yourself."

She slapped him. Bruce did not respond. Rachel slapped him again, and again and again.

Bruce shoved the gun into a jacket pocket.

Rachel stared down at her lap for a full minute, crying silently. She wiped her eyes on her sleeve and said, "Just another coward with a gun. Your father would be *ashamed* of you."

Without replying, Bruce opened his door and got out of the car.

He watched the taillights of Rachel's car vanish around a corner and then turned to orient himself. He was in the harbor area. Bulky shapes of freighters and tankers were silhouetted against a sky brightened by the reflection of the city's lights and there was a mingled odor of oil and salt in the air. Bruce walked to the water, his footfalls echoing hollowly on the boards of a pier. He took the gun from his pocket and held it up to let the stern lights of one of the ships shine on it. He turned it slowly, squinting, as though he were examining some unimaginably alien artifact, then flung it into the water.

He walked from the pier back onto the street, his shoes crunching on broken glass, and went to the CLUB sign and down the stairs beneath it. He passed through a metal door and gasped: the air was a brew of smoke, sweat, perfume, cologne, and alcohol. Bruce wiped his suddenly watering eyes on his sleeve and stood, trying to acclimate himself to the noise of a hundred conversations, a hundred raucous laughs. He had never seen so many people jammed into such a small space.

Falcone was not hard to spot. He was at a corner

table surrounded by men in suits and women in cock-tail dresses, spreading his hands, making a point.

Bruce crossed and stood in front of him.

"You're taller than you look in the tabloids, Mr. Wayne," Falcone said in a surprisingly pleasant voice.

A burly man in jeans and a blue jacket appeared at Bruce's side and ran his hands over Bruce's body. The man looked at Falcone and said, "Clean."

Falcone said, "No gun? I'm insulted."

"Only a coward needs a gun," Bruce replied.

Falcone gestured to a chair and the man in the blazer pulled it away from the table. Bruce sat.

"Coulda just sent me a thank-you note," Falcone said to Bruce.

"I didn't come here to thank you. I came to show you that not everyone in Gotham is afraid of you."

Falcone laughed. "Just those that know me, kid. Look around. You'll see two councilmen, a union of-ficial, a couple off-duty cops, a judge . . ."

Bruce recognized one of the men who had been at the hearing sitting at a nearby table. When Bruce re-turned his attention to Falcone, he was looking at a silver pistol aimed at his chest.

"I don't have a second's hesitation blowing your head off in front of them . . . that's power you can't buy. The power of fear."

"*I'm* not afraid of you."

"Because you think you've got nothing to lose. But you haven't thought it through . . . you haven't thought about your lady friend from the D.A.'s . . . or that old butler of yours . . ."

Falcone slid the gun beneath his jacket. "People from your world *always* have so much to lose. That's why they keep me in business. I stop the desperate heading uptown the way Joe Chill did. You think because your mommy and daddy got shot you know the ugly side of life, but you don't. You've never tasted desperation—you're Bruce Wayne, Prince of Gotham. You'd have to go a thousand miles to meet someone who didn't know your name. So don't come down here with all your anger . . . trying to prove something to yourself. This is a world you'll never understand. And you'll always fear what you don't understand."

Falcone nodded and the man in the jacket punched Bruce in the face, knocking him off his chair. Two other men hauled Bruce to his feet and it began: a brief, savage beating, perpetrated in front of a hundred club-goers. The room quieted, and for a while the silence was broken only by grunts and the sound of blows.

"Enough," Falcone said and the man who was hitting Bruce stopped. Falcone rose and came close to Bruce. "You got spirit, kid, I'll give you that. More than your old man, anyway. In the joint, Chill told me about the night he killed your parents . . . said your old man begged for mercy. Begged. Like a dog."

Falcone jerked a thumb in the direction of a rear door and the thugs dragged Bruce through it and flung him into the street.

Bruce pushed himself to his feet and staggered to a wall. He leaned against it and wiped the back of his hand over his mouth, tasting something copper, recognizing it as blood, wondering if he was going to lose any teeth.

All those people, watching me be beaten . . . What had Falcone said? "That's power you can't buy. The power of fear."

He shoved away from the wall and walked toward the dock, aware that he was being observed from doorways and alleys. He approached an oil barrel with flames licking out of its top.

A man huddled near the barrel, warming himself, said, "Maybe ya shoulda tipped better."

Bruce drew closer; the glow of the flames revealed a face with grime in deeply etched lines and a splotchy beard. Bruce stared thoughtfully into the flames as the man rubbed his hands over them.

"You have a name?" Bruce asked the homeless man.

"Name's Joey. Last name's none a' your business."

Bruce removed his wallet and gave a wad of money to the homeless man.

"For what?" Joey asked.

"Your jacket."

Bruce dropped his wallet into the fire. Joey laughed. He shrugged out of his overcoat and bundled it into a ball.

"Let me have it," Joey shouted. "That's a good coat."

They traded: a nine-hundred-dollar, fawn-colored, cashmere overcoat for a frayed and torn Navy pea coat that had cost some sailor a ten spot when it was new three decades ago.

"Be careful who sees you with that," Bruce said. "They're going to come looking for me."

Joey was buttoning the overcoat. "Who?"

"Everyone."

Bruce smiled, saluted Joey with two fingers, and walked onto the pier, threading his way among stacks of freight containers. A horn blared, deep and loud, and Bruce looked toward one of the ships, its hull trembling as its engines churned the water. Bruce ran toward it.

FROM THE JOURNALS OF RĀ'S AL GHŪL

Early this morning, I walked as far as the nearest dune and back again, breathing in the clean desert air and rejoicing in it. Here, in the heat, and in the mountains, on the glacier, I can remember the planet as it once was before the stink of the greed of man made it a purgatory that is quickly becoming a hell.

I begin to feel the rigors of age, as I have so often before. Soon I must descend again into the Pit to rejuvenate myself. The rejuvenation will be followed, as it always is, by a period of insane rage and violence. Once, I hoped to find a cure for this inevitable consequence of my chemical bath, but apparently there is none. Everything has a price.

I have also decided to abandon my attempts to alter my genes in such a way as to allow me to sire a male child. The reason for my long inability to generate a boy apparently has to do with my Y chromosome that, once damaged, does not repair itself as does the heartier X chromosome. Not having a son is the greatest personal burden I bear. It is a consequence of my visits to the Pit that keep me alive. I have made a strange bargain with the universe.

I am as always sustained by the righteousness of my mission and the realization that I am humanity's savior. In another man these might seem like boastful words. I am not like other men. My long life has proven this, if nothing else.

We will soon relocate our domicile to the building above the glacier. I think that is a strategically desirable location for the next phase of my efforts. I will augment my army and bring the League of Shadows to its greatest strength in three hundred years. I will continue to seek an adequate leader, someone to replace me in the event that I never create my own replacement.

The experiment in Gotham City was at best a qualified success. I have given long consideration as to the means I shall use next in my crusade to save humanity and I may have come to a conclusion. I have decided against nuclear bombs. To use enough nuclear power to rid the earth of the eighty percent of its human inhabitants would be to render the planet inhospitable to most life forms and this has never been my wish. Neither can I use the environmental outrages humanity has already perpetrated for they, too, could leave the earth a barren cinder. Microbes and other biological means are also difficult choices for in the amounts I require they are almost impossible to control. I sense that the answer I seek is one I already possess. My problem is to recognize it.

During my few moments of tranquility, I reflect on the irony of my plans for the mass eradication of Homo sapiens. For the first century of my life, I devoted all my efforts to furthering human existence. I ministered to the ill in the lowest hovels and the grandest palaces alike, with no thought except to ease suffering. Even after the slaying of my wife, I continued to ply my altruism. Only slowly, over dozens of decades, did I come to realize that there are occasions when to heal, a physician must first harm. This is a lesson my daughters seem unable to absorb. I am certain a son would have no difficulty understanding it.

Our task grows urgent and our time short. Every day the earth becomes still more toxic. Within a generation or two at most it will reach the point of no return. I must succeed before it does, and I will.

4

Throughout the long, snowy winter that followed, Gotham's glitterati wanted to know what had happened to that handsome young Bruce Wayne. There were no shortage of rumors:

—*I heard he was wintering on the Riviera.*

—*My cousin saw him in Charlotte Amalie.*

—*I know it was him playing baccarat in Monaco. He was in disguise—bald and short, but it was him, all right.*

—*Bruce Wayne? Skiing in Gstaad.*

—*The real truth is, the death of his parents drove him mad. They have him in an asylum.*

—*Well, wherever he is, you can bet that he's enjoying himself.*

By spring, however, Bruce Wayne's name was not being mentioned so much. There were other matters to discuss: the antics of that divine Ms. Fitzgerald— *when she jumped into the fountain, we thought we'd die*—and, of course, the summer fashions and vacation plans . . . Oh, and crime. *Isn't that situation down by the docks getting* dreadful?

* * *

Bruce had just been beaten senseless for the third time. His first week on the ship had not been bad. The captain was willing to take on a new hand, one without experience or papers, provided the new hand was not choosy about where he slept, what he ate, or what kind of work he did. So Bruce slept on rags in a corner of the engine room, ate whatever was left when everyone else had eaten, and worked harder than he had known it was *possible* to work: lifting heavy crates, pulling at heavy cables, scraping paint off the ship's hull, cleaning foul-smelling gunk from the bilges. At the end of each fifteen-hour day, he dropped onto his rags, every muscle aching, but particularly the muscles in his back and calves, and drifted off to sleep despite the roar of huge machines only feet away. But despite the toil and discomfort, the first week was bearable because the crew pretty much ignored him.

The second week was bad. He was not ignored; he was tormented. It began when a wiry man, a bosun's mate, motioned for Bruce to join him on the ship's fantail. Bruce smiled, thinking that he was finally going to make a friend.

The bosun grinned and said, "I am Hector."

Still smiling, Bruce neared the bosun and was kicked in the groin. He doubled over, falling to the deck, and without a word the bosun kicked him on the top of his head. Bruce fell into a whirl of eddying color and awoke hurting.

The following day, a member of the black gang hit him with a garbage-can lid, and as Bruce reeled against a bulkhead, he tossed the lid aside and punched Bruce, twice in the chest and once in the face. When Bruce opened his eyes—a minute later? an hour?—his attacker was gone.

Bruce went to the toilet and turned on a rusty faucet. He splashed cold, salty water on his bruises and tried to understand what was happening to him. An initiation? Maybe that, but probably he was being hit because he was a stranger and life aboard ship was boring. Okay, he'd accept this reality and take what he could from it. He didn't like being punched and the color of his own blood held no delight for him, but there were lessons to be learned here, and Bruce was determined to learn them.

The bosun initiated the third attack. This time, Bruce was ready and managed to land a blow before being knocked out. Bruce awoke with water in his face. He looked up and saw the bosun standing over him with an empty pail.

"I teach you," the bosun said.

And he did—in odd, five-minute intervals between jobs, he educated Bruce in dirty fighting. The lessons amounted to this: trust no one, hit first, preferably with something harder than a fist, and then hit or kick again, until your enemy can no longer resist. Then hit him once more. Or kick him. Or stomp him.

Bruce had an idea of his own. Hector, and a lot of his other shipmates, were bigger and more powerful than he—the hard labor he'd been doing for months they'd been doing for years. But none of them seemed particularly bright, including Hector. By contrast, Bruce *was* smart, as a whole battery of IQ tests had proven.

Okay, I can't outmuscle them, but I can outthink them . . .

When they were within sight of land, Bruce asked the captain about his salary. Salary? The captain chuckled. Bruce was a stowaway and stowaways did not get paid.

After the ship was off-loaded and the crew had gone ashore, the bosun, Hector, invited Bruce to the fantail. "Let's see how good I teach you," he said.

Okay, pal, you asked for it . . .

While Bruce was thinking about his first move, Hector knocked him down and began kicking him senseless.

Every morning Alfred Pennyworth waited by Wayne Manor's main gate, next to the mailbox, until the postman arrived in his odd, three-wheeled vehicle with the day's delivery, and every morning Alfred thumbed through the envelopes, hoping for a letter from Bruce. But there were only bills, and occasionally a postcard from his niece in London.

Something brand-new was happening to Bruce, something he could not have imagined eighteen months ago, when he was the soft and pampered scion of a wealthy family. He was starving. He knew that his body had exhausted its store of fat and was consuming its muscle and that soon he would collapse and would probably lay in the filthy street until he died, unnoticed unless someone decided his rags were worth stealing. How long since he had eaten? At least three days. It had been a cup of undercooked rice and Bruce had gulped it down almost without chewing.

He sat with his back against a tree. He raised his eyes and looked out over the African marketplace. There were dozens of tents and tables heaped with fruit, vegetables, curried meats, and a throng of colorfully clad shoppers inspecting, haggling, buying, and hurrying off to feed their families.

Bruce forced himself to his feet and joined the throng. He stopped by a fruit vendor, and as the old woman behind the table eyed him suspiciously, he picked up a mango in his right hand and made a show of examining it as with his left hand he stole a plum from the table and dropped it into his pocket.

He hurried into an alleyway and bit into his plum and almost fainted from joy—the sweetness of it, the juiciness—nothing had ever tasted so good. Nothing *could* ever taste so good.

He heard something, the slightest stirring, and saw a child, about four, squatting in a doorway. The child, a boy, was naked and covered with grime. His ribs stretched his skin and his eyes, wide and glazed, were in hollows above his cheeks.

Bruce gazed down at the half plum in his fingers— *the wonderful plum!*—and then handed it to the boy.

Bruce could probably get more food. The boy probably could not.

Later, Bruce was able to steal a handful of dates, and eat them, greedily sucking the last bits of flavor from the pits.

I've committed my first crime. I'm a criminal. Well, well, well . . .

The next day, Bruce got himself hired by a tramp steamer and in the following months saw a lot of Africa and some of Asia. He jumped ship in Marrakesh, slept under a bridge for a couple of nights, and signed onto a tanker bound for the United Kingdom.

He hung around London long enough to learn something about stealing cars from the ship's cook, then shipped out on a freighter and found himself in Shanghai. One of the deckhands from his last ship had a way to make some quick, easy money, and Bruce was interested. This was yet another opportunity to do what he had been trying to do for months, to understand the kind of human being who had deprived him of all he cherished—the Joe Chill kind. He went with the man, whom he had nicknamed "Stocky," and together they traveled by taxi to an airport terminal at the edge of the city. There, they sat on a bench across the street and watched laborers fill a truck with crates. That night, Bruce felt fear, the fear of one preparing to commit a crime, and perversely, he was exhilarated by it.

Stocky and Bruce hijacked the truck: no problem, the driver was not about to be a hero. After the job was done and they were speeding down a dark road,

Stocky driving, Bruce suddenly began to laugh. Soon he was laughing and gasping and pounding the dashboard and Stocky, who was behind the wheel, began laughing, too.

"We *did* it," Bruce said in English, then repeated himself in Mandarin.

Stocky drove into a warehouse near the docks. The two men climbed down from the truck's cab, still laughing.

In Mandarin, Bruce asked Stocky, "Where is your friend? The man who is supposed to meet us?"

"Not a friend," Stocky replied. "The friend of a friend."

Something in Stocky's tone of voice, in his body language . . . Bruce knew he was being lied to and began looking for an exit. He was considering a run at a side door when it slammed open and at almost the same second every other door in the warehouse opened and uniformed policemen with guns and truncheons ran through them, shouting in Mandarin. The policemen surrounded Bruce and several other men who had been in the warehouse when he arrived, pointed guns at them, handcuffed them, and shoved them down to sitting positions on the floor. Stocky had vanished. Obviously, he had made a deal of some kind, traded Bruce for his own freedom. The policemen began unloading the truck and stacking the crates near where Bruce sat.

One of the policemen, a young man with cold eyes, asked Bruce his name in English.

Bruce considered telling him and decided against it.

He did not want to tarnish his family's reputation, but more important, he did not want anyone in Gotham hearing about what happened and sending help. Whatever Bruce was doing—and he still was not sure what it was—he knew he had to do it alone.

"I would rather not tell you," Bruce said in Mandarin.

"Fool, what do I care what your name is? You are a criminal."

"I am not a criminal."

"Tell that to the guy who owned these," the policeman said, kicking a crate bearing a Wayne Enterprises logo.

Bruce expected a formal internment procedure: a reading of his rights, an appearance before a judge, perhaps even a phone call. Because he continued to refuse to give the policemen his name, he got none of that. Instead, he was put into a cell with four other men. After a few days behind bars, someone got him released. He never learned the identity of his benefactor, but he was met outside the jail by a small Asian man wearing a Brooks Brothers suit and a diamond ring on his right index finger who asked him if he might be interested in some work in Bhutan. It seemed to be a given that the work would be illegal.

Why not? I'm already a criminal . . .

He was taken to a small airstrip in a rural area and put on a World War Two vintage aircraft, a refitted old DC 6, with smoking engines and no passenger amenities, and flown over the Himalayas to a similar airstrip in southwestern China. He never learned what he was supposed to do there because a company of soldiers armed with automatic weapons erupted from the surrounding woods as soon as the plane's engines had stopped and placed Bruce and the two pilots under arrest. Obviously, another deal had been made, somewhere, by someone, with Bruce as a bargaining chip.

As in Shanghai, Bruce refused to give the authorities his name. He was taken to a prison near some farmland and told he would remain there until he cooperated.

Was this the time to reveal his identity? To summon Alfred or a Wayne Enterprises lawyer and go home? No. He still didn't know whatever it was he had to learn. He had a hunch, though, that his next lessons would be painful.

The first night, in the mess hall, as Bruce was carrying a metal bowl of gruel to a table, one of the inmates stuck out a foot and tripped him. Bruce broke his fall with his left hand and the bowl skittered across the floor. The man who had tripped Bruce drew back a foot to kick. Bruce grabbed the man's other leg and yanked and as the man was falling Bruce threw an awkward punch and caught the man under the chin. The man's head snapped back and struck a chair and he lay still. Bruce got up and looked around: the guards, who had not moved from their places along the wall, were grinning. Apparently they enjoyed a good fight.

Bruce waited, without supper, until he was returned to his cell. He slept fitfully that night.

He awoke to find his cellmate, a man who looked

to be at least eighty and was almost as skinny as the child Bruce had shared his plum with in Africa, staring at him. Already, the corridors of the prison rang with shouts and the occasional scream.

The next incident happened during the afternoon recreation break in the yard. The day was bleak. A cold drizzle was falling, turning the tan dust on the ground to a dark brown mud. Bruce was walking toward the cover of a tower when someone grabbed him from behind in a choke hold. Bruce drove his elbow into his attacker's ribs, twice, and reached back, grabbed the man's hair, pulled forward, and then got his shoulder under the attacker's chest and heaved. The attacker, a young man whose skin was mottled and flaking, fell into the mud.

Bruce continued to the tower and hunkered down, scanning the yard, aware that he was being stared at. *This is bad,* he realized. Life had been hard on the ship and he had acquired a few scars, but none of the crewmen had actually wanted to kill him. They tormented him because they were bored, and sometimes drunk, and they did not know how else to amuse themselves. But here, these men . . . they were full of hate and rage and he was a stranger, not of their kind, and so he was their natural enemy, and enemies died.

FROM THE JOURNALS OF RÃ'S AL GHŪL

A young man from the United States has come to my attention. He is of wealthy parentage but seems to have retained a modicum of character despite a privileged upbringing. At this time he is in a Chinese prison. I can change that quite easily, as the warden of the prison has long been a paid ally of ours. It may be that I will investigate this Bruce Wayne further, although he will undoubtedly prove to be as disappointing as his many predecessors.

Bruce and his ancient cellmate were in the mess hall, waiting to have gruel plopped into their bowls.

"They are going to fight you," the old man said.

"Again?"

"Until they kill you."

The cook dumped a ladle full of gruel into Bruce's bowl. "Can't they kill me *before* breakfast?"

Bruce moved toward a table. He stopped. His way was blocked by an enormous man with dozens of knife scars on his face and arms. Five other prisoners stood behind him. None seemed friendly.

The scarred man spoke English in an accent Bruce could not identify. "You are in hell."

He punched Bruce in the face and Bruce fell.

"I am the devil," the scarred man said.

Bruce got to his feet and smiled as he brushed dust from his shirt. "You're not the devil—you're practice."

The scarred man swung. Bruce caught the fist, kicked the man's knee, and as the man fell, Bruce kneed his face.

The scarred man's five companions all charged at once—a mistake, because they got in each other's way.

Bruce fought, using everything he had learned on the ship, everything he had seen in back-alley brawls, and some things he did not know he knew.

Then the familiar sound of two boards being slapped together instantly chilled Bruce. He had heard its like before, outside an opera house, and immediately Bruce's attackers stood back and dropped their fists to their sides. A guard holding a pistol stepped in front of Bruce. Two other guards grabbed Bruce's arms.

"Solitary," the guard with the gun barked.

Bruce made a show of being indignant. "Why?"

"For protection."

"I don't need protection."

"Protection for *them*."

The guards dragged Bruce from the mess hall and down a steep flight of stone steps. They flung him through a door and slammed it shut. Bruce could see very little of where he was. The only light was from a small gap high in the wall that cast a crack of sunlight onto the dirt floor. The air was dank and stank of human waste. Bruce tasted blood and touched a split on his lower lip.

"Are you so desperate to fight criminals that you lock yourself in to take them on one at a time?"

The voice had come from the shadows—a richly civilized voice, deep and mellifluous.

"Actually, there were seven of them," Bruce said.

The source of the voice stepped into the light. He was tall, powerfully built, wearing an impeccably tailored gray suit.

"I counted *six*, Mr. Wayne."

"How do you know my name?"

"The world is too small for someone like Bruce Wayne to disappear"—the newcomer swept his arm in a semicircle—"no matter how deep he chooses to sink."

"Who are you?"

"My name is Henri Ducard. But I speak for Rā's al Ghūl. A man greatly feared by the criminal underworld. A man who can offer you a path."

"What makes you think I need a path?"

"Someone like you is only here by choice. You've been exploring the criminal fraternity . . . But whatever your original intentions—you've become truly lost."

Bruce moved closer to the stranger, this Ducard, and examined his face: prominent bones, a prominent nose and chin—a strong, highly resolute face. "What path does Rā's al Ghūl offer?"

"The path of one who shares his hatred of evil and wishes to serve true justice. The path of the League of Shadows."

Bruce turned his back on Ducard and snapped, "Vigilantes."

"A vigilante is just a man lost in the scramble for his own gratification. He can be destroyed or locked up." Again, Ducard swept his arm to indicate the cell around them. "But if you make yourself more than a man . . . if you devote yourself to an ideal . . . if they can't stop you . . . then you become something else entirely."

"Which is?"

Ducard strode to the door. "A legend, Mr. Wayne."

The door swung open and a guard moved aside to let Ducard pass.

"Tomorrow you'll be released," Ducard said. "If you're bored of brawling with thieves and want to achieve something, there's a rare flower—a blue poppy—that grows on the eastern slopes. Pick one of these flowers. If you can carry it to the top of the mountain, you may find what you were looking for in the first place."

"And what was I looking for?"

"Only you can know that."

The door slammed shut behind Ducard. Bruce pushed against it: locked. He lay down on the dirt and stared up at the sliver of light until sometime, many hours later, he slept. He dreamed of bats exploding from a crevice and tearing at him . . .

5

Before dawn the following morning, Bruce was escorted from his cell, given a breakfast of gruel and a chunk of stale bread. A guard handed Bruce a canvas jacket with frayed sleeves and took him to where a rusty army truck was waiting, its ancient engine coughing and sputtering. Bruce climbed into the back of the truck, which left the prison grounds and bumped along a rutted road for an hour. The sun was bright in the eastern sky when the truck screeched to a halt. An Asian man in military fatigues came to the tailgate of the truck and barked at Bruce in a language he did not understand. In the next instant it became clear as he was thrown from the truck. As he picked himself up he watched it speed away.

Bruce shivered; it was snowing and incredibly windy and cold. He pulled the jacket's collar tighter around his neck and scanned his environment. There was a glacier far off in the distance, and Bruce set off in its direction. He walked for a very long time, and eventually he found himself in the foothills of the Himalayas, at the edge of a field of exquisite blue poppies. He stooped and picked one, studied it, and put it in his breast pocket. He trudged to the foot of the nearest slope and began the hike upward.

The sun was almost directly above, and the snow and wind had increased in pitch by the time he topped a steep, twisting trail and saw a cluster of huts a few hundred yards away. He hurried toward them; he had been climbing for hours in thin, frigid air. He needed food, rest, warmth. He saw two men and a woman near one of the huts and waved to them. They scurried into the hut. He ran toward them, yelling. All the doors were closed. He pounded on one with his fist. No answer.

Maybe the flower is some sort of signal . . .

He took the poppy from his pocket and held it high over his head.

"No one will help you."

Bruce turned: a young child, a boy around eight years old, had spoken in English and was pointing to the flower.

"I need food," Bruce said.

An old man came around the corner of the closest hut, stood beside the child, and said, also in English, "Then turn back."

Bruce waited for the old man to say more. When he did not, Bruce continued up the mountain.

At about midafternoon, by Bruce's estimate, clouds had completely covered the sun and the mountainside was colder and windier. The upward slope had grown steeper and snow hit him constantly. Bruce was panting as he climbed to the top of an icy ridge. The rest of the mountain was covered in clouds, snow, and mist. Bruce clamped his teeth together to stop their chattering, but he could not control the shivers that racked his body. Wind howled down the slope, driving gusts of snow into Bruce's face and eyes. He blinked, wiped his face on his sleeve, and struggled on.

At the next level clearing, Bruce flopped down into the snow. The sky was almost dark and the wind felt like a razor slicing his face but he did nothing to shield himself. He was completely exhausted. He could go no farther.

This is where it ends . . .

Something was visible through the snow, the silhouette of . . . what? A building? Bruce rolled to his hands and knees and tried to stand. He could not; his legs refused to stay straight.

Bruce crawled across a stone patio, making furrows in the snow behind him, and up a small flight of wide steps to a tall wooden door. He struck the wood with his fist feebly. He struck again, harder, and again, harder still. There was a creaking and a grinding sound, and the door scraped open.

Bruce pulled himself inside and, leaning against a wall, got to his feet. He was in a huge, vaulted hall lit by torches set into iron brackets on the stone floor, forming pools of flickering firelight that melted into surrounding shadows. There were thick, supporting pillars every few yards.

The door creaked and scraped and thudded shut.

Bruce squinted, adjusting his sight to the semidarkness. At the far end of the hall, at least half a city block away, there was a raised platform. On it sat a robed figure, a man whose features, in the dim glow of the torches, seemed vaguely Asian, but only vaguely.

Despite the subzero temperature outside, the long chamber was warm and humid. Bruce felt his body recovering from its ordeal as it warmed. He unbuttoned his jacket and shuffled forward.

"Rā's al Ghūl?" he called.

A dozen men emerged from the shadows behind the torches. Their clothing was a mix of ethnic dress and modern combat garb. As they moved toward Bruce, they brandished daggers and short swords.

"Wait!" someone commanded. The armed men stopped and became as still as stone.

Ducard stepped around a pillar. Bruce reached into his breast pocket and pulled out the blue poppy. He held it out, his hand shaking.

Rā's al Ghūl spoke in what Bruce thought was Urdu. Ducard translated: "What are you seeking?"

Bruce's lips were numb and he found it difficult to answer. "I . . . I seek . . . the means to fight injustice. To turn fear against those who prey on the fearful."

Ducard moved to stand in front of Bruce, and took the flower.

Rā's al Ghūl spoke again, and again Ducard translated: "To manipulate the fears of others you must first master your own." Ducard placed the poppy in a buttonhole and asked Bruce, "Are you ready to begin?"

Bruce felt himself trembling with fatigue. "I . . . I can barely . . ."

Ducard kicked him and Bruce fell to the floor.

Fists on hips, Ducard looked down at him and said, "Death does not wait for you to be ready."

Gasping, Bruce struggled to his feet and Ducard punched him in the ribs. Bruce staggered backward.

"Death is not considerate, or fair," Ducard said. "And make no mistake—here, you face death."

Ducard pivoted 340 degrees and aimed a kick at Bruce's neck. But Bruce raised his right forearm and blocked Ducard's foot. Ducard smiled.

Bruce put his left leg forward and shifted his weight onto his left, and put his flattened, crossed hands at chest height: a martial arts stance he had learned aboard ship. He forced himself to remember everything else he had learned on the ship, and in all the dark alleys and filthy bars where he had fought, and won, and been defeated. Ducard attacked and Bruce responded: punches, kicks, blocks, jabs, chops—a smooth flurry of continual motion.

Ducard said, "You are remarkably skilled. But this is not a dance."

Ducard smashed the top of his head into Bruce's face and immediately kneed him in the groin, driving his flat palm up into Bruce's chin. Bruce fell backward and tried to rise, but could not.

Ducard crouched over Bruce. "And you are afraid. But I sense that you do not fear *me*." Ducard pulled the blue poppy from his buttonhole and dropped it onto Bruce's chest. He put his lips close to Bruce's ear. "Tell us, Wayne . . . what *do* you fear?"

And Bruce remembered: *screeching bats exploding from the crevice and tearing at him . . .*

FROM THE JOURNALS OF RÃ'S AL GHÛL

I feel like Michelangelo must have felt when he found the block of marble that became his *David*. Thus far, Bruce Wayne has not disappointed me. He may be the raw material of my masterpiece. Evolution has been kind to him. He is of huge mental capacity with an intelligence quotient I believe to be among the highest ever recorded and an eidetic memory. Everything that he sees or hears he can recall with total accuracy and he is able to absorb new information of any kind with speed. He is also a splendid physical specimen with what appears to be an optimum balance between fast and slow muscle fibers, a large lung capacity, unimpeded circulation of blood, a responsive nervous system, and excellent proportions, so much so that the artists of ancient Greece might well have used him as a model for the statues of idealized humans they were fond of creating. Bruce Wayne is still ignorant and cannot access all that nature has given him, but those are conditions that I can remedy.

6

The following morning, Ducard and Bruce, now wearing cold-weather gear, stood on the balcony of the monastery. The sun glared on a vast sheet of ice, a glacier that lay below them. Bruce had just finished telling Ducard the details of his parents' deaths. He was silent for perhaps ten minutes, enjoying the cold, clear air flowing into his body, and the sight of the hard blue sky above them.

Ducard broke the silence by asking Bruce a question. "Do you still feel responsible for your parents' deaths?"

"My anger outweighs my guilt," Bruce replied.

Ducard nodded, seemingly satisfied with the answer. He led Bruce into the monastery's main chamber, where Bruce had first entered the building. Groups of warriors, perhaps fifty men in all, were training: sparring, shadow boxing, leaping, and kicking. Ducard and Bruce walked to one of the pillars, where a ninja was hanging upside down. Ducard motioned the man to come down and when he did, Ducard showed Bruce the secret of the feat: spikes spaced along a gauntlet that the ninja had driven into the pillar.

"The ninja is thought to be invisible," Ducard explained. "But invisibility is largely a matter of patience."

Bruce and Ducard climbed a short flight of steps to a mezzanine full of stacked boxes and bottles. Several ninjas were pouring powders into packets, obviously making compounds. Bruce knew that the ninja's art had originated in Japan, but these ninjas were a mixed lot: Asians, East Indians, some Caucasians.

Ducard took a pinch of gray powder from an open box and threw it down. There was a flash of light and a loud *bang*. Bruce flinched and Ducard smiled.

"Ninjitsu employ explosives," Ducard said.

"As weapons?"

"Or distractions. Theatricality and deception are powerful agents. You must become *more* than just a man in the mind of your opponent."

Bruce took some powder from the box and, with a snap of his wrist, dashed it on the floor. This time Bruce did not flinch at the flash and the noise.

After a lunch of rice and vegetables, Ducard gave Bruce a straight-bladed Chinese sword and a pair of gauntlets similar to those the ninja had worn.

Ducard equipped himself identically and led Bruce down the steep, snowy path to the glacier.

"You're training me to fight with a blade?" Bruce asked. "Why not a gun?"

"The man who killed your parents—he used a firearm?"

"Yes."

"Was he a great warrior? Was he even an efficient killer?"

"No, he was a thug, but—"

"The weapon is nothing, the man who wields it everything. Guns are crude and impersonal and a blade is not. With a blade, you do more than learn combat. You develop character."

Ducard unsheathed his sword, held it in front of himself, and said, "I suppose 'en garde' would be appropriate here."

Bruce and Ducard circled each other. Suddenly Ducard's blade flashed forward, aimed at Bruce's chest. Bruce deflected the blow with his gauntlet-sheathed arm. Ducard glided to his left, frozen breath streaming from his nostrils. Bruce, sliding to his right to again face Ducard, heard the ice beneath him creak and shift. And the muted gurgle of running water.

"Mind your surroundings, always," Ducard said.

They fenced. Bruce thrust and Ducard parried, Bruce thrust again and Ducard turned aside the point of Bruce's blade with his own. Their faces were inches apart; Bruce could feel the heat of Ducard's breath on his cheek.

"Your parents' deaths were not your fault," Ducard said conversationally. "It was your father's."

This remark consumed Bruce with rage. He abandoned all pretense of skill and swung his sword. Ducard caught Bruce's blade in the scallops of his gauntlet and rotated his arm, wrenching Bruce's sword from his grasp. The sword skidded across the ice.

"Anger will not change the fact that your father

failed to act," Ducard continued, as though he was discussing the weather.

"The man had a gun," Bruce blurted.

"Would that stop *you*?"

"I've had training—"

"The training is nothing. The will is everything. The will to act."

Ducard slashed downward at Bruce, who blocked the strike with his crossed, gauntleted forearms. Then Bruce dropped and dove between Ducard's legs, sliding to where his sword had stopped its skid. He grabbed it and pivoted, his legs sweeping toward Ducard's lower body. Ducard jumped straight up and Bruce grabbed Ducard's left foot and yanked. Ducard fell onto his back as Bruce scrambled to his feet and aimed his sword at Ducard's bare throat. The point stopped only inches from Ducard's flesh. Ducard lay still, his arms at his sides.

"Yield," Bruce commanded.

"You haven't beaten me," Ducard replied. "You've sacrificed sure footing for a killing stroke."

Ducard tapped the ice beneath Bruce's feet with the flat of his sword. There was a loud *crack* and the ice tilted and splintered and Bruce plunged into the freezing water.

Ducard watched Bruce flounder for almost a full minute, then reached down to help him up and out.

Later that evening, next to a blazing campfire near the glacier, Bruce shed his jacket and shirt and rubbed his arms, trying to control the violence of his shivering.

"Rub your chest," Ducard told him. "Your arms will take care of themselves."

Bruce began to rub his torso.

"You're stronger than your father," Ducard said.

"You didn't know my father."

"But I know the rage that drives you . . . that impossible anger strangling your grief until your loved ones' memory is just poison in your veins. And one day you wish the person you loved had never existed so you'd be spared the pain."

Bruce stopped what he was doing and looked at Ducard as though he had just found something amazing.

"I wasn't always here in the mountains," Ducard continued. "Once, I had a wife. My great love. She was taken from me. Like you, I was forced to learn that there are those without decency, who must be fought without pity or hesitation. Your anger gives you great power, but if you let it, it will destroy you. As it almost did me."

Bruce took his shirt from where it had been drying near the fire and slipped it on. "What stopped it?"

"Vengeance."

"That's no help to me."

"Why not?"

FROM THE JOURNALS OF RĀ'S AL GHŪL

I now know what my weapon must be. Men commit folly after folly because they are afraid. Fear was once mankind's most powerful ally, giving enormous potency to the instinct for survival. Now, fear has become mankind's greatest enemy, and such is the obtuseness of my race that its members do not realize it is the most powerful element of human existence. It is what drives them to embrace leaders who offer nothing more than false promises of security and doctrines that assure them that they are exempt from the inevitable consequences of being born, and to destroy the earth with insane consumption that does nothing more than distract them from their own mortality. They venerate charlatans and deny what is necessary to their own well-being because they are afraid. The situation is exacerbated by one of evolution's cruelest jokes, the capability to deny to themselves what they are doing even as they are doing it.

I have long taught my followers that to overcome fear they must first face it. As the American psychologist Rogers observed, one cannot change until one has accepted oneself fully. Long ago I learned that embrace of any dread that dwells within is necessary to fulfill one's potential. I have also instructed my minions in manipulating an enemy's fear, in the use of fear as a tactical weapon. I am woefully late in realizing that fear can also be a strategic weapon and I can base my whole campaign upon it.

Fear is my weapon. I shall use fear.

7

Bruce was aware that the months of brute labor on ancient ships had physically changed him, coarsened his rich boy's palms and thickened the muscles of his arms, chest, thighs. He had thought that by the time he was locked in the Chinese prison, the change was complete. But at Rā's al Ghūl's monastery, he realized that his months at sea had only begun his transformation. He learned a different kind of power, one that came from the knowledge and efficient use of his body's parts, not just raw, untutored strength. His mind, too, was altering. He was coming to depend on a relaxed alertness rather than reasoned thought, which was sometimes slow and not always reliable.

His training, of both mind and body, was of a kind he could not have imagined possible, and he reveled in it. He slept, with a dozen others, on a thin futon placed on the floor of a chamber below the monastery's main hall; he knew that there were other sleeping chambers both inside the monastery and in outbuildings.

The monastery itself was divided into three tiers.

The bottom, where Bruce slept, was barracks-style living quarters, food storage facilities, a kitchen, and a dining area consisting of several long, uncovered tables with backless benches along either side. The ground floor was almost completely occupied by the huge main hall, where Bruce had first entered, and included Rā's al Ghūl's throne, which was seldom in use. At its rear were two locked doors—a storage area of some kind, Bruce guessed. Once, he spotted a line of workers carrying crates that bore red warning signs in four languages into one of the forbidden chambers: explosives. Bruce wondered what use they might possibly be put to.

The top floor of the monastery was, on three sides, a mezzanine, with exits to the balcony that overlooked the glacier. The fourth side was another forbidden area: the living quarters of Rā's al Ghūl and Ducard. There were several outbuildings that, Bruce concluded, were for storage.

Almost every day Bruce arose before dawn, wakened by the striking of a gong—*almost,* because sometimes he and his mates were not roused until the sun was high above the neighboring peaks. No explanation for the delay was ever given. After an hour's running along the ridge on which the buildings stood, often through dense snow and icy winds, he ate the first of two daily meals, usually vegetables and rice, or a grain Bruce could not identify. To drink, there was a small cup of tea.

At irregular intervals, the morning run was canceled and Bruce and his mates picked their way down the trail to the hamlet Bruce had passed through on his way to the monastery. There, they found stacks of boxes and sacks: supplies. They each lifted something and, sliding and stumbling, struggled back up the mountain. Once, Bruce saw the little boy he had spoken to, peeking around the corner of a hut. At other times, during the warmer summer months, he and his mates were put to work in vegetable gardens near the hamlet.

"It is important that you feel a connection to what sustains you," Ducard once explained.

The regimen was not unlike what he knew of how religious communities and, for that matter, military boot camps operated. After breakfast, the group disbanded and each of the trainees did something unique to himself. In Bruce's case, this was what he later realized were exercises and techniques designed to increase his flexibility and litheness. He did yoga stretches and trained on gymnast's gear: rings, rails, parallel bars, and vaulting horses. Gradually, his bulky muscles grew smaller and sleeker and he was able to stretch and bend and twist his limbs in ways he would have once considered impossible, if not freakish.

Then, for several months, he did very little that was physically demanding. Ducard would give him puzzles, or using cards, flash a random series of numbers and shapes in front of his eyes and demand he reproduce them on paper. Or ask him to work arithmetic problems mentally. Or have him sit in certain positions for hours, or just stand alone in a dark room or on the glacier. He was told that he was in the process of learning what he already knew and that this was not a conundrum, just a simple fact—one of the few times any explanation of any kind was offered.

When Bruce resumed his physical training, he was swifter and stronger than ever.

FROM THE JOURNALS OF RĀ'S AL GHŪL

Bruce Wayne apparently thinks that his training here is akin to the training he would receive at a military or religious installation. Such is his intelligence that he will surely come to realize that what most military and religious leaders do is to minimize individuality and maximize sameness in their charges. Indeed, that is what we do with most of those we recruit so their actions and effectiveness become both optimal and predictable.

However, for centuries the League of Shadows has known that one must deal with extraordinarily gifted individuals differently. We seek to plumb their depths and discover all the strength within them, both physical and mental. We next devise a plan to allow them to access and increase their innate powers. Most of their weaknesses we ignore, for if they are as intelligent as we know they are, they will compensate for most of their weaknesses with no help from without. Fear is always the great exception to this. Fear is usually the last enemy a man conquers and to do so he must be forced to do whatever is necessary. It is unfortunate that most men fail this ultimate test.

At noon each day, Bruce joined his fellow trainees for the day's second and final meal, usually identical to what they had had for breakfast, but occasionally spiced with a sliver of fish or smoked meat. There was no tea at this second meal, just water from the glacier. Bruce had eaten in the world's premier restaurants with his parents, both at home and in Europe and Asia during family vacations, had dined on the finest efforts of the finest chefs, and had never enjoyed any food so much as Rā's al Ghūl's starkly simple fare. Not because of the food itself, though it was inevitably fresh and well prepared, but because he was learning to really taste what went into his mouth.

After lunch, more exercises. At dusk, another run outside and then, as the sun was vanishing below the mountains and long shadows spread across the glacier, to bed.

Bruce was always asleep within seconds of touching the futon. If he had dreams, he did not remember them.

He sensed that nothing was done randomly—that every activity, however inconsequential, was part of a carefully planned curriculum.

He had been in the monastery for months before he was taught actual combat. His tutors were not kind. On the contrary. Ducard and the ninjas who taught Bruce were unrelentingly critical and showed absolutely no tolerance of blunders. And blunder he did. He often felt as though he were wearing cardboard boxes for shoes and concrete gloves. He had imagined himself well versed in martial arts from his shipboard ordeals and the adventures he had had in ports of call, and in fact, after the first humiliating months, he had won most of his fights. But against the opponents he faced in the monastery, he was clumsy, oafish, more clown than combatant.

But he learned. And he did not make the same mistake twice.

For a long period, he was physically challenged to his utmost, forced to defend himself until his breath exploded from his lungs and he could feel the adrenaline coursing through his veins and sweat coating his entire body. Then, abruptly, Ducard would stop the combat and have Bruce do breathing and visualization exercises. And then he would again be attacked. Eventually, Bruce decided that the purpose of this drill was to teach him to be as calm during combat as he was afterward—to train him never to allow body chemistry to impair his judgment. Ducard, as usual, neither confirmed nor denied Bruce's conclusion.

FROM THE JOURNALS OF RĀ'S AL GHŪL

Many years past I thought I had lost my capacity for amazement at about the same time that I lost my capacity for affection. I was mistaken. Bruce Wayne amazes me every day. He has already developed far beyond any student I have ever had and there seems to be no limit to his potential.

I have begun to have thoughts that disturb me because they fill me with what I fear is a false hope. They concern my daughter Talia and Bruce Wayne. Talia is of an age to reproduce and carry my lineage forward into the new world I shall create. No man I have ever met until now has been worthy of mingling his genes with mine nor worthy of the company of my daughter. Bruce Wayne may be an exception to this unhappy rule.

If I have a son of my own I will not need Bruce Wayne and Talia may then devote herself entirely to my comfort and convenience. But none of my consorts have given me the male offspring I desire. A noble son-in-law may in the long run prove to be as satisfactory as a noble son.

Bruce Wayne may yet prove unworthy of the beneficence I contemplate bestowing upon him. There is yet ahead of him the ultimate test that he like the others will surely fail. If he does not fail it I will summon Talia.

Bruce seldom saw Rā's al Ghūl and wondered if their mysterious host even lived at the monastery. Sometimes, though, Rā's appeared on his raised platform, or on the balcony overlooking the glacier, and watched, erect and motionless, his hands hidden in his sleeves. He never spoke, nor made any kind of sound at all, but his presence was always palpable. Rā's was on the platform the morning Bruce, bare-chested and wearing shorts, was fighting with a bald Japanese man of his own size and build. Someone shouted his name and for perhaps a half second Bruce was distracted. Could he have been called by Rā's himself? No, the voice had been Ducard's. His opponent struck twice, to the chest and jaw, and Bruce dropped.

When Bruce fully regained his senses, Rā's was gone.

Ducard stepped forward and looked down at Bruce with disgust. "Childish, Wayne."

"Resume!" Ducard ordered, motioning to the Japanese man who had knocked Bruce down, and a few seconds later, Bruce was punching, blocking, kicking, ignoring everything except the opponent in front of him.

So intent was he on his training, so involved in the tasks Ducard set for him, that Bruce all but forgot that months were passing, that the color of the sky and the angle at which the sun hit the glacier changed and the air both inside and outside the monastery was warmer, then colder.

Later, he reckoned that he had been at the monastery just under a year and that, after the initial period of adjustment, he was happy in the rambling building above the glacier. He forgot his old life, in Gotham and on campuses and the jet-set watering holes of the world and, eventually, his memory of his parents also dimmed. What was the color of his father's hair? Of his mother's eyes? How did they sound in the morning? At bedtime? He could summon the memories by force—he had learned that he could summon *any* memory by force—but they did not come unbidden into his dreams now. But the sight of them sprawled in the street amid bloody pearls—that did not diminish, nor did the hot bite of hate that inevitably accompanied it.

He never learned the names of his fellow trainees, and there had been hundreds of them. Ducard had made it known that any unnecessary fraternization would be severely punished and no one doubted him. But Bruce felt close to these anonymous men of varied nationalities, closer than he had ever felt to anyone except his mother and father and Alfred. They may have been nameless, but they were pieces of something of which he, too, was a part and that gave him a commonality with them that often felt like affection.

None of them stayed for long. A new group seemed to arrive every few weeks or so, receive instruction, and leave. Only Bruce remained, although his skills were plainly superior to those of everyone except Ducard. He would ask, "Does Rā's al Ghūl have something special in mind for me?" and Ducard would turn away, refusing to answer.

Eventually, he stopped asking.

Ducard remained aloof, always the savagely forthright instructor, never the friendly mentor, but a bond grew between him and Bruce regardless. Bruce could not have given it a label, or even described it. In neither his personal experience nor his reading had he encountered anything like it. But he knew it was there, as he knew he had blood in his veins.

Was it possible to love a man who did little more than brutalize one? Was Bruce Wayne, this pampered child of privilege, suffering from some form of the Stockholm syndrome, becoming emotionally attached to his enemy? He had questions he could not possibly answer, at least not yet, not here. He did not forget them, but he did not worry about them, either.

There was a scream from the far end of the monastery. Bruce saw two warriors dragging the man who had screamed toward an iron cage.

"Who is he?" Bruce asked, getting to his feet.

"He was a farmer. Then he tried to take his neighbor's land and became a murderer. Now he's a prisoner."

The portly farmer was locked in the cage and the cage was winched ten feet off the floor.

"What will happen to him?" Bruce asked.

"Justice. Crime cannot be tolerated. Criminals thrive on the indulgence of society's 'understanding.' You know this."

Bruce nodded, staring at the man in the cage.

"Or when you lived among the criminals . . . did you make the same mistake as your father?" Ducard asked. "Did you start to pity them?"

Bruce remembered the feeling of a hollow belly and a wide-eyed child in an alley and the taste of a ripe plum.

He said, "The first time you steal so that you don't starve, you lose many assumptions about the simple nature of right and wrong."

FROM THE JOURNALS OF RĀ'S AL GHŪL

The agony of suspense I have endured this past year will end within twenty-four hours. Though he himself has no inkling of it, Bruce Wayne will face his final trials very soon. His skill will be tested and also his courage and his resolve. We will learn if fear still dwells within him and how he has confronted it if it does. We will finally come to know if he has what weak men call ruthlessness. For if the world is to be saved it will be saved by those willing to do all that may be necessary. There will be a time for weeping and lamenting and even regret that draconian measures were needed, but that time will be later when we have accomplished our tasks and can afford the luxury of the weaker emotions.

I actually have little doubt that the blood of Bruce Wayne will leak onto the floorboards of the monastery and we will use fire to dispose of his remains. He will die as his dozens of predecessors have died and in dying prove himself to be at last unworthy.

If he continues to breathe two days from now I will allow myself to rejoice and I will summon Talia to return from Switzerland.

It would be good to see my daughter once more.

That night, as Bruce lay down on his futon, Ducard, clad in a ninja uniform, a short sword slung across his back, came to the doorway and spoke his name.

Bruce rose, dressed, and followed Ducard across a moonlit courtyard to the throne room. Inside, they went to a workbench set against a wall, and Ducard said, "You traveled the world to understand the criminal mind and conquer your fear."

Ducard took from his pocket a dried flower, the shriveled blue poppy Bruce had long ago carried to the monastery. Ducard put it in a stone mortar and used a stone pestle to grind it to dust. "But a criminal isn't complicated," he said. "And what you really fear is inside yourself. You fear your own power. Your own anger. The drive to do great or terrible things . . . You must journey inward."

Ducard poured the dust into a small brazier, struck a long wooden match, and set it aflame. A thin column of smoke rose, twisted, curled. Ducard motioned Bruce closer. "Drink in your fears. Face them. You are ready."

Bruce understood without further instruction. He inhaled the smoke and shook his head. Time roiled and shifted inside his skull and he saw:

. . . himself falling into the well . . .

. . . screeching bats exploding from the crevice and tearing at him . . .

. . . Father staring down at a red splotch on the snowy white shirt that spread outward from a small, black hole . . .

. . . bloody pearls spilling past Bruce's face and clattering lightly on the pavement . . .

Bruce shook his head violently and blinked his eyes. *So real, the visions are so real . . .*

Ducard tugged a ninja mask over his head. He pulled a second mask from under his jacket and handed it to Bruce.

"To conquer fear you must become fear," he said as Bruce put on the mask. "You must bask in the fear of other men . . . and men fear most what they cannot see."

Ducard raised a hand and a dozen ninjas congealed from the shadows: not the trainees Bruce had come to know by sight, if not by name—no, although these warriors were completely covered by their uniforms and masks, Bruce somehow knew they were fully trained, and he had no doubt that they were ruthless.

"It is not enough to be a man," Ducard said. "You have to become an idea . . . a terrible thought . . . a *wraith*—"

Suddenly Ducard drew his sword and slashed at Bruce's throat—a strike that would have decapitated Bruce if it had connected.

It did not: Bruce had spun out of its path.

The ninjas closed on Bruce, surrounding him. Then they parted to reveal a long, wide, flat wooden box: a coffin for a giant? Bruce gazed at it, still disoriented from the smoke he had inhaled.

From the darkness, Ducard spoke: "Embrace your worst fear . . ."

Cautiously, Bruce approached the box, lifted the lid, and peered inside. For a moment, he heard the flapping of leathery wings—

And the scene that was still echoing in his memory became real: screeching bats tearing at him . . .

Bruce dove away from the box, rolled, staring at the bats, blinking and flinching . . .

"Become one with the darkness," Ducard said from some great distance.

The ninjas attacked.

Bruce should have been terrified. These men were killers and all had survived the ordeals that had been visited on Bruce and they outnumbered him at least twelve to one. They were armed, and his only weapon was his body. They were alert and he was still groggy from the smoke.

He should have been terrified, and immediately killed, and if he had taken even a second to think about his situation, he would have been. But he did not. No, he merely did as, without knowing it, he had been learning to do all these years. He became fully in the moment and let a wisdom deeper and vastly quicker than thought guide his movements.

A ninja jabbed. Bruce pivoted and kicked the man's arm, and as the sword flew from the man's grasp Bruce sent a palm strike to the man's chin and caught the sword as it fell.

A blade ripped Bruce's sleeve and the skin beneath it. Bruce retaliated by swiping his blade against his attacker's arm and leaping over and behind the box.

In the rafters, bats flapped and screeched.

On the floor, Bruce whirled and leaped, pivoted, thrust, parried, moving as silently as fog among the black-clad assassins.

Ducard leaped forward into the center of the ninjas. He kicked the face of a ninja with a torn sleeve.

The man fell to his knees and Ducard put his sword to the man's throat.

"Your sleeve, Wayne," he said. "Bad mistake. You cannot leave any sign."

From behind Ducard, Bruce said, "I haven't."

The edge of his sword was against Ducard's throat.

Ducard glanced at the ninjas. Five of them had slashed sleeves. He gestured and the ninjas fell back, lowering their weapons.

From across the chamber there came the sound of clapping. Rā's al Ghūl sat on his throne, watching and slapping his long palms together.

"Impressive," Rā's said in English. It was the first time Bruce had heard him in months.

Bruce pulled off his mask and bowed his head in acknowledgment of the compliment.

The ninjas sat. Ducard escorted Bruce to the platform on which Rā's sat and stood beside him. Rā's rose, his robes rustling, and led Bruce and Ducard to a smoking brazier with a branding iron sticking from the glowing coals. Then Rā's began to speak in Urdu.

Ducard translated: "We have purged your fear. You are ready to lead these men. You are ready to become a member of the League of Shadows."

Rā's again struck his palms together, not in applause but command. Two ninjas dragged the portly, frightened prisoner from a doorway and shoved him down next to the brazier. Bruce recognized him immediately: the farmer, the murderer who had been caged.

Rā's pointed a thin, straight finger at the prisoner

and spoke. Ducard translated: "First you must demonstrate your commitment to justice."

Ducard handed Bruce a sword. Bruce looked at the
prisoner, whose eyes were pleading pools of terror.

"No," Bruce said, addressing Rā's. "I am not an
executioner."

Ducard said, "Your compassion is a weakness your
enemies will not share."

"That's why it's so important. It separates me from
them."

"You want to fight criminals. This man is a murderer."

"This man should be tried."

"By whom?" Ducard demanded. "Corrupt bureau-
crats? Criminals mock society's laws. You know this
better than most."

Rā's al Ghūl stepped forward and in thickly ac-
cented English said, "You cannot lead men unless you
are prepared to do what is necessary to defeat evil."

"Where would I be leading these men?" Bruce
asked him.

"Gotham City. As Gotham City's favorite son you
will be ideally placed to strike at the heart of crimi-
nality."

"How?"

"Gotham City's time has come. Like Constanti-
nople or Rome before it—grounds for suffering and
injustice—it is beyond saving and must be allowed to
die . . . This is the most important function of the
League of Shadows. It is one we have performed for
centuries. Gotham City must be destroyed."

Bruce turned to Ducard. "You can't believe this."

"Rā's al Ghūl has rescued us from the darkest corners of our own hearts," Ducard replied. "What he asks in return is the courage to do what is necessary."

Bruce said, "I'll go back to Gotham. And I'll fight men like this. But I won't be an executioner."

Ducard's reply was whispered, almost a plea: "Wayne, for your own sake . . . there is no turning back . . ."

Bruce raised his sword. The prisoner raised his gaze to Bruce and his lips moved soundlessly.

Bruce struck downward, his blade missing the prisoner's neck by inches and hitting the white-hot branding iron, flipping it off the brazier. It arced high into the air and spun into the door of the room where explosives were stored. The door instantly smoldered and tiny tongues of flame appeared where the iron had struck.

"What are you doing?" Ducard shouted.

"What's necessary," Bruce said and hit Ducard's head with the flat of his sword.

Rā's al Ghūl had a Chinese sword in his hands almost instantly. He thrust at Bruce and Bruce deflected the blade with his own. Bruce returned the attack, driving Rā's backward and off the platform.

An explosion shook the hall and flaming debris spouted from the explosives room.

Rā's ignored the fire and noise and renewed his assault. Bruce's eyes stung and he coughed; he could barely see Rā's through the smoke. He was aware of men running past him, scrambling toward the doors.

But he dared not join them: the moment he turned his back, he knew, Rā's would kill him.

For an instant, fear intruded into Bruce's consciousness: *This is Rā's al Ghūl! This is the master! I cannot possibly defeat him!*

But even as this thought flitted across his mind, Bruce knew it was wrong. The man before him was formidable, true, but only highly skilled, not superhuman. Bruce had fought tougher opponents, Ducard among them. Perhaps Rā's had erected a reputation and was hiding behind it. Perhaps it was more illusion than reality.

Then Bruce stopped thinking and again became one with the moment.

He blinked and saw Rā's again charging at him. A second explosion shook the hall and suddenly a slab of roof, fully ablaze, fell onto Rā's, burying him.

I didn't want him to die . . .

The back of the monastery was a holocaust. Bruce ran for the front, jumping over chunks of wood and broken furniture that littered the floor.

Ducard lay directly in his path, between him and the exit. In the flicker of the flames, Bruce could see that Ducard's head was bloody and his hair was partially burned away.

Bruce knelt and shouted Ducard's name: no response. Bruce got his shoulder under Ducard's and hoisted the unconscious man into a fireman's carry. But he could go no farther; a sheet of flame was now between him and safety.

He looked around, trying to see through the dense

smoke. The steps to the mezzanine were still intact. Bruce, with Ducard over his shoulders, ran up them. He went onto the balcony. A third explosion rocked the boards beneath his feet and some of them tore free of their moorings. In a second or two, the balcony would collapse.

There was fire directly below, gushing from the explosives room. If they fell into it, they would be incinerated.

Bruce kicked aside the balcony railing, took two steps back, ran forward, and leaped. His trajectory carried him and Ducard over the flames and down a steep slope covered with ice. They landed with a jolt and Ducard slipped from Bruce's grasp. Both men slid toward a cliff, a four-hundred-foot drop to the glacier below. Bruce's groping hand found a rock and closed around it. His momentum halted. But Ducard's did not; his rotating body was gaining speed.

Bruce released his hold on the rock, pivoted on his stomach, straightened, and hands clasped in front of him, he dove headfirst down the slope. Only inches from the edge of the cliff, Bruce caught Ducard's upper arm. Both of them continued to slide. Bruce raised his gauntlet-clad forearm and smashed the bronze scallops into the ice. He and Ducard stopped, with Ducard's legs dangling over the cliff.

Bruce allowed himself a minute to calm his breathing before digging the scallops on his other arm into the ice, a bit farther up the slope.

This will take a while . . .

Some time later, he dragged Ducard over the lip of

the slope and onto flat ground, slushy from melted ice. Nothing much was left of the monastery, just the stone foundation and a few gaunt, blackened timbers, bits of flame dancing along them, silhouetted against the afternoon sky. Despite the ice, there had been neither rain nor snowfall for weeks. The monastery had been dry as kindling. The snow around the ruin was trampled, some tracks leading to the trail down the mountain, others to the path to the glacier. Bruce wondered if the ninjas had a planned escape route or if they had merely run from the inferno.

Bruce saw no one. He considered going into the remains of the monastery to see if he could find Rā's al Ghūl. But Rā's was surely dead and Ducard might soon be if he did not get help.

He shook Ducard: no response. He hoisted Ducard onto his shoulders and went to the trail leading to the hamlet. Now trembling with exhaustion, Bruce descended it. He arrived as the sun was reddening the eastern peaks. As usual, the tiny settlement seemed to be deserted. He pounded the door of the first hut he came to and it immediately opened. Inside stood the old man Bruce had spoken to on his initial trek up the mountain. Bruce entered and, heeding the old man's gesture, lay Ducard down on some straw mats. The old man wiped blood from Ducard's temple, put his ear to Ducard's chest, felt Ducard's pulse. He nodded. For a moment, Bruce and the old man stood on either side of Ducard, looking at each other. Then Bruce shrugged and went to the door.

"I will tell him you saved his life," the old man said in English.

"Tell him . . . I have an ailing ancestor who needs me." Bruce flattened his palms in front of his chest and bowed his head.

The old man pointed to a stain on Bruce's jacket. "It is blood. Do you wish to clean it?"

"Not necessary."

Bruce left the hut. He looked up at where he had come from and saw wisps of smoke rising against the evening sky, and then down, at the trail to the village and prison. Which way? No choice, really. He started toward the trail. The door to another of the huts opened and the little boy he had seen during his first visit ran out, carrying a bundle wrapped in sackcloth. He handed it to Bruce and, without saying anything or waiting to be thanked, vanished into the hut and closed the door. Bruce unwrapped the bundle enough to see what was inside: a clay bowl full of rice with a chunk of brown bread and two crude chopsticks on top. Lunch. Bruce bowed to the boy's hut and moved down the trail.

The air was chilly, but not cold, as it had been on the mountaintop, and the next morning, bright sun gradually warmed Bruce. When it was directly overhead, he perched on a boulder, opened the bundle, and ate the rice and bread.

The sun was low when he finally reached the trailhead and continued past it on the road the army truck had taken a year earlier to the town—or small city?—near the prison. His plan, such as it was, was to beg for food and money until he had enough for a telephone call to the United States—to Gotham City and Wayne Manor and Alfred. It might take days, but it would probably be faster than finding a berth on a ship bound for America.

But he got lucky. As he was hunkering down at a roadside near the marketplace, now almost deserted as darkness inched over the area, he met an old shipmate, a bosun's mate, who was accompanied by a slender woman whose eyes were downcast and whose whole demeanor was one of extreme shyness.

"Hello, my old shipmate," the bosun yelled in breath laden with rum. "Remember me—Hector. I beat you up plenty."

"I still bear the scars," Bruce answered, grinning and shaking Hector's hand.

"Guess what? I am husband now. How you like that?"

"Congratulations."

Hector said that he and the woman had just gotten married, that very afternoon, mere hours ago, and were celebrating and did his dear old shipmate want for anything, anything at all in this blessed world? In the end, after more hand-shaking and much backpounding, the bosun's mate gave Bruce the money he needed and, with promises that they would get together soon, put his arm around his new wife's shoulders and stumbled toward a nearby inn.

Bruce located a merchant who offered long-distance telephone service and persuaded him to remain open long enough for Bruce to make his call.

There was no answer. Perhaps Alfred was having one of his weekly nights away from the big house. Bruce left a message on the answering machine and, thanking the merchant for his kindness, left to seek a place to sleep.

He finally settled for a culvert. He put a thin layer of dried grass on the rounded bottom and lay on it. He was cold and uncomfortable and seven years ago that would have been a problem. But now, he simply accepted the cold and the discomfort, instead of fighting them, and slept for the five hours he needed.

The next morning, just after sunrise, he walked around, seeking food. He was not discomfortingly hungry, not yet, but he had eaten only the boy's rice and bread in the last day and his body would need fuel soon. He saw a mendicant monk, barefoot and wearing an orange robe, going from house to house and holding out a bowl into which householders put a morsel of food. Bruce approached the monk, who seemed to immediately guess what Bruce might want, and gave him half of what was in the bowl.

At about eight, Bruce returned to where he had made the call to Alfred. The merchant was waiting for him. Alfred had already returned the call and made the necessary arrangements, which the merchant read to Bruce from a sheet of lined paper. Again, Bruce thanked the merchant and began to follow Alfred's instructions.

Two days later Bruce was in Kathmandu, standing at the end of an unpaved landing strip. There was a corrugated steel shed at the other end, with a pole flying a windsock, and nothing else. A dot appeared in the eastern sky, black against a huge, billowing cloud, and grew larger and resolved itself into an airplane, which landed and taxied to a stop. It was a Wayne Enterprises jet, gleaming and in perfect condition.

Bruce ran toward it. The exit hatch opened and a small set of steps thudded to the dirt. Alfred, immaculate in a pressed suit, descended and, when Bruce stopped in front of him, said, "Master Bruce. It's been some time."

Bruce smiled. "Yes. Yes it has."

It had been seven years since he had last looked at Alfred Pennyworth, and in some fundamental ways Bruce was not the same man who had left America as a stowaway on a tramp freighter. But he felt recognition and a familiar, immense affection for the elegant, courtly gentleman who stood before him.

Alfred looked at Bruce, scanning him from hairline to feet. Bruce knew what he was seeing—a long-haired, bearded, sooty man wearing black rags. "You look rather fashionable," Alfred said. "Apart from the dried blood."

Bruce followed Alfred into the aircraft. The hatch closed and the engines revved and within seconds they were airborne. The interior of the plane was well appointed, with leather seats, a padded bulkhead, and first-class food service. Alfred gave Bruce a glass of orange juice, which tasted as though it was fresh-pressed, and settled into a seat across from him.

"Are you coming back to Gotham for good?" he asked.

"As long as it takes." Bruce sipped the orange juice. "I'm going to show Gotham that the city doesn't belong to the criminals and the corrupt."

Alfred leaned back in his chair and said, "During the depression your father nearly bankrupted Wayne Enterprises combating poverty. He believed that his example would inspire the wealthy of Gotham to save their city."

"Did it?"

"In a way . . . your parents' murder shocked the wealthy and powerful into action."

Bruce nodded. "People need dramatic examples to shake them out of apathy. I can't do this as Bruce Wayne. A man is just flesh-and-blood and can be ignored or destroyed. But a *symbol* . . . as a symbol I can be incorruptible, everlasting."

"What symbol?"

"I'm not sure yet. Something elemental. Something terrifying."

"I assume, sir, that since you're taking on the underworld that this 'symbol' is a persona to protect those you are about to endanger from reprisal?"

Bruce nodded again. "You're thinking about Rachel?"

"Actually, sir, I was thinking of myself."

"Have you told anyone that I'm coming back?"

"I haven't figured out the legal ramifications of raising you from the dead."

"Dead?"

"It's been seven years."

"You had me declared dead?"

"Actually, it was Mr. Earle. He wanted to liquidate your majority shareholding. He's taking the company public. Your shares brought in an enormous amount of capital."

"Good thing I left everything to you, then."

"Quite so, sir." Alfred closed his eyes. "You're welcome to borrow the Rolls, by the way. Just bring it back with a full tank."

The plane refueled once that day, and twice more before flying over a Gotham City whose spires were catching the gold of first morning light. Bruce peered from his window down at a place he had not seen in a long time, and wondered what dramas were occurring in its streets.

PART II

BATMAN

8

Bruce considered making a big show of his return to Gotham but decided against it. Oh, he would certainly reveal himself with all appropriate bells and whistles sooner or later, and probably sooner, but first he wanted to accomplish a few things without being scrutinized by every gossip hound on the East Coast.

The first item on Bruce's agenda was to find out just who and what he had spent the last year of his life with. Neither Ducard nor any of the trainees explained the exact nature of the League of Shadows, much less any of its particulars—when it had originated, how it was financed, and most important, what its purpose was.

Bruce asked Alfred for help and so Alfred spent five days in various Gotham City libraries, and another day telephoning professors at the local universities. Unfortunately, he learned very little.

On the morning of Bruce's sixth day back, he and Alfred met in the library after a late breakfast. Alfred flipped back the cover of a notebook and said, "I'm afraid I must disappoint you, Master Bruce."

"You never have, Alfred."

"Then you are about to experience an historic first. All I managed to glean regarding this 'League of Shadows' is that no one believes it ever really existed. It seems to be a chimerical organization like the Illuminati or the Order of St. Dumas. There are a few scattered legends concerning it, but according to my sources, not a scrap of genuine evidence."

"Nothing written down? Memoirs, business papers . . ."

"Absolutely nothing."

"Well, I hate to contradict the experts, but they're wrong with a capital W. I didn't *imagine* the monastery, Ducard, Rā's al Ghūl, and all the rest."

"I am reminded of something the French poet Charles Baudelaire once wrote. 'The devil's deepest wile is to persuade us that he does not exist.' "

"Alfred, I had no idea you were so erudite."

"I'm not. I was dusting a book of French verse one day and it happened to fall open and . . ." Alfred tilted his head to one side and shrugged, as if to say, *What is one to do? These things happen.*

Bruce thanked Alfred, borrowed the notebook, and drove his Lamborghini Murciélago toward the city. He was sure that Alfred had been thorough, but he was still not satisfied.

It won't kill me to find out what I can learn on my own . . .

The one thing he had liked when he had taken his few liberal arts courses was doing research papers. There was something about pursuing a fact and finding it despite obstacles that he found deeply satisfy-

ing. He remembered a grad student at Gotham U.:
Sandra Flanders. When he was a freshman, she had
once pointed him in a fruitful direction and, at the
time, confessed that she wanted nothing more from
life than to be a research librarian. He remembered
reading somewhere—the alumni newspaper still sent
to his father?—that Sandra had, indeed, done exactly
that. She was now the university's chief researcher.

Bruce parked the Lamborghini in the visitors' lot
amid a cluster of huge SUVs and walked across a
quadrangle toward the administration building. The
campus had deteriorated since his last visit. The grass
was badly in need of mowing, the sidewalks were
cracked and uneven, the paint on the walls of the
buildings was faded and peeling. But the coeds he
passed were pretty and the male students certainly
seemed energetic. Three of them were throwing a
Frisbee around. One of them missed a catch and the
disk spun toward Bruce. He caught it and sent it
back—a bit too hard. It struck a young, blond-haired
man in the chest and almost knocked him over.

"Sorry," Bruce shouted, and wondered to himself:
Could those things be adapted to weapons?

He entered the admin building and wrinkled his
nose. Was that *urine* he was smelling? Could it *possibly* be? He went through a door marked INFORMATION and spoke to a middle-aged man whose trim
haircut and pressed suit were in marked contrast to
his surroundings. He was polite and helpful and able
to direct Bruce to Sandra Flanders's office.

Bruce recrossed the quadrangle to the library, climbed a flight of stairs off the main lobby, and found Sandra Flanders behind a large wooden desk, surrounded by thousands of shelved books, peering at a computer screen. The place smelled of old leather and old paper—a *nice* smell, this was, unlike what he had sniffed in the admin building. It reminded Bruce of the library in Wayne Manor. When he entered, Sandra raised her eyes and smiled a welcome. She was in her late thirties, with dark brown hair, regular features, and a trim figure. Bruce wondered if he should tell her his real identity, but decided against it. He and Alfred had yet to sort out what Alfred had called "the legal ramifications of raising you from the dead."

But would she remember, and recognize, him? *One way to find out . . .*

Bruce extended his hand. "Ms. Flanders? I'm . . . Gene Valley."

"You remind me of someone . . . Bruce. Bruce Wayne?"

"My cousin. Some say the resemblance is uncanny." He sighed. "Poor Bruce."

"What happened to him? I heard he just vanished."

"Yes. Several years ago. Perhaps he'll turn up someday . . . But I need your help *now.*"

"What can I do for you?"

Bruce told her about the League of Shadows and saw that she was immediately interested. Obviously, Ms. Flanders enjoyed a challenge. She proceeded to dazzle him. He had not known there were so many ways to pursue facts and five hours later he had filled

Alfred's notebook with information—enough for him to make several good guesses about the League of Shadows.

"One more thing," Bruce said as Sandra pushed back from her computer.

"Yes?"

"Can you find anything on Rā's al Ghūl?"

"Well, he's mentioned in one of the references. Let's see what else there might be." Sandra returned to her computer and reference books and, after another hour had passed, gave Bruce more information.

As Bruce was leaving Sandra's office, he thanked her and asked if there was anything he could do for *her*.

"Well, as you may have noticed, things have gotten a bit shabby around here . . . I realize that you're probably not as well off as your cousin . . ."

"I'll send a check." *And it will be a large one.*

Back at the manor, Bruce sank into his father's favorite easy chair in the library and opened the notebook. As Alfred had said, solid information about the League of Shadows was sparse. The earliest recorded mention of it was appended to a piece of parchment dating to the fourteenth century, copied by a monk in an Irish monastery. According to this fragment, the League had already been in existence for hundreds of years. The next reference was in a letter, again just a fragment, sent from Paris to Berlin in 1794, at the height of the French Revolution. Then another, more cryptic message concerning the League sent from a clothier in London to a Manchester sea captain; there was no month or day on it, but the year was 1866.

In the early twentieth century, an Oxford don had done a monograph on what he termed "secret societies" that was mostly concerned with the Masons, the Ku Klux Klan, the Knights Templar, the Order of St. Dumas, the Illuminati, and the League of Shadows. The learned academic dismissed the latter three as "very likely the turbulent fabrications of overwrought imaginations," and did not bother to list the sources he had consulted, an omission Sandra Flanders apparently considered grievous.

"But," she had concluded, "despite his pedagogical slovenliness and his turbulent and overwrought prose style, I guess he was right. There doesn't seem to have been a League of Shadows."

"Do you always say things like 'pedagogical slovenliness'?"

"Only when I'm tired or trying to impress someone. I'll let you decide which applies here."

As for Rā's . . . there was even less information about him than about his League, and what there was Bruce found hard to believe. The name itself was easy: Sandra had found a meaning a few minutes after she'd accessed a lexicographical database. In Arabic it meant: "Head of the Demon." And that was about the extent of what Bruce considered reliable data.

So that leaves me . . . where?

The telephone rang, a loud jangling from an old-fashioned phone on Thomas Wayne's desk that seemed to shake the walls of the library.

"I've got it, Alfred," Bruce yelled, picking up the receiver.

The caller was Sandra Flanders. "I've come across something," she said.

"I'm all ears."

"There was an eccentric collector named Berthold Cavally who got very interested in the kinds of things that seem to interest you. Amassed quite a collection of artifacts of all kinds, but he had a special interest in lost civilizations, cults, secret societies, and the like. He died in a fire in 1952 and his collection burned up with him."

"Very interesting, Sandra, but how does this . . ."

"Wait. There's a bit more. A nephew found one of Cavally's notebooks in the ashes along with a badly charred fragment of a parchment. Both items had been partially burned, but a lot of it survived. Apparently, it contains Cavally's translation of a parchment he acquired in North Africa and it mentions this Rā's al Ghūl character."

"And how might an earnest young fellow get a look at this notebook?"

"Well, if he's earnest *and* rich, he might buy it. The nephew got wiped out in a dot-com fiasco and is selling everything he can get his hands on."

"Where and when?"

"I hope you have a bag packed. The items are up for sale at an auction tomorrow at ten in New York City, at a place called the Olympus Gallery."

"I'll be there—if you'll give me an address."

Sandra recited an address on Madison Avenue and Sixty-first Street. Bruce thanked her again and began to call airlines.

Alfred volunteered to learn something about the Olympus Gallery and made a few calls. He reported that it had once been a prestigious venue for acquiring antiquities, but lately had become "decidedly second-rate."

Bruce thanked him and moved toward the door.

"Another moment?" Alfred asked. He held up the bloodstained clothes Bruce had been wearing at the airstrip in Kathmandu.

"Let's hang on to them."

"I doubt they'll ever be clean again, Master Bruce."

"They're souvenirs. Souvenirs don't have to be spotless."

"Souvenirs of what, if I may ask?"

"Most people get a diploma when they complete their schooling. I got a sooty, smoky, bloody ninja suit. I think I got the better deal."

"I doubt that the diploma manufacturers are a bit worried."

For the next fifteen minutes, Bruce busied himself making more telephone calls. The one he considered most important was to the Wayne Enterprises offices in Wayne Tower. A chirpy-voiced receptionist told him that Mr. Earle was not in and was not expected, but would return from his vacation in a few days and perhaps the gentleman would like to leave his name and

call back at that time. The gentleman said he would
prefer *not* to leave his name, thank you, but would be
happy to call again.

Bruce wandered into the kitchen where Alfred,
wearing a white apron, was feeding something into a
blender. When Bruce explained what his problem
was, Alfred took a credit card from his wallet. Bruce
thanked him and returned to the library and his phone
calls. Using Alfred's card number, he made a round-
trip plane reservation to New York City for the following day and a hotel reservation at the Plaza in
Manhattan.

At six twenty-five the next morning, Bruce was
walking through a terminal at La Guardia Airport in
Queens, New York. He remembered liking airports
when he and his family had passed through them on
vacations, en route to Paris, London, Hong Kong,
Buenos Aires, the Caribbean Islands: a different desti-
nation every year, and all of them enchanting to a
wide-eyed little boy. But *this* airport, *now* . . . maybe
his time with Rā's al Ghūl had changed his tastes, or
maybe the years he had lived since childhood did. For
whatever reason, he found La Guardia at six-thirty in
the morning to be depressing. His fellow passengers
mostly walked with their heads down, as though moving into a ferocious wind, and carried their tote bags
and suitcases and attachés as though they were the
burdens of the damned.

It's early. Maybe they'll cheer up later on . . .

Bruce was far from chipper himself. He was not a morning person—that was one of the many lessons he had learned at the monastery. It was not a matter of character, as some of his high school teachers had apparently believed, but of the body's natural circadian rhythms. But he had also learned that willpower, judiciously applied, could trump lethargy. If he *had* to be wide awake and fully functioning in the morning, he could be.

The will is everything . . .

He was traveling light today, with nothing but the clothes on his back and a wallet full of currency. He stood in line for twenty minutes before he could get a taxicab, another indication that he had not yet fully readjusted to being the wealthy scion of a wealthy family: a wealthy scion would have had a limousine waiting. He gave the driver the Madison Avenue address and watched the scenery go by. The cab merged with an army of automobiles, all inching toward the distant Manhattan skyline.

Once the cab had actually crossed the East River into Manhattan, Bruce amused himself by looking at New York City and comparing it to Gotham: the buildings were, on the whole, taller, yet here there was none of the oppressive cavernous quality that characterized downtown Gotham. Sunlight actually reached the sidewalk in Manhattan.

Ninety minutes after it had left La Guardia, the cab stopped in front of a brownstone house that Bruce estimated to be at least 150 years old and was obviously built by someone who was wealthy—a friend of his grandfather's, maybe? He paid the fare and climbed the steps to the front door. A tasteful brass plate above the doorbell was etched with the words OLYMPUS GALLERY.

The door opened and a pretty young brunette in a pantsuit gave Bruce a catalog printed on vellum and escorted him to a long, wide chamber obviously converted from several smaller rooms. The woman did not recognize him, which relieved Bruce, but did not surprise him. Thomas Wayne had discouraged journalists from publishing photos of his family; the last picture of Bruce to grace the public prints was taken when he was barely fourteen, before he had even attained his full growth, much less been hardened by his travels. He no longer looked much like that cherubic adolescent.

The room was crowded with rows of chairs occupied by a diverse array of men and women, all well dressed, most of them speaking in murmurs to companions. At the far end was a raised platform and a lectern, flanked by paintings on easels and a few statues. The young brunette offered Bruce coffee, tea, chocolate, scones, and pastries. Bruce asked for coffee. A minute later she returned with some in a dainty china cup. She told him that the rooms around them had an interesting variety of works of art and suggested that he might want to examine them after the auction. Bruce thanked her, both for the coffee and the suggestion, and received a carefully crafted smile in return.

A tall, cadaverous man with thick glasses and a few

wisps of brown hair combed over his dome moved behind the lectern and welcomed everyone.

He tapped a microphone and winced when a shriek of feedback filled the room, and said, "Before we begin today's proceedings, I have a regrettable announcement to make. On page eleven of your catalogs—" There was a rustling as the gallery patrons turned pages. The tall man continued. "You see listed there an item offered by James Cavally, a parchment accompanied by his uncle's translation of its contents. Unfortunately, we are not able to offer this to you today."

"Why not?" someone asked.

"I regret to say that Mr. Cavally perished in an airplane crash last night and the items described in the catalog were destroyed with him. We, of course, convey our deepest sympathy to his family and friends on their loss. Now, if there are no further questions . . . we begin the auction with lot seven . . ."

Bruce was pretty sure he was not interested in the oil paintings of sunsets or the marble statues of nymphs or anything else the Olympus Gallery would sell that day. He got up and made his way to the door, aware that the brunette was frowning at him, and left the house. He had a return ticket to Gotham in his pocket and he knew of no reason not to use it as soon as possible. He waved down a passing cab—

And stopped, gesturing to the cabbie to keep going. He turned and remounted the steps. By the time he reached the door, he knew why he had not gotten into the cab, what was nagging at him.

Too much of a coincidence . . . the guy with the

*Rā's al Ghūl information dying the night before it
went on sale. That might mean that there's something
in the old manuscript actually worth knowing, and
that means I shouldn't give up so easily . . .*

With an exasperated look on her face, the brunette
again showed him to a seat. She did not offer him coffee, and her smile this time was glacial.

Bruce sat through an hour's tedium; he had not
been so bored since that day in the classroom when
the professor had droned on and on about Jungian
archetypes. Toward the end of the auction, Bruce out-
bid everyone else and found himself the owner of a
marble nymph. He thought that maybe taking the
monstrosity off the auctioneer's hands would incline
him to be friendly.

He had no idea what he would do with it. It was
too big to be a paperweight . . .

When the sale was finally over, and the art lovers
had left, still murmuring to each other, Bruce paid for
the nymph, approached the auctioneer, and intro-
duced himself.

"I'm Wesley Carter," the auctioneer said, shaking
Bruce's hand. "I must congratulate you on your ac-
quisition. A truly fine piece. What do you plan to do
with it, if I may ask?"

"It will occupy a place of honor," Bruce said and
added to himself: *In a swamp somewhere.* "I wonder
if I might have a word with you in private."

Wesley Carter scrutinized Bruce and clearly ap-
proved of what he was seeing. He almost certainly
recognized that the casual clothing his visitor wore

had cost several thousand dollars and told himself that a person who could afford such plumage was a person who could also afford expensive art. "If you'll come with me, Mr. . . ."

"Valley. Gene Valley."

Bruce followed Wesley Carter up a steep flight of winding stairs to a small office on the second floor, probably a maid's room originally. Bruce settled into a leather chair and told Carter what he wanted.

When Bruce had finished, Carter said, "Let me be certain I understand you. You're asking if there is any way to learn the contents of Mr. Cavally's uncle's translation."

As Carter spoke, his eyes shifted down and to the left, briefly but unmistakably.

"That's it exactly."

"Well . . . Mr. Cavally was an extremely cautious person. That's why he insisted on bringing the items himself. But I couldn't offer them to our clients without some knowledge of them—our patrons are *most* discerning. So Mr. Cavally photocopied both the original parchment and his uncle's work on it and forwarded the photographs to us last week."

Again, the darting glance down and to the left.

"I can't tell you how happy I am to hear that," Bruce said. "I'd like to buy those copies."

"I'm afraid that's out of the question."

"I'd be willing to let you name your own price."

"Mr. Valley, I would love to be able to accommodate you, I truly would. But until I hear from Mr. Cavally's lawyers . . ."

"When will that be?"

"Well, these matters seldom proceed rapidly. I would guess two to three months, at the earliest."

"Did I mention you can set your own price?"

"Yes you did," Carter said, his tone now frosty. "And did *I* mention that it's out of the question?"

Bruce rose and extended his hand. "Sorry to have taken up your time."

"No trouble, Mr. Valley."

They shook, and Bruce said he could find his own way out. He descended the winding staircase and, in the short hall leading to the exit, noticed another door. He glanced around. Nobody was near. He opened the door and was looking at another short flight of steps leading to a cellar.

Oh-kayyy . . .

He left and walked around the block, mentally noting everything about it, from the kinds of awnings the shops had to the placement of fire hydrants. When he was satisfied with his reconnaissance, he strolled downtown on Madison Avenue, allowing himself to be a tourist and merely enjoy the sights. At Sixtieth, he cut across a corner of Central Park to the Plaza Hotel. He registered and before going up to his room, asked the concierge for some store suggestions.

He got the photo supplies he needed on Forty-seventh Street and the clothing on Sixth Avenue. He briefly visited a luggage shop on Broadway, and at a large drugstore near Rockefeller Center, he bought a pair of rubber gloves and a penlight. He made his final purchase at a hardware store in Greenwich Village.

He returned to the Olympus Gallery at four that afternoon, now dressed in a black silk shirt, a black silk tie, dark blue trousers, and very expensive black sneakers, carrying an alligator attaché case with gold fittings.

He nodded pleasantly to the brunette. "Saw some things this morning I might like to have. Going to have another peek at them, if that's all right."

The brunette replied with an excessively wide smile and said certainly, he could take his time, but they *did* close at five.

Bruce browsed through several of the galleries, trying to look like a really avid art lover, but really checking the security arrangements. There was one video camera in the lobby and nothing else that he could see. He waited until he was momentarily alone, then dashed to the cellar door and scrambled down the steps.

The cellar was almost totally dark, but light from a place where paint had chipped from a window that had been painted over was enough for him to see by. He was in a low-ceilinged basement filled with crates and what must have been paintings wrapped in brown paper. At the rear, behind all the clutter, he could see an old-fashioned coal bin, which was also full of crates. He went into it and crouched in a dark corner and waited.

Waiting was no problem. It was something Ducard

had insisted he learn and Ducard had taught him
well.

He heard footsteps on the floor above him, and
muffled voices calling good-byes. Then silence.

He waited, aware of all the noises in the old house
and the darkness around him, alert but still.

When the faintly luminous dial on his Rolex said
8:25, he put on the rubber gloves, crept from his hiding place, ascended the steps, and slowly, carefully
opened the door, just a crack.

*There must be guards. I'd rather not run into
them . . .*

He listened: the creakings and groanings of any old
house, and somewhere, the whine of an electric engine. He crept into the carpeted hall. The only light
was from a red EXIT sign. Careful to stay out of the
scanning area of the single video camera, which was
really no problem, he went up the winding staircase
until he reached the upper landing and heard someone coughing. A flashlight beam struck the wall just
ahead of him; someone was in an adjoining hall, coming his way. Whoever it was would be facing him in
two or three seconds.

With neither hesitation nor conscious thought, he
swung over the railing and hung from the floor of the
landing, his legs dangling down into a gallery below,
the handle of the attaché in his teeth. A uniformed
man, with a belly that drooped over a belt festooned
with a small radio and a can of Mace, lumbered past,
sweeping a flashlight beam ahead of him. His right
shoe sole came within an inch of Bruce's fingers.

By the time the man had reached the top of the stairs, Bruce had vaulted over the railing. He moved as he had been taught to move, swiftly and in absolute silence, to the door of Wesley Carter's office. He tried the knob and found it unlocked. Wesley was a trusting soul, bless him. Bruce entered and crossed to the desk. He opened his attaché and removed the small crowbar he had purchased in the Greenwich Village hardware store. Carter had twice glanced at the top left-hand drawer of his desk while discussing the photocopies, so that was where Bruce would start his search. He was prepared to hate himself for using a crowbar on such a fine piece of furniture, but he did not have to; like the door, the drawer was open. Carter was a *very* trusting soul. Or he did not think the contents of the drawer were worth stealing, and maybe he was right.

Bruce removed a small camera from his attaché and lay the photocopies flat on the desktop. For the next ten minutes, he photographed the photocopies, hoping that the tiny flash from his camera would be visible neither under the door nor to anyone outside the room's single window.

He replaced the original copies in the drawer, stepped to the door, and pressed his ear against it: no lumbering footsteps.

Now to figure out an exit strategy . . .

The sidewalk in front of the house would still be busy at this time of night; like Gotham, New York was a city that never slept, and he did not want to chance being seen leaving and be arrested for burglary. The rear faced the backyards of private homes and a few tony businesses, some of which would certainly have dogs and security cameras.

That left the roof.

He glided down the hallway to a window and took the penlight from his pants pocket. He quickly ran the light beam over the edges of the window: no tape. So no security alarm. He lifted the window, slowly, to make as little noise as possible, and stood on the sill, the back of his body facing the yard below, the handle of the attaché again gripped in his teeth.

Okay, now the hard part . . .

He bent his knees and jumped straight up. His gloved fingers curled around the edge of the roof and he flexed his arms and lifted himself until he could roll over onto the rooftop.

From here on, it would be easy. During his earlier reconnaissance, Bruce had noted the location of a tall tree, three doors south of the gallery. So: over the roofs, a short jump to the tree, a brief wait until no one was near, then down to the sidewalk and back to the hotel. Piece of cake.

Twelve hours later, Bruce was in the sunny kitchen of Wayne Manor finishing his breakfast.

"I trust your meal was satisfactory," Alfred said from the sink, where he was rinsing out some cups.

"Absolutely," Bruce said. "What could be better than the blood sausage and eggs Benedict you've been giving me?"

Alfred finished with the cups and sat across the

table from Bruce. "You seem pensive this morning, Master Bruce. Anything you'd like to share?"

"I'm rehashing yesterday. Trying to make sense of it, I guess."

"What about it puzzles you?"

"For one thing, I *liked* it. Almost all of it. Dangling like a Christmas tree ornament, running across those rooftops . . . it felt *right*, somehow."

"The thrill of danger, perhaps?"

"I know that thrill, and this wasn't it. This was . . . more. Like I was finally doing something I *should* be doing."

"Really? Are you aware that the career opportunities for cat burglars are severely limited? And the benefits are disgraceful. No health insurance, no parking space . . ."

"Okay, Alfred, point taken. May I change the subject?"

"Certainly, sir."

"I've got some pictures to be developed and I'd rather not trust the drugstore. Any ideas?"

"My friend in Gotham has photographic equipment."

"Is your friend discreet?"

"Completely."

Bruce went into the library and returned with the alligator attaché case.

"They're in here. Your friend can keep the attaché case."

"I'm sure she'll put it to good use. By the way . . . what use was it to *you*?"

"It carried my tools and it was a pain in . . . the teeth. I'm not sure a shoulder bag would have been much better when I was rooftop hopping. Something like a tool belt . . . I could have used night-vision lenses, too, and an infrared flashlight might have been useful."

"The next time you commit a felony, we will equip you properly."

"I certainly hope so."

Ten minutes later, Alfred drove his Bentley away and Bruce was left to wonder what to do with himself. Well, what *do* people do when they don't have to run across glaciers, repulse armed ninjas, or commit burglary?

Watch television, of course.

Except for occasional moments aboard ship, when the vessel he happened to be on was in position to receive commercial broadcasts, Bruce had not watched TV in over seven years. He went into the den and switched on a large flatscreen monitor.

He watched. *Had there always been this many commercials?* He grew bored until he made the watching an exercise in patient awareness. He was still and he waited and was aware of the sight and sound of the television set, which was tuned to an all-news channel.

On the screen: several fire trucks outside a burning brownstone.

From the speaker: . . . *officials say the fire was apparently started when a boiler in the basement of the 150-year-old building exploded. A night watchman,*

*Henry Billeret, is believed to have died in the confla-
gration, although his body has not yet been recov-
ered. Mr. Billeret was a retired New York City police
officer . . .*

The brownstone housed—*had* housed—the Olympus Gallery. So the owner of the Rā's al Ghūl documents and the documents themselves were destroyed
in a plane crash and two days later the place for which
they were bound burns to the ground. Could it possibly be a coincidence?

Alfred returned late in the afternoon bearing a
large bound album. In the center of each heavy brown
page was a photograph of writing, about half of which
was in English, the other half in a calligraphy Bruce
did not recognize.

"Do we owe your friend anything?" Bruce asked
Alfred.

"She has her favorite charities. Perhaps a dona-
tion?"

"You decide the amount, I'll sign the check. After
I'm declared legally alive, that is."

Bruce took the album into the library and settled
into the leather easy chair. He began reading, first the
translator's notes and then the English translation of
the mysterious calligraphy. The story seemed like a
fairy tale, real "once upon a time" stuff.

. . . a man-child was born during a terrible storm.
It was a time of madness. It was a time of the mingling of things that should remain forever apart.

For at noon the light died and darkness claimed the oasis and the sky above roiled and split and jagged blades of lightning slashed the earth below, and the very desert itself lifted and rode the screaming wind to strike anything in its path. Thus day assumed the guise of night. Water and sand allied.

Then from the whirling insanity of a world in torment came a man. A hermit was he who for the past forty years had lived alone in a place without mercy. Some said he was a prophet. Some said he was a demon. All agreed that he had long ago abandoned that which makes a creature human.

He entered the birthing room and suddenly the storm quieted. And in the stillness could be heard the wail of a newborn infant. The gaze of the new mother and her two sisters fastened on him in fascination and they trembled as he spoke in a voice that rasped and rumbled: Give him to me.

The man from the storm lifted the newborn and he spoke: His will be a life lit by lightning. His years will be many stretching beyond the farthest dreams of age and it is his destiny to be either mankind's savior or to destroy all that lives upon the earth.

The man from the storm returned the infant to his mother and spoke: My task is finished.

And as the mother looked upon her son only minutes from the womb she was afraid.

Bruce looked up from the manuscript. The sky outside had darkened and a bat fluttered past the library window. Bruce saluted it, switched on a lamp, and started to read again.

There was a gap in the story. Obviously, many pages, perhaps a hundred or more, had been lost. As the narrative resumed, the infant had grown to manhood, had married, had mastered such healing arts as existed, and had somehow become a favorite of the local ruler, known as the Salimbok, and his son, Runce. Bruce skimmed several pages that seemed to concern things like trade routes and the size of dwellings, until he came to an account of the Physician's falling-out with the bigwigs, the Salimbok and Runce.

It began with a race. The Physician and Runce were tearing through the town, mounted on a couple of stallions, when an old woman got in their way. The story resumed in the middle of a sentence.

ancient was she and blind and her soul was locked within itself no longer touching the world around her. She heard but did not heed the pounding of hooves as they approached her. She fell and was trampled into the dust.

The contestants crossed the finish line and were joyously greeted by the Salimbok who declared the race truly excellent.

The Salimbok spoke: The Physician is a superb horseman. He rides as well as he heals. But my son rode as swiftly as the wind. I declare my son and heir the victor.

The Physician's wife called Sora approached him.

He spoke to her out of wounded pride: It seems that once again your husband bows to his better.

She spoke: It is the will of the Salimbok that it be so. But I am still proud of my husband. Later when we are alone I will demonstrate the extent of my pride.

Runce approached them. He spoke: What of me, fair Sora. Do not I merit any of your demonstration?

Runce embraced Sora while her husband stood by in helpless rage.

The Salimbok approached and spoke to his son: The victor's feast awaits you. Such food as will delight your tongue and women too. Lovely girls in the first blush of maturity.

Runce spoke: There are none so lovely as the wife of the Physician.

The Salimbok spoke to the Physician: He is young and impetuous. You must forgive him.

The Physician quelled the rage and pride within him and spoke: Yes, Excellency.

The Physician and his wife retired to their quarters and conversed regarding the son of the Salimbok. The Physician spoke: He is young. Years and responsibilities will teach him decorum.

Sora doubted this and reminded her husband that Runce was no younger than he. The Physician replied that his studies had aged him beyond his years.

What studies were those? Bruce wondered. *And where did he study? Who were his teachers? Most of all, what, exactly, did he learn?*

"Is this a good time for an interruption?" Alfred asked from the doorway. He was carrying a tray with a teapot and two cups. "I thought you might be ready for some refreshment."

"What are we having? Earl Grey?"

"I've brewed some of the green tea you seem to favor since your sojourn abroad. I must admit that it's growing on me."

"That was not, I hope, a pun."

"Perish forbid." Alfred filled the cups, gave one to Bruce, and sat with his own cup in an adjoining chair. "Is it too early to ask how the reading progresses?"

Bruce sipped his tea and said, "It progresses fine, I guess. I could do with a few more punctuation marks—the guy seems allergic to commas and quotation marks—and a little less quasi-poetic diction would be okay, and a couple of hard facts now and then would be nice. But on the whole, no complaints."

"Have we added 'literary critic' to our portfolio?"

"Hardly. But I do know what I like."

"We shall make an educated man of you yet, Master Bruce."

"Don't hold your breath."

Alfred stood. "I shall leave you to it. Dinner at the usual time?"

"Sure. Whatever's good for you."

Bruce drained his cup and picked up the manuscript. He reentered the story at the point where the Physician went to see the old woman who had been trampled.

Brandishing a knife the son spoke to the Physician: You are not welcome here. I shall show you just how unwelcome.

The Physician spoke: I understand your anger and I do not blame you for it. But before you slice me open allow me a moment with your mother.

The wish of the Physician was granted and he tended to the old woman whose sightless eyes were closed. Her son inquired as to her condition and the Physician spoke: She is old and her injuries are grievous. There is little I can do. The Great Enemy will soon claim her.

The son wished to know the identity of this Great Enemy that he might be slain before the death of the mother.

The Physician spoke at length: The greatest and final enemy of mankind. The merciless felon who is always lurking nearby ready to snatch from us all we hold dear. The mocker of our aspirations and dreams and hopes. Our cruel master. Death. How I hate death.

The Physician gave a pouch full of herbs to the son of the old woman. He explained that the herbs would not save the old woman but would ease her passing. The son was touched by the kindness of the Physician and cast his blade to the ground.

A messenger from the Salimbok entered the dwelling and reported that Runce the son of the ruler had fallen gravely ill and was in need of the Physician.

The Physician and the messenger hurried to the

royal dwelling. The Physician found Runce to be grievously ill. His skin was pale and his brow burned.

The Salimbok inquired as to the cause of the illness. For had not Runce been victorious in a race mere hours earlier? The Physician confessed that he had no certain knowledge but he supposed that the illness came from merchants who had recently visited the area and were themselves ill. The Salimbok wanted to know how this could be. The Physician replied that certain of his researches indicated that disease could move from one person to another and promised to exhaust himself in seeking to cure Runce.

The Physician was sorely troubled. He mounted the animal he had ridden in the race and rode into the desert. In the distance silvered by moonlight a cloud of dust and sand were sure signs of the nomads who preyed upon travelers. But either they had not seen him or they were indifferent to plunder this night.

He dismounted at the place where he had been born and immediately he felt the energy that surges from the very earth itself. Here he could think and dream those dreams that are often the better of mere thought. The wind murmured and then howled and then shrieked and a thousand shapes began to shimmer on the boundary of sleep. Monsters welled up from unimaginable abysses to surround the Physician and fill him with dread. But he did not shrink from them as he had in the past. He faced them and called them by their names and the names he called

them were the names of Death. It was in facing
them that he came to see how he might defeat them

The narrative broke off. More missing pages. Bruce
allowed himself a flicker of annoyance. *Just when I
was getting to the good part . . .*

He put down the manuscript and carried his empty
cup into the kitchen. Something was bubbling on the
stove and something else was in the oven, and both
smelled rich and highly caloric. He could hear the
sound of a Louis Armstrong solo from another part
of the house and knew that Alfred was listening to his
favorite music while waiting for whatever he was
cooking and baking to be done. Ever since Bruce's return from abroad, Alfred had been outdoing himself
as a chef. Every night there was a different meal and
every one was sumptuous.

Bruce did not know how to tell his friend that every
one was also making him queasy.

He brewed himself another serving of green tea and
went back to the library and his reading.

The narrative resumed with the Physician riding
home and passing a corpse lying on the road. He
reached the gate of the city and was greeted by a guard
who told him that during the night the nomads had
attacked. The marauders had been repulsed, but not
without cost. Many men had been wounded.

The gatekeeper spoke: All that is of no consequence. The son of the Salimbok is dying and you
must attend him without delay.

The Physician went to the royal dwelling immediately and found that Runce was indeed close to death. The Salimbok implored the Physician to save his son and promised the Physician gold and slaves and even his kingdom itself. But the Physician wanted none of these things and told the ruler that Runce was already beyond the reach of the healing arts.

The Physician spoke: It may be that last night a knowledge beyond medicine came to me in the guise of a dream. I will need laborers to dig a pit and a tent and other supplies.

The kingdom was scoured to provide what the Physician needed and before the sun had set all was in readiness. The wife of the Physician confessed that she was troubled for much of what her husband had requested was poisonous and deadly to the human body.

The Physician spoke: If my theory is correct the poisons can be curative provided they are used under exactly the right conditions. In this place where we stand I sense great energy. Perhaps it is the energy of the earth itself. This combined with the other agents will either cure young Runce or hasten his inevitable demise.

The Salimbok came forth and implored the Physician to accompany him to the shrine of Bisu who was the foremost deity of the people. The Physician protested that he was a man of science and had no belief in gods and would not worship them

Here, again, there was a gap in the story. But someone, almost certainly the younger Cavally, had inserted into the folio a sheet of paper bearing some notes typed on a machine that had needed a new ribbon.

Bisu . . . desert god. Not worshiped in the usual ways. More demon than god? Fitting for a harsh place? Living conditions shape local idea of godhood? (Cf volkergedanken.)

Human sacrifice? Would answer some questions.

Maybe it would answer some of his *questions,* Bruce thought. *Doesn't do a thing for* mine, *though. And what's this word in parentheses . . . "volkergedanken"? German word, looks like. Mean anything important? Probably not, but better find out.*

He would call Sandra Flanders in the morning—her or the university's German department. (Surely, it *had* a German department.)

A bit wearily, Bruce resumed reading. Whatever the Physician did about worshiping, or not worshiping, Bisu had happened in the missing pages. The narrative began in midsentence:

confess to a dislike of Runce as strong as yours, my wife. But he is a man and none who can be called so are blameless. And his father has been generous to us.

In the tent the Physician made ready his preparations and commanded that Runce be lowered into the pit that seethed and boiled and made a horrible stench. Runce no longer gave breath and all who were present thought the Physician had failed. But with a terrible roar Runce rose up from the pit and his eyes were filled with madness and his gaze was cast upon the fair wife of the Physician. And he grasped her. The Physician tried to intervene but Runce was as strong as ten men and flung the Physician aside. And such was his embrace of Sora that her neck snapped and she fell lifeless.

The madness left the eyes of Runce and he called out to his father. Others who had heard the tumult entered the tent and saw the lifeless form of Sora and the Salimbok lied to save his son from disgrace and blamed the death of Sora on the Physician.

Bruce lowered the manuscript. *This is getting positively biblical . . .* He had a sudden need to do something physical; he could finish his research later. He put the manuscript in a drawer, went to his room, and changed into a sweat suit.

In the garden behind the house, he began a series of dancelike martial arts moves designed both to hone his combat skills and improve his overall conditioning. Within minutes, he was sweating and panting and feeling fine. The moon was directly overhead and quite bright; Bruce had all the light he needed.

A car passed the gate, almost a quarter of a mile away, going too fast for the narrow road. Bruce glanced at its headlights and stopped in midmotion.

If I can see the car, maybe the car's occupants can see me. Do I want the world to know that Bruce Wayne is alive and a wannabe Bruce Lee?

Okay, no martial arts, not where he could be seen. But he still felt the need to exert himself. So—he could run. Running is something anyone might do and if anyone came close enough to see him, Bruce would stop, and rest his palms on his knees, and pant, and pretend to be exhausted.

He ran. Out the gate and left on the road and all the way to the freeway ramp, two and a half miles south, and back to the house. It felt wonderful to be stretching his legs, muscles sliding and locking, moving smoothly and gracefully under the moon and stars of a glorious early summer night. After a while, the rhythmic slap of his shoe soles on the asphalt became pleasantly hypnotic but he resisted letting his attention relax. A lesson learned at the monastery: Always be alert—always. But that did not preclude his enjoying himself.

He met no one.

As he was going up the stairs to shower, Alfred called from the kitchen that dinner was almost ready.

Five minutes later, hair still wet, dressed in a sport shirt and chinos, Bruce joined Alfred at the big table in the dining room.

Alfred was apologetic. "I'm afraid the pheasant might be a trifle overdone and I couldn't get the really good truffles . . ."

"It'll all be wonderful," Bruce assured him and began putting food in his mouth. "Delicious."

"I sense a certain insincerity in the compliment," Alfred said. "You sound rather like a little boy who's found socks under the Christmas tree instead of toys. I've detected a lack of enthusiasm for my other culinary productions, as well."

Bruce dabbed at his lips with a napkin. "Alfred, the food really *is* good, and I appreciate the effort you put into it. But I guess my tastes got simplified while I was abroad. A bowl of rice and a serving of vegetables tastes as good to me as filet mignon now, and I don't leave the table feeling weighed down after eating them."

"So I'm to serve only the simplest fare?"

"Sometimes, when you're in the mood, sure—knock yourself out. But every meal doesn't have to be a feast." Bruce pushed back from the table. "I don't mean to offend you . . ."

"Master Bruce, I cannot tell you how *little* you've offended me. On the contrary . . . I haven't felt so relieved in years. I've been spending half my time in the kitchen, and the other half at the market. Tomorrow night, rest assured, you will be given the *best* bowl of rice in the county. And not a morsel more."

"I look forward to it."

Bruce went into the library and picked up the manuscript. He heard Alfred leave by the side door and, a minute later, his Bentley driving down to the gate. This was Alfred's night out. From hints Alfred had dropped, probably intentionally, Bruce guessed that Alfred spent these weekly trips to the city in the company of a woman, a doctor who operated a clinic in

one of Gotham's less savory neighborhoods. Bruce
did not know the exact nature of the relationship, nor
did he want to. Alfred had earned his privacy, a thousand times over.

Bruce settled deep into his father's chair and finished
his self-assigned reading.

Where was I . . . ?

. . . The Salimbok lied to save his son from disgrace and blamed the death of Sora on the Physician.

The Physician was confined until the Salimbok
pronounced sentence upon him.

Acting on advice from Runce the Salimbok commanded that the Physician be confined in a metal
cage with the body of his dead wife and the cage
be lowered into a pit in the desert sand. For three
nights the Physician suffered in silence. On the fourth
night the man whose mother had fallen beneath the
hooves of the horses slew the guard at the site of the
grave of the Physician and drew forth the cage that
imprisoned him. He gave the Physician cool water
to drink and bathed the wounds the Physician had
suffered and together they escaped into the desert

Another bunch of pages missing. The last fragment
was only a couple of dozen words long. Like the pre-
vious one, it began in midsentence:

who had once been known as the Physician rose
howling from the pit with eyes filled with madness
and when the madness had subsided Rā's al

That's where it ended, again in midsentence.

Bruce dropped the book onto the rug beside the chair and leaned back. *So is Rā's the Physician? Apparently. And I'm supposed to believe that his dunking-in-noxious-chemicals trick works and gives him incredible longevity . . . that he's a healthy four hundred years plus. All very hard to swallow.*

Bruce got up, stretched, and walked out into the moonlit night. *Okay, let's stick with what I know. I know the League exists, unless I imagined everything that happened at the monastery, and I didn't. And it seems to surface at times of social upheaval. What else? What exactly does it do? And what did Rā's want with me? Interesting questions. I wish I had some interesting answers. But at least I'm way ahead of where I was a couple of days ago, and for that I owe the nice librarian.*

He got up, went to his father's huge old oak desk, and got a checkbook from the top drawer. He wrote a check to Gotham University, filled in a number, hesitated, and added another zero. Then he began addressing an envelope, though he would not be able to actually send the check until he was declared among the living. He really should do something about that. He had done enough reconnaissance to know there was nothing unexpected waiting for him in Gotham and he was sure he had all the information about his former mentor that he needed. So the time had come to ruin William Earle's day.

*   *   *

Bruce did not feel it necessary to revisit the university the next day, nor was it. He telephoned the school's general number and was patched through to the German department, where he spoke to a Professor Liam O'Shaugnessy.

"You're surprised that somebody with my name teaches German, am I right?" O'Shaugnessy asked in an accent that Bruce guessed was a mixture of Dublin and Brooklyn.

"Mildly, Dr. O'Shaugnessy."

"Only 'mildly'? Knocks most people out of their socks. What can I do for you? Got a question?"

Bruce asked for the meaning of the word "volkergedanken," the word in the younger Cavally's notes, and started to spell it.

"Hold the spelling bee. Don't need it. Word's kinda hard to wrap your head around but it means something like 'local ideas.' I think it was popularized by a guy named Adolph Bastien. He was a mythology guy. The idea is, basic myths are changed by local conditions. Anything else?"

Bruce said there was not and thanked the professor. The conversation had not yielded much useful information. Okay, Rā's's people created a mean deity because their living conditions were mean. Interesting, maybe, but irrelevant. Bruce still did not know much about the man who had been his mentor and now, perhaps, had been his enemy.

But maybe he knew enough.

*   *   *

Sergeant James Gordon squirmed in the front seat of the unmarked police car, and looked out the driver-side window at his partner, Flass, standing in front of a liquor store and shaking hands with its owner. It was late afternoon and they should have been back at the station house, but Flass had this stop to make.

Flass crossed the street, got into the driver's seat, and held up a wad of currency.

"Don't s'pose you want a taste?" he asked Gordon.

Gordon stared at Flass.

Flass grinned and began counting the money. "I keep offering 'cause who knows, maybe one day you'll get wise."

"Nothing wise in what you do, Flass."

"Well, Jimbo, you don't take your taste, makes us guys nervous you might decide to roll over."

Gordon let his irritation creep into his voice. "I'm not a rat, Flass. If I were, I'd still be in Chicago. Besides, in a town this bent, who's there to rat to?"

Flass laughed, started the car, and screeched down the street. Fifteen minutes later he braked in front of the station house. Gordon got out of the car and, his body sagging with weariness, watched Flass drive away.

Standing in the doorway of a tailor shop that was closed for the night, Bruce Wayne watched Gordon as Gordon had watched Flass.

*   *   *

Jim Gordon went up a flight of steps to the detective division on the second floor of the precinct house, ignoring the screaming from the ragged woman who had just been led to the front desk and the ever-present stink of smoke and stale humanity. He had a little paperwork to get done before he climbed into his ten-year-old sedan and drove home. Barbara would have a decent meal waiting, even if it was a meal that came from cans, and she'd ask him how his day went and he'd say fine. Like always. If it wasn't too late, Jim would read his daughter a story and tuck her in. Maybe then he and Barbara would watch some TV.

Or maybe they'd argue. The same old argument. Barbara would tell Jim that there was no future in the Gotham PD and no future for him in any police work, not since Chicago, and Jim would probably lose his temper. What had happened in Chicago hadn't been his fault, even if he took the heat for it, and Barbara knew that and why the hell did she keep bringing it up?

But later, lying in bed, he'd admit to himself that his wife was right. He was only in Gotham because, after Chicago, the Gotham force was the only one that would hire him. He'd had to return to his hometown with his tail between his legs. But, dammit, he was a *cop*. That's all he had ever been. Even in the Marines, he'd been assigned to a shore patrol unit.

He pulled a standard form from the stack on the

corner of the desk and began writing a report that no one would ever read—hell, that probably wouldn't even get filed.

9

Rachel Dawes sat in the courtroom for forty-five minutes, listening to Dr. Jonathan Crane's testimony. Much of what the thin, bespectacled psychiatrist said was the medical equivalent of boilerplate, filling up air and time without communicating much, but two sentences caught Rachel's attention. As she listened she twisted a handkerchief in her lap and bit her lip.

"In my opinion," Crane told the court, "Mr. Zsasz is as much a danger to himself as others."

The doctor looked at Victor Zsasz, a bulky man with a completely bald head wearing an orange jump-suit who sat beside his lawyer at a long table.

"Prison is probably not the best environment for his rehabilitation," Crane concluded. "But he would be a welcome addition to our group at Arkham."

When the hearing was over, Rachel ran down the long, curving marble steps and caught up with Crane in the lobby.

"Dr. Crane!" she called breathlessly.

Crane stopped by the door to the portico and said, "Yes, Miss Dawes?"

"Do you seriously think that Victor Zsasz shouldn't be in jail?"

"I would hardly have testified to that otherwise, would I, Miss Dawes?"

Together, they went through the door and began walking in the portico toward an adjoining building.

Rachel said, "This is the third of Carmine Falcone's thugs that you've seen fit to have declared insane and moved into your asylum."

"You shouldn't really be surprised," Crane answered. "The work offered by organized crime has an . . . attraction for the insane."

"And the corrupt."

Crane stopped in midstep, turned to Rachel, and spoke over her shoulder: "Mr. Finch, I think you should check with Miss Dawes here. Just what implications has your office authorized her to make? If any."

Crane stalked away as Rachel watched her boss approach. Carl Finch took Rachel's arm and said, "What are you doing, Rachel?"

"What are *you* doing, Carl?"

"Looking out for you."

Finch guided Rachel to an alcove before speaking again. "Rachel, Falcone's got half the city bought and paid for . . . drop it."

"How can you say that?"

"Because much as I care about getting Falcone . . . I care more about you."

"That's sweet, Carl. But we've been through all this."

Rachel stood on her toes and gave Finch a sisterly kiss on the cheek.

Across the street, sitting on a bus stop bench, a man wearing a baseball cap and sweat clothes that were old and frayed, watched Rachel kiss Finch and hurry toward the parking lot. Then Bruce walked down the block and behind a greeting-card store, where Alfred waited in the car.

Several hours later, shaved, showered, and dressed in jeans and a Gotham U. sweatshirt, Bruce sat on the floor of his library shuffling through papers and photographs. He paused at a picture of Rachel leaving the court, taken with a telephoto lens. He heard a chittering sound and dropped the photo, stood, and strode into the mansion's main hall. He squinted and stared upward, trying to see clearly a shadowy thing that fluttered just outside the window.

Alfred, holding a silver tea service, spoke from the doorway to the kitchen: "Another blessed bat again, sir. They nest somewhere on the grounds."

"Yes, they do."

Ten minutes later, Bruce, wearing a long overcoat, with a coil of rope over one arm, walked past the greenhouse. The long, low building where Bruce and Rachel had played together as children had not fared well: glass was cracked or completely missing; paint was peeling from the wrought-iron frame. Bruce continued to the old well shaft; it was almost completely overgrown with weeds.

Bruce wrenched loose the boards covering the well and tossed them aside. He tied one end of his rope to a nearby tree and began lowering himself into the dark, chilly shaft. When he reached the bottom, he felt air blowing on his face. He unclipped a flashlight from his belt and shone its beam into a crevice. He remembered an old panic . . .

. . . bats tearing at him . . .

He stooped and pulled stones from the well's curving wall until the crevice was wide enough to accommodate him. Then, on his hands and knees, the flashlight wedged between chin and shoulder, he crawled.

Within a few yards, the crevice widened into a low-ceilinged chamber. By bowing his head, Bruce was able to stand. He heard running water. Crouching, he inched forward. The angle of the stone under his boots changed. In the flashlight beam, he saw that the chamber floor was tilting downward. Bruce lay on his back and slid, slowly lowering himself into—

Someplace huge—Bruce sensed that. He got a chemical torch from inside his coat, cracked it, and threw it. The harsh metallic glare revealed a vast cavern, long, tapered stalagmites rising from its floor, equally long stalactites jutting from above.

The torchlight glinted on a wide gap full of running water that roared and sprayed white foam in the center of the cavern.

I wonder if I'm the first person ever to see this place . . .

He swept his flashlight beam upward, to the darkness between the stalactites, and saw a flicker of movement. A second before they descended—thousands and thousands of flapping, chittering, screeching bats—

Bruce realized what they were and knelt and covered his head and face with his arms. He felt hot panic—

Then he remembered the bats that had swarmed from Rā's al Ghūl's box and felt himself grow calm. His moment of terror, he knew, had been created by the memories of someone who no longer existed— who had not existed since he saw his parents' blood spilling over pearls in a Gotham street alleyway. Bruce had a secret that child had not yet learned: *Embrace your worst fear* . . .

He threw back his arms and stood calmly in the midst of the fluttering maelstrom, smiling.

10

It was midnight and the Friday evening crowd in Carmine Falcone's club was getting rowdy. Falcone listened to the raucous laughter and occasional shouting, intermixed with the feeble efforts of the jazz combo, through his office wall. Sitting behind his mahogany desk, he was leaning back in his overstuffed leather chair and contemplating the thin, bespectacled man who stood before him, shifting his weight from foot to foot.

"No more favors, Falcone," Jonathan Crane said. "Someone's sniffing around."

"Hey, Doc. Remember how it works? I scratch your back, you scratch mine. I'm bringing in your shipments."

"We're paying you for that."

"Maybe money isn't as interesting to me as favors."

Crane leaned forward. A moment ago, he seemed nervous. Now, he did not. "I'm aware that you're not intimidated by me. But you know who I'm working for and when he gets here—"

Falcone straightened in his chair. "*He's* coming to Gotham?"

"And he's not going to want to hear that you've endangered our operation just to get your thugs out of jail time."

Falcone stared at his desktop for a minute. "Okay, who's bothering you?"

"There's a girl in the D.A.'s office—"

Falcone shrugged. "We'll buy her off."

"Not this one."

"Idealist, huh? Well, there's an answer for that, too."

"I don't want to know."

"Yes. You do, Dr. Crane."

Most of Gotham's businesspeople were just straggling into their offices, pouring their first paper cupful of company coffee, logging onto their computers, strategizing about how to get through their day. But William Earle believed in early starts and so, although the clock on the boardroom wall indicated that it was not yet nine, the Wayne Enterprises staff meeting had been in full session for over an hour. A young, smartly dressed blond man in a tailored suit named Barry McFraland was standing, a sheaf of papers in his hand, addressing the ten other executives in the room.

"We're showing very healthy growth in these sectors," he was saying.

An older man named Joseph Fredericks spoke without getting up. "I don't think that Thomas Wayne would have viewed heavy-arms manufacture as a suitable cornerstone of our business."

From his seat at the head of the table, Earle said, "I think, Fredericks, that after twenty years we ought to be at a point where we stop asking ourselves what Thomas Wayne would have done. Thomas Wayne wouldn't have wanted to take the company public, either, but that's what, as responsible managers, we're going to do."

Fredericks stared down at the yellow legal pad in front of him and said nothing.

At that moment, about fifty feet away, down a heavily carpeted hallway, Bruce Wayne emerged from an elevator, looking quite debonair in a business suit and tie, and walked briskly to the reception desk where a young woman was arranging some reports in a folder.

"Good morning," Bruce said through a wide smile. "I'm here to see Mr. Earle."

The woman dropped the reports and brought up the visitors' list on a computer screen. "Name?"

"Bruce Wayne."

The woman began to scan the list, then stopped and looked up, her eyes widening.

The phone at her elbow buzzed.

"You can answer that," Bruce said pleasantly. "I'm in no hurry."

The woman put the receiver to her ear and heard Earle bark, "Jessica, get me that prospectus . . . never mind, I'll get it myself."

Thirty seconds later Earle came from the hallway. "Jessica—" He stopped in midstride and stared at Bruce.

"Good morning, Mr. Earle," Bruce said. "You may not remember me. We met years ago, when I was a kid."

Earle seemed to have a problem speaking. But finally he said, "We thought you were dead."

"Sorry to disappoint."

Twenty minutes later, Bruce and Earle sat in Earle's large office with windows overlooking all of Gotham City's downtown area, and with a view of twenty miles or more, stretching beyond the suburbs. Jessica poured coffee into china cups, set them on a low, marble table in front of Earle and Bruce, and asked, "Will there be anything else?"

"Not at the moment," Bruce said. "Later—who knows?"

"I suppose you know that we've taken the company public," Earle said.

"I *did* hear something about that."

"You realize, Bruce, that the public offering is a done deal."

Bruce sipped coffee and sighed. "Excellent. What is it—Kona? From Hawaii?" He sipped again. "Wherever it comes from, it's first-rate . . . Where were we? Oh, yes. The public offering. I understand I'll be handsomely rewarded for my shares."

"Very handsomely indeed."

"I'm not here to interfere, Mr. Earle. Actually, I'm looking for a job." Bruce paused, and put his cup on the table. "I just want to get to know the company that my family built."

"Any idea where you'd start?"

"Applied Sciences caught my eye."

"Lucius Fox's department? Perfect. I'll make a call."

"Thank you." Bruce rose and moved toward the door.

"Oh, and, Bruce?" Earle called after him. "Some of the assistants and so on . . . because of your name they may *assume* . . ."

Bruce held up a flat hand. "Not to worry. I'll be absolutely clear with everyone that I'm just another humble employee."

Bruce was curious about Lucius Fox. His father had once called Fox "the best hire I ever made. The man's darn near a universal genius. Doctorates in both engineering and chemistry before he was twenty-five and only a thesis away from another doctorate in physics." How would a universal genius with a couple of PhDs react to a world-class college dropout?

Bruce asked Jessica where the Applied Sciences Department was and, following her directions, took an elevator to the sub-basement level and went through a heavy metal fire door into a windowless chamber. There was a single lightbulb hanging from a wire over a battered steel desk. A wiry African American man in his fifties, wearing a rumpled suit and a bright red bow tie, sat behind it and contemplated Bruce over the top of his glasses.

"You're Bruce Wayne?" he asked in the laziest drawl Bruce had ever heard.

"Guilty."

"Lucius Fox." Fox came around the desk and shook Bruce's hand. Nothing about how he moved was as lazy as his drawl. "What did they tell you this place was?"

"They didn't tell me anything."

Fox chuckled. "Earle told me *exactly* what it was when he sent me here—"

Fox flicked a switch on the wall, the sudden light revealing that they were standing in a massive warehouse. Crates and boxes and bales, many under dust covers, were stacked everywhere.

"—A dead end," Fox continued, "where I couldn't cause any more trouble for the board."

"You were on the board?"

"Back when your father ran things."

"You knew my father?"

"Sure. Helped him build his monorail. Want to see some of our more interesting stuff?"

"Sure."

Fox led Bruce around a stack of crates to a steel box and pulled from it what looked like a small electric drill and a coil of thin wire. "If you're a climber, you'll like this. Pneumatic. Magnetic grapple."

Bruce lifted the gear and bounced it on his palm. "Light."

"Strong, too," Fox said. "Monofilament tested to 350 pounds."

Bruce picked up something else. "This go with it?"

"Yep. A harness. Try it on."

Bruce slipped his arms through the shoulder straps and tightened a wide belt around his waist, then shoved the pneumatic gun into the belt buckle. It clicked into place.

"What use did you have in mind for this stuff?" Bruce asked.

"Your father's philosophy was, if you have an idea for a gadget, build it first, figure out what it's good for later."

"A variation on 'if you build it they will come.'"

"I guess."

Bruce shed the harness and followed Fox deeper into the jungle of crates.

"Beautiful project, that elevated train of your father's," Fox reminisced. He had apparently forgotten what they had been talking about. "Routed the tracks right into Wayne Tower, along with the water and power utilities. Made Wayne Tower the unofficial heart of Gotham. Course, Earle's left it to rot . . ."

Fox stopped and peered at the stenciled lettering on a narrow, upright crate. "Found it. Knew it was here someplace."

He lifted the lid up and set it aside. A dark bodysuit hung inside the crate. "The nomex survival suit for advanced infantry. Kevlar bi-weave, reinforced joints . . ."

Bruce rubbed the fabric between thumb and forefinger. "Tear resistant?"

"This sucker'll stop a knife."

"Bulletproof?"

"Anything short of a direct hit with a large-caliber slug."

"Why didn't they put it into production?"

Fox sighed. "The bean counters figured a soldier's life wasn't worth the three hundred grand."

"I'd like to borrow it. For spelunking. You know, cave diving."

Fox shrugged and put the lid back on the crate. "You get a lot of gunfire down in those caves?"

Bruce smiled. "Never hurts to be ready for the worst. Listen, Mr. Fox, I'd rather Mr. Earle didn't know about me borrowing . . ."

"Mr. Wayne, the way I see it"—Lucius Fox swept his arm in a wide arc—"all this stuff is yours anyway."

"I have another request, Mr. Fox."

"Fire away."

"I'm in need of a kind of . . . tool belt, I guess you could call it. Do you think I could keep the harness and belt as well?"

"Of course."

Bruce smiled. He would never again have to hold an attaché case between his teeth.

11

At nine the next morning, Alfred telephoned the *Gotham Times* Society Page editor to report that Bruce Wayne, son of the late Dr. and Mrs. Thomas Wayne, had returned from an extended sojourn abroad and had taken up residence at the ancestral Wayne Manor.

By one that afternoon, eleven other news organizations had called and three local television stations had sent reporters and camera crews to interview Bruce, who took the calls and met with the newspeople. He smiled, chatted, showed them around the estate.

All the local papers ran brief items about Bruce's return, though none of them were in the main news sections, and most of the local radio stations mentioned it during their hourly news breaks. One of the television outlets ignored the story completely and the other two ran it as thirty-second items right after the weather forecasts.

A television reporter named Kassie Cane told her boyfriend why Bruce Wayne's return got so little play.

"There was no way we could make a story of it," Kassie said. "I mean, I wanted to . . . good-looking guy, richer than Croesus, return of the prodigal, all that . . . But I swear, talking to him is like talking to a wall. The lights are on but nobody's home. He was nice, even kind of sweet, and he obviously wanted to please us, but there was no personality there."

"Who's Croesus?" her boyfriend asked.

At eleven-thirty that night, Bruce thumbed the off button on the remote and the television screen he and Alfred had been watching went dark.

"Your fellow Gothamites seem remarkably unperturbed by your reappearance among them," Alfred said.

"They *do* seem to be containing their excitement. One has to admire their self-control."

"I take it that all has gone as you wish."

"The old 'hide in plain sight' ploy. Still one of the great ones."

Bruce, wearing the climbing harness and belt that Fox had sent to Wayne Manor, hung thirty feet above the cave floor, hammering a bracket into the stone. A line of industrial lamps hung from the bracket and an electric wire ran from the lamps to a generator below.

"Okay," Bruce shouted. "Give it a try."

Alfred threw a switch and the lamps flickered on, dimly lighting the length of one wall and hundreds of bats hanging from the ceiling.

"At least you'll have company," Alfred said, staring up at a throng of bats.

Bruce rappeled down, unhooked his rope, moved to a wrought-iron spiral staircase at one end of the cavern, and shook it.

"This was grandfather's?" he asked.

"Great-grandfather's. During the Civil War he was involved with the underground railroad. He secretly helped transport escaped slaves. I suspect these caverns came in handy."

Bruce shone a flashlight beam on the small river and then on the place where the water disappeared under rocks. He stepped over the rocks and continued following the river around a bend until he stopped and stared at what his flashlight beam was revealing: a beautiful curtain of water.

"Alfred, come here," Bruce shouted, and his words echoed throughout the cavern. He hopped over slick, glistening rocks and reached out to touch the waterfall.

The following day, Bruce was back at work in the cave. He brought a few items down with him: tools, lumber, some apples, and the sooty, bloody ninja suit he'd brought from Kathmandu—his first trophy. He had fashioned a rough worktable by putting a board between two sawhorses and laid on it two bronze gauntlets, the ones he had salvaged from Rā's al Ghūl's monastery. He picked up a battery-powered paint sprayer and gave them a matte-black finish. Next, he lay the combat suit he had gotten from Lucius Fox on his makeshift trestle and sprayed *that* black.

"Ohhh-*kay*," he murmured.

Alfred descended the spiral staircase carrying an armful of rolled papers. He spread them onto the table and said, "I believe I have our problems solved."

"Tell me," Bruce said.

Alfred pointed to a diagram. "If we order the main point of this . . . cowl? If we order that from Singapore—"

"Via a shell corporation."

"Indeed. Then, quite separately, place an order through a Chinese manufacturer for these—"

He pointed to a drawing of what looked like a pair of horns.

Bruce nodded. "Put it together ourselves."

"Precisely. Of course, they'll have to be large orders to avoid suspicion."

"How large?"

"Say, ten thousand."

"At least we'll have spares." As Bruce was refolding the schematics, he said, "The cave still needs a lot of work to be what I want it to be."

"And what exactly is that, Master Bruce?"

Bruce hesitated, gazing up into the darkness at the top of the cavern. "A workshop, of course. A laboratory. A place to store things. A garage and . . . a place to be who I'm becoming. A place fit for a *bat man* to live. And some other stuff . . . TV cameras to scan all the roads in the area so I don't get surprised coming or going. And I think we should have a second way in and out in case something blocks the pantry. We'll need carpentry, masonry, electronics, maybe hydraulics . . . a lot of skills we don't have."

"Perhaps not yet. But the world is brimming with information and we have access to most of it."

"So you're saying we can do the work ourselves?"

"We managed the lights, didn't we?"

"That we did, Alfred. That we did."

12

It was a few minutes after ten and already Falcone's club was filled to capacity. The air was dense with smoke and liquor fumes and occasionally the hoot of a ship's horn could be heard from outside, over the sound of the three-piece jazz combo that was mostly ignored by the clubbers.

Judge Faden sat between two young women who wore satiny cocktail dresses; he had a drink in one hand and a green cigar in the other. Carmine Falcone stopped next to the judge and put a friendly hand on his shoulder, then moved away.

"Carmine," the judge shouted. "Where are you going?"

Falcone looked back over his shoulder. "Duty calls. You have yourself a good time, Judge."

The judge assured Falcone that he would, finished his drink, and whispered something to one of the young women. He and the woman rose and threaded their way to the front of the club, went up the flight of steps and across the neon-lit sidewalk to a waiting limousine. Faden opened the door, bowed ceremoniously, and guided the woman into the car. A stooped man, obviously a street person, scurried from where a fire burned in an oil barrel nearby, leaving a companion who was wearing a fawn-colored, cashmere overcoat to continue warming himself at the flames. He went to the limo's rear door and, with a foot, prevented Judge Faden from pulling it shut.

"Help a guy out?" he asked the judge.

"Get away," the judge said, and the woman giggled.

The homeless person seemed to slip and fall halfway into the car. He was muttering an apology when the uniformed driver grabbed the back of his collar and yanked. The driver flung him to the sidewalk and kicked him.

The second man by the fire shouted, "Leave him alone. Let him be."

The limo sped off, bumping on the rough pavement toward a beltway that led out of the city. The man who had been kicked smiled and straightened and looked at a tiny video receiver he was holding waist-high. On it, in grainy black-and-white, were the images of Judge Faden and his companion sitting in the backseat of the limo.

"The picture's not great," Bruce said. "But it will do. It will certainly do."

Detective Flass entered Falcone's club by a side door and sat across from the mob boss.

"I need you at the docks tomorrow night," Falcone said.

"Problem?"

"Insurance. I don't want any problems with this last shipment."

"Sure," Flass said. "Word on the street is you got a beef with someone in the D.A.'s office."

"Is that right?"

"And that you've offered a price on doing something about it."

"What's your point, Flass?"

"You've seen this girl? Cute little assistant D.A. That's a lot of heat to bring down, even in this town. Even for you, Carmine."

"Never underestimate Gotham. Besides, people get mugged on the way home from work every day."

Across the street, Bruce Wayne stood in a doorway, adjusting a directional microphone hooked under his ear and hearing the end of Falcone's conversation with Flass. "*Sometimes,*" Falcone was saying, "*it goes bad.*"

Bruce switched off the microphone and got into his car parked nearby. He was wearing the black bodysuit and gauntlets. He drove three miles uptown and parked in an alley across from Gotham's Central Police Headquarters and pulled on a ski mask. He climbed a windowless wall, using the spikes on the gauntlets to pull himself up, topped the balustrade, and ran silently over tar paper until he reached the front parapet. Then he waited. A few minutes later he saw James Gordon park a police sedan in front of the headquarters and enter the building.

Gordon walked past the desk sergeant and up a flight of rickety stairs to the detectives' area on the second floor and into his office. He slammed the door behind him and slumped into a chair, his back to the single dusty window. He removed his glasses, wiped them on his tie, switched on the desk lamp, and pulled a stack of reports from an in-box.

Suddenly the light went out and someone very close behind him said, "Don't turn around."

Something was suddenly pressing against the back of his neck—something that felt like a gun.

"What do you want?" Gordon asked, his voice level, conversational.

"You're a good cop. One of the few."

Gordon narrowed his eyes, puzzled. If this were a hit, he would be dead by now. So what kind of caper *was* it?

The person behind him continued. "Carmine Falcone brings in shipments of drugs every week. Nobody takes him down. Why?"

"He's paid up with the right people."

"What would it take to bring him down?"

Should he answer? Why not? He was not saying anything that every beat cop in the city did not know. "Leverage on Judge Faden . . . And a D.A. brave enough to prosecute."

"Rachel Dawes in the D.A.'s office." It was not a question.

"Who *are* you?"

"Watch for my sign."

"You're just one man?"

"Now we are two."

"*We?*"

Gordon felt the pressure on his neck ease and waited for a reply. Finally, he turned around; the room was empty. He ran to the open window and looked down at the street, empty except for parked cars. He looked up and glimpsed a figure silhouetted against the night sky vanishing onto the roof.

He moved, racing across the floor to the stairwell, drawing his pistol as he went. Two uniformed patrolmen saw him and followed, reaching for their holsters.

Gordon, with the two cops only a few steps behind, ran onto the roof and saw someone dressed in black near the parapet. He knew the space between police headquarters and the parking garage next door was too far to jump. He aimed his pistol and yelled, "Freeze!"

The figure sprinted forward and jumped.

Gordon reached the parapet in time to see the man—he guessed it was a man—hit the side of the garage a few feet beneath the roof edge and fall and grab a fire-escape balcony below, then somehow melt into the shadows.

Gordon lowered his weapon.

One of the patrolmen asked, "What the hell was *that*?"

"Just some nut."

Yeah, Gordon thought, *some* nut . . .

*   *   *

It was not yet eight o'clock the next morning when Bruce Wayne, wearing an expensive, tailored suit, entered Wayne Tower and smiled at everyone he passed. He took the elevator to the basement and entered the Applied Sciences Department. Lucius Fox was already behind his desk.

Fox smiled. "What's it today? More spalunking?"

"*Spee*-lunking," Bruce said. "And no, today it's base-jumping."

"Base-jumping? What, like parachuting?"

"Kind of. Do you have any lightweight fabrics?"

Fox looked at Bruce over his glasses. "Oh, yeah. Wait here."

Fox went behind a stack of crates and, a minute later, emerged holding a sheet of black cloth. He gave it to Bruce and asked, "Notice anything?"

Bruce ran the cloth through his fingers and shook his head.

Fox put on a thick canvas glove. "Memory fabric. Flexible, ordinarily, but put an electric current through it—"

Fox pressed a button on the glove and there was a faint *buzz*. The fabric instantly changed shape and became a small tent.

"The molecules align and become rigid," Fox concluded.

Bruce pressed his fingers on the fabric tent. It did not bend. "What kind of shapes can you make?"

Fox again touched the tent with the electrified glove and the tent reverted to being a square of black cloth.

"It could be tailored to any structure based on a rigid skeleton."

"Too expensive for the army?"

"Yeah. Guess they never thought about marketing to the billionaire base-jumping, spelunking market."

"Look, Mr. Fox, if you're uncomfortable . . ."

"Mr. Wayne, if you don't tell me what you're really doing, then when I get asked, I don't have to lie. But don't treat me like an idiot."

"Fair enough. Anything else a billionaire, base-jumping, spelunking wastrel might want to see?"

Fox gestured to something covered by a tarpaulin. "I could show you the Tumbler . . . but nah, you wouldn't be interested . . ."

"Show me."

They had the Tumbler loaded onto a flatbed truck and followed it in Fox's car to a test track near a small airfield, where the Tumbler was downloaded. Fox, with a bow and a flourish, swept away the canvas cover to reveal the strangest vehicle Bruce had ever seen.

"It looks like a cross between a Lamborghini Countach and a Humvee," he said to Fox.

Bruce and Fox climbed into the Tumbler and Fox began explaining the controls. When he was finished, he said, "She was built as a bridging vehicle. You hit that button—"

Bruce put his forefinger out and Fox shouted, "Not *now*!"

Bruce jerked his finger back.

"It boosts her into a rampless jump," Fox continued. "In combat, two of them jump a river towing cables, then you run a bailey bridge across. Damn bridge never worked, but this baby works just fine."

Bruce settled into the driver's seat and tested his reach to the various buttons and levers. The fit was perfect; it was as though the Tumbler had been built for him.

"Would you like to take her for a spin?" Fox asked.

Bruce pushed the ignition button, eased the stick into first gear, and toed the gas pedal. The Tumbler shot forward. To Bruce it seemed like the first bend in the track was in his windshield immediately. He tapped the brake pedal and the Tumbler skidded to a halt.

"I forgot to tell you," Fox said. "She's kinda peppy. What do you think?"

Bruce inched the Tumbler forward and smiled. "Does it come in black?"

Three days later Bruce and Alfred were in the cave below the mansion, bent over a workbench they had installed, examining what looked like a batter's helmet. As Bruce watched, Alfred picked up a baseball bat and slammed the helmet-thing, breaking it in two.

"Problems with the graphite mixture," Alfred said. "The *next* ten thousand will be up to specifications."

"At least they gave us a discount," Bruce said.

"Quite. In the meantime, might I suggest you try to avoid landing on your head?"

"Good idea." Bruce moved to where the utility belt and grappling gun were hung on a mannequin. "Time to begin testing."

He removed the utility belt, now freed of the harness, from the mannequin and strapped it on, shaking the gun to be certain that it was firmly nestled in its buckle holster. He went back to the bench and put on a pair of gloves, one with electric contacts in the fingers and a tiny but powerful battery on the underside of the wrist. Each glove had scallops like those on the gauntlets he had worn at Rā's al Ghūl's monastery.

"Devilishly handsome, if I may say so, Master Bruce," Alfred commented.

"Emphasis on the 'devilish,' I assume."

Bruce lifted a curved metal object from the bench, hefted it, and threw it at a stalactite. It whistled across the cave and bit deep into the stone.

"Your boomerang did not come back," Alfred said.

"It's not supposed to, unless it misses what I'm aiming at. By the way, Alfred, I'm thinking of calling these things 'Batarangs.' What do you think?"

"*Devilishly* clever," Alfred said.

The following morning there was a small item buried in the local gossip column of the *Gotham Times*. It told

the world that Bruce Wayne, newly returned to the
city, was leaving again for a brief vacation in northern
California. He planned to see the sights in and around
San Francisco and was considering a few days' hang
gliding at Mount Tamalpais.

Reading the snippet on a westbound plane, Bruce
thought it a mistake to have leaked the part about
hang gliding because it might call attention to abili-
ties he wanted to remain hidden.

He was living and learning.

He returned from Mount Tamalpais a week later
by commercial carrier. He told the perky young woman
behind the airline's ticket counter that his wallet with
his credit cards and ID had been stolen but, fortu-
nately, he always carried emergency cash in his sock
and would five hundred be enough for passage to
Gotham? It was highly irregular and the perky ticket
seller had to confer with her supervisor, but finally
Bruce was allowed to board the plane.

He arrived at Gotham International at four in the
morning, his only concern that he might run into someone he knew in the terminal. He did not want anyone
to know he was back yet because his alter ego was
about to reappear and he was afraid that someone—
that smart cop Gordon, for example—might connect
Bruce Wayne's return with the mystery man. Sooner or
later, he would make a big, clumsy deal of the wastrel's
homecoming—do something stupid, maybe.

He need not have worried. No one was in the terminal except a few indifferent maintenance workers, and the following night no one saw him enter several of Carmine Falcone's habitats and vehicles and install tiny microphones.

At his last stop, an apartment Falcone owned near the theater district, Bruce placed his bug and went up the fire escape to the roof. He waited, a small receiver in his ear, until the sky began to lighten.

Time to pack it in . . .

Through his earpiece, he heard the sound of a door opening, the clink of glass against glass, and two voices. He recognized Falcone's: "Tomorrow night, pier fourteen. Tell your guys."

A second voice: "Don't worry, Mr. F. They'll be there."

Tomorrow night. Pier fourteen. It's a date . . .

An icy wind was blowing off the bay. Already, the dock area was chilled; soon, the wind would chill the entire city. A wispy mist blurred the streetlamps and softened the edges of the large cargo container, one of dozens of similar containers.

Bigger, Alfie, and Steiss were finally working, unloading boxes, and it was about time. They had arrived at pier fourteen at eight-thirty, as Mr. Falcone insisted, and then waited around for three hours until the huge overhead crane had swung a cargo container from the deck of a freighter onto the dock. The night was growing cold and Steiss and Bigger pulled the zippers of their jackets higher. Suddenly headlights from an approaching sedan lit the scene and the three stopped and for several seconds did not move.

Detective Flass got out of the car and strode briskly to one of the unloaded boxes. He parted its flaps, reached inside, and brought out a stuffed bear. He tossed it onto a nearby pile of bears. Next to the bears was a pile of stuffed rabbits.

"Cute," he said.

He went to where a limousine was parked at the curb and let himself into the backseat. Carmine Falcone was already there, a stuffed rabbit in his lap.

"Looks fine out there," Flass said. "So the bears go straight to the dealers—"

"And the rabbits go to our man in the Narrows," Falcone said.

"What's the difference?"

"Ignorance is bliss, my friend. Don't burden yourself with the secrets of scary people."

"Scarier than you?"

"*Considerably* scarier than me."

Outside, the work of unloading the containers continued beneath a single overhead lamp. Steiss handed a box to Bigger, who took it away down a narrow passageway between the stacked containers. Steiss turned back to the darkness in the open container and was yanked inside.

A moment later, Bigger heard a muffled groan. He set the box down and called, "Steiss?"

There was no reply. Bigger pulled a gun from under his jacket and nodded to Alfie, who was coming from the docks.

Bigger said, "Come on, we gotta—"

Alfie drew his own gun and together they moved toward the open container.

Behind them, something whistled from the shadows and the overhead lamp shattered. The two men jerked around, raising their weapons. The thing that had hit the lamp fell to the ground and Alfie lifted it, trying to see exactly what it was in the darkness. His gaze went past it to the huge crane that loomed against the sky and the winged shape that hung from it.

The shape moved.

Alfie blinked and whispered, "What the hell . . ."

The winged shape dropped and its wings whipped out and became rigid. The shape—was it a man?—somersaulted and enveloped Alfie.

Bigger ran, his arms pumping, the breath exploding from his mouth. He charged down the narrow passage between the stacks of containers, came to a corner, slowed and rounded it, and raced toward the street. A blackness with wings descended on him and he screamed.

In the limo, Falcone and Flass heard the scream. Flass got out of the car, pulled an automatic from a shoulder holster, and eyes scanning the area, moved toward the docks.

"Where the hell're the lights?" he muttered.

He slipped into the passage between the containers and his foot hit something soft that moaned. He knelt, struck a match, and saw Bigger, alive but unconscious.

Flass ran to the limo, jerked open the door, and

told Falcone, "Call the club. Get some more men. Tell 'em to bring guns."

Less than five minutes later, eight men bolted up the steps from Falcone's club and, puffing, ran to the docks, a block away. Falcone, cradling a shotgun, waited for them beside the limo. He told them that somebody was around who did not belong and to find that person and kill him.

As they crept toward the containers, guns leveled ahead of them, the smallest of the gunmen whispered, "I wish we didn't haveta do this."

His nearest companion said, "Shut up, Jimmy."

"I didn't mean nothing, Willy, only . . ."

"Shut up," Willy repeated. Willy turned to a third man. "You got any idea what we should do, Lou?"

"You heard the boss," Lou replied. "Find something and kill it."

"Maybe we oughta split up," Willy said.

"That ain't such a good idea . . ."

This time Lou said, "Shut up, Willy."

They separated, Willy going into the passage between the containers, Lou and Jimmy circling around to the loading area, the other five creeping through the narrow spaces between the stacks of containers.

A dark shape fell on Willy and then Willy fell, unconscious.

Lou inched onto the dock, saw nothing, returned to where the containers were stacked. The dark shape leaped from the passageway. An arm flashed into view and yanked Lou back into the shadows.

Jimmy saw Lou and the shape vanish from where

he had been standing forty feet away. He lifted his gun. The shape reappeared and Jimmy fired at it. The dark shape darted across the space between two crates and Jimmy fired again and kept firing until the hammer of his gun fell on an empty chamber.

He fumbled in his coat pocket for a fresh clip and, his voice edged with panic, shouted, "Where are you?"

He heard a whisper in his ear: "Here."

Jimmy turned his head and was looking into a masked face, inches from his, hanging upside down. Something closed over him and he fell to the ground.

Flass was still outside the stacks of containers and crates, his gun held loosely at his side. He was listening, hard, and he heard only the lapping of water and the distant rush of traffic. He went to Falcone's limo, opened a rear door, and poked his head inside.

"What the hell's going on?" Falcone demanded.

"You've got a *problem* out there."

"Yeah? Then I'll *solve* it."

Falcone, gripping his shotgun by the stock, left the limo and he and Flass went into the stacks and separated. Falcone lifted his shotgun to waist level, aimed the barrel ahead of himself, and curled a forefinger around the trigger.

He heard noises coming from the containers: grunts, groans, the dull thud of blows. He just stood, shotgun half raised.

After fifteen minutes, Flass rejoined Falcone and together, guns stuck out in front of them like the prows of ships, they searched for and found their men. All were unconscious except for Jimmy, who was babbling about a big black bird. They did not bother to help their fallen employees.

"What do you think?" Flass asked.

"I think we get the hell out of here until we know what's going on."

They returned to the limo and Flass continued on to his own car. Falcone got in the back, tapped on the Plexiglas partition between the passenger compartment and the driver's seat, and said, "Let's go."

There was no answer. Falcone lowered the partition and shook the driver, who fell forward onto the steering wheel.

The limo shook as something landed on the roof. Falcone's head whipped around and he peered up out of the sunroof window at the silhouette above him.

"What the hell are you?" Falcone murmured.

For a moment, there was stillness.

Then the glass sunroof shattered and a pair of black-clad arms grabbed Falcone by the lapels and yanked him up through the opening until his face was level with another face, one hidden by a mask.

"I'm Batman," the masked man said.

A block away, Joey, hugging his cashmere coat around him and warming himself at his blazing oil barrel, heard a stifled shout. Cautiously, he left his fire and crept up the block, keeping himself against the walls, scurrying past the island of light from the street-lamps. He reached the docks and gasped—could not *help* but gasp—when he saw a tall figure in black, with a scalloped cape blowing behind it, standing on the roof of a limousine.

"Nice coat," the figure told Joey and vanished—upward into the night sky!

Joey looked down at his coat and back to where the figure had been. "Thanks," he said.

13

Rachel Dawes sat in the monorail car, alternately staring out the window at the lights of the city blurring past and back into the car at the graffiti that covered virtually every surface. She was alone except for a thin man who sat at one end of the car, head bent, speaking into a cell phone.

Rachel allowed her head to fall forward and closed her eyes. She was exhausted. She had just finished a sixteen-hour day at the office where she had achieved nothing except frustration. It sometimes seemed as though all of the city's criminals except jaywalkers were immune from prosecution. So much disappointment in her life right now . . .

Rachel was not one to feel sorry for herself, but she had to admit to a chronic low-level depression. She had grown up assuming that she and Bruce Wayne would go through high school and college together and then get married and begin having it all—children, friends, and careers, a lifetime spent improving Gotham City. But Bruce had been gone for years, only resurfacing recently. Yet he had made no effort to contact her or see her. She could not help but feel stung by this.

As for improving Gotham City—big laugh. You could not improve the unimprovable. Rachel had graduated at the top of her Harvard law class and had been besieged with offers from the big-bucks firms in New York, Chicago, Los Angeles . . . If she had accepted any one of them, by now she'd be pulling down two-fifty k, easily, driving a Beemer, living in an expensive apartment, dating congressmen. Instead, she'd chosen to return to Gotham and take a job in the D.A.'s office that barely paid the rent on a cramped studio apartment in a borderline neighborhood and kept her eating the tuna salad that was her main sustenance. She'd kept that job a lot longer than she expected she would, despite an unblemished record of successes. In Gotham, apparently, there was no such thing as a deserved promotion.

Because, dammit, she wanted to make a difference! She'd seen the law as a bulwark against life's chaos and a way to create meaning and harmony, not the endless succession of compromise and sleazy dealmaking that was her daily lot.

And her love life? Another laugh. Oh, sure, she'd dated a few guys, some lawyers, some junior entrepreneurs, but after an hour either they bored her or seemed intimidated by her. She was aware that her boss's interest in her was more than professional, but although Carl was a sweetheart, he did nothing for her. After a while, she tired of being hit on by the courthouse crowd—the lawyers, cops, even some judges.

The train rounded a bend and slowed to a halt, breaking her thoughts. They had arrived at her station. Rachel moved out onto the platform, unlighted because its lamps had been broken for months, and stepping through litter, descended the staircase, dimly aware that the thin man had also left the train and was somewhere behind her. That made Rachel uneasy, but almost everything in Gotham made her uneasy these days. Instinctively, she hugged her bag to her chest.

Halfway down the stairs to the parking lot, a large man appeared, blocking her way. Rachel's unease became alarm and she scanned the area, seeking help. But the station was deserted and the parking lot empty except for her car and a black SUV parked near the exit. The thin man was descending toward her. She ran down the remaining steps and tried to push past the large man. He grabbed her arm, but she slammed her bag into his head. Reaching inside it, she brought out a Taser, and aimed it at the man she had just hit.

"Hold it!" she yelled.

The thin man was only a couple of yards away and her weapon needed to be reloaded after every use. If she shot the large man the thin man would be on her . . .

In the dim light from a distant streetlamp, she saw the large man's expression change as he looked past her, over her shoulder. She heard a rustling sound and chanced a glance back. She saw a black shape enveloping the thin man, tearing him off his feet and into the shadows.

The large man spun and lumbered off.

"You'd *better* run," Rachel shouted after him.

Rachel turned and caught her breath. A black, demonic shape was crouched on a railing, a dark cape billowing behind it. Rachel did not hesitate; she shot the Taser. A projectile, trailing two wires, struck the demon-thing and, Rachel knew, hit it with fifty thousand volts of electricity. Sparks danced around the projectile and in their flicker she saw a masked face calmly regarding her.

The masked man casually pulled on the wires, tugging the projectile from his chest.

He said, "Next time, try Mace." The voice was low and hoarse, possibly disguised.

"Are you with . . . him?" Rachel asked, pointing to the thin man, who had tumbled to the bottom of the steps.

"No. Falcone sent him to kill you."

"Why?"

"You rattled his cage."

The masked man produced some photographs from somewhere under his cloak and tossed them to Rachel. She held the photos to let the light from the distant lamp strike them. They were compromising pictures of Judge Faden and some woman. Rachel would even call them damning.

"What's this?" she asked.

"Leverage."

"For what?"

"To get things moving."

Rachel stepped closer to the masked man and tried to peer at his face. There was something familiar about him . . . "Who are you?"

"Someone like you . . . Someone who'll rattle the cages."

A train pulled onto the platform above them and for a moment Rachel was blinded by its headlight. When her vision cleared, she was alone. But not exhausted, as she had been only minutes earlier. No, now what Rachel felt was something akin to excitement.

Jim Gordon sipped coffee from a paper cup. Lousy coffee, already cold. He dropped the half-full cup into a trash container, buttoned his trench coat all the way up, and walked onto the dock to where a uniformed cop was shining his flashlight onto six men whose backs were against a cargo container. All six were unconscious and bound with nylon rope.

"Tell me," Gordon said.

"We got a call, anonymous," the cop said. "Found a coke shipment in the container worth maybe four mil on the street."

Gordon gestured to the men on the ground. "These guys?"

"I'm not sure, Sergeant. Maybe Falcone's men?"

Gordon shrugged. "Does it matter? We'll never tie them to him anyway."

"I wouldn't be too sure of that." The cop pointed at a harbor light, normally used to help ships navigate the narrow entrance to the piers at night. Its beam had been redirected from the water and was shining into the sky. Carmine Falcone, unconscious, was strapped to it, his arms spread, his coat ripped and hanging from his arms; Falcone's shadow was cast onto the clouds.

"Looks like a big bat," the cop said.

"Cut him down," Gordon said.

He needed time to think. He started back toward his car. Two reporters from the *Times* tried to block his way and a photographer ran past him.

"Sergeant Gordon," one of the reporters called, extending a small tape recorder.

"Not now," Gordon growled.

A block away, he saw something blowing from the side of a building. A black flag? No, a man wearing a cape, perched on a ledge, watching . . .

Rachel did not want another adventure in the monorail parking lot, at least not right away, so the next morning she drove her car all the way into downtown Gotham and spent about a third of what she would earn that day to park in a private garage. Leaving the garage, she glanced around nervously and, inside her purse, gripped the Taser.

No, she told herself. *If they scare you, they win.*

She released the Taser and sauntered on.

Outside her office, she dropped two quarters into a machine and grabbed a copy of the *Gotham Times*. She paused to scan the front page, and then grinned.

Ten minutes later, she dropped the paper onto her

boss's desk and grinned again as she watched Finch take in the picture of Falcone strapped to the harbor light.

"No way to bury it now," Rachel said.

Finch raised his eyes. "Maybe so, but there's Judge Faden . . ."

"I've got Faden covered."

"And this 'bat' they're babbling about . . ."

"Even if these guys'll swear in court to being thrashed by a giant bat . . . we have Falcone at the scene. Drugs. Prints. Cargo manifests. This bat character gave us *everything*."

Finch straightened the knot in his tie and said, "Well, then. Let's get frying."

At that moment, a block away, in the fortress-like stone edifice that housed Gotham Central Police Headquarters, Commissioner Loeb was holding up the *Gotham Times* and shouting to a conference room full of captains, sergeants, and lieutenants, including James Gordon.

"Unacceptable. I don't care if it's rival gangs, Guardian Angels, or the Salvation Army, get them off the street and off the front page."

A captain named Simonson said, "They say it was only one guy . . . or thing."

"Some nutcase in a costume," Flass added.

Gordon raised his hand. "This guy *did* deliver to us one of the city's biggest crime lords."

Loeb glared at him. "No one takes the law into their own hands in *my* city, understand?"

Everyone nodded solemnly.

Alfred Pennyworth pulled open the curtains on the window of Wayne Manor's master bedroom. The afternoon sun shone on the bed and the man lying in it.

Bruce Wayne blinked and said, "Bats are nocturnal."

"Bats, perhaps," Alfred said. "But even for billionaire playboys, three o'clock is pushing it. The price of leading a double life, I fear."

Alfred picked up a tray from a sideboard and set it down on a table next to the bed. On it was a health shake, a bunch of grapes, an orange, a small knife, and that day's *Gotham Times*.

Alfred unfolded the paper and displayed the photo of Falcone strapped to the light. "Your theatrics made quite an impression."

Bruce looked at the photo. "Theatrics and deception are powerful weapons, Alfred. It's a start."

He threw aside the bedding, rose, and stretched.

Alfred peered at the bruises on Bruce's bare chest and arms. "If those are to be the first of many injuries . . . it would be wise to find a suitable excuse. Polo, for instance."

"I'm not learning polo, Alfred."

"Strange injuries, a nonexistent social life . . . these things beg the question of what, exactly, Bruce Wayne does with his time. And his money."

Bruce sipped from the health shake. "What *does* someone like me do?"

"Drives sports cars, dates film actresses . . . Buys things that aren't for sale."

"Uh huh." Bruce put the glass onto the tray and without pausing dropped to the rug and began doing push-ups, two per second.

"Economy of effort?"

Without stopping his push-ups, Bruce replied, "Not a good idea to waste anything, *including* effort."

"You learned that abroad?"

"Among many other useful things."

Alfred watched him for a while and then said, "Enjoyment was obviously not one of them. If you start *pretending* to have fun, you might even have a little by accident."

"You think?"

That afternoon, Bruce backed a rented Chrysler into an airport fence. He told the security men that somehow he had lost control of the darn thing and that he was just back from Mount Tamalpais and had they ever been to the West Coast?

14

It was only seven forty-five in the morning and already William Earle was having a bad day. He had lost a bundle when overnight the Tokyo markets nose-dived, his espresso machine was on the fritz, and he had a dull, throbbing ache in his temples.

Then Barry McFraland bustled into his office and things got worse.

McFraland planted himself in front of Earle's desk and blurted, "We have a situation."

"What kind of situation?"

McFraland plopped down in a chair and scooted it close to the desk. "The Coast Guard picked up one of our cargo ships last night. Heavily damaged. Crew missing, probably dead."

"What happened?"

"The ship was carrying a prototype weapon. A microwave emitter."

"Which does what, exactly? Cook frozen pizza?"

McFraland uttered a single *ha*, acknowledging his boss's joke but not really laughing, and continued. "It's designed for desert warfare. It uses focused microwaves to vaporize the enemy's water supply."

"And?"

"It looks like someone fired it up."

"What caused the damage?"

"The expansion of water into steam created an enormous pressure wave and everything exploded—pipes, boilers, drains . . ."

"Where's the weapon?"

"That's the *really* bad part. It's missing."

Bruce Wayne guided his Lamborghini Murciélago into the semicircular driveway of Puccio's, a restaurant that occupied the top floor of the Gotham Arms. His turn was too wide and the car's right tires went onto the curb and knocked over a potted plant. He jolted to a stop at the valet's station. A uniformed attendant opened the driver's door and Bruce emerged.

"They really ought to make these drives wider," he said.

"Yessir, Mr. Wayne," the attendant said. "Nice car."

"You ought to see my *other* one."

Another attendant opened the passenger door and two young women who called themselves Kiki and Sooze got out. They were petite, one brunette and one blond, spike-heeled, and both were wearing very short floral-print dresses.

Kiki took Bruce's left arm while Sooze took his right and the trio entered the building through a revolving door dedicated to Puccio's clientele and went up a modern glass elevator. They rode up to the fortieth floor and stepped into a glittering place of white linen, crystal, and silver tableware, and the aroma of richly sauced dishes. Floor-to-ceiling windows gave the diners a view of downtown Gotham City's millions of lights. A sculptured fountain with a pool at its center ran along one whole side of the establishment. There was a low murmur of conversation and the *plink* of spoons and forks against china.

A tuxedoed maitre d' led Bruce, Kiki, and Sooze to William Earle's table, where dinner was already under way.

Earle and four other people, two men and two women, were already enjoying their appetizers.

Bruce smiled a hello as he and the two women sat.

There was an animated conversation already in progress between an expensively dressed, middle-aged man and the much younger woman who was obviously his wife. For several minutes, Bruce joined the chitchat, which eventually turned to the crime situation in Gotham and the mysterious vigilante newly arrived in the city. Everyone except the young wife seemed to think that this masked do-gooder was a nutcase.

"Well, he may be . . . *unorthodox,*" the young wife said. "But at least he's getting something done."

"Bruce, help me out here," her husband said.

"A guy who dresses up like a bat clearly has *issues,*" Bruce said.

"But he put Falcone behind *bars,*" the young wife protested.

"And now the cops are trying to bring *him* in," the husband said. "What does *that* tell you?"

"They're jealous?" the wife asked sweetly.

As Bruce and the other dinner guests conversed, Kiki and Sooze quietly left the table and headed to the fountain. The two women slipped out of their dresses and lowered themselves, giggling, into the pool.

The horrified maitre d' hurried toward Bruce. "Sir, the pool is for *decoration* and . . . your friends do not have swimwear."

"Well, they're European," Bruce explained.

The maitre d' looked around, as though seeking help, and said, "I'm going to have to ask you to leave."

Bruce took a checkbook from an inner pocket, uncapped a gold fountain pen, and began writing.

"It's not a question of money," the maitre d' protested.

Bruce tore a check from the book and gave it to the maitre d'. "Take this to your boss. I just bought this hotel—and as of now, I'm making some new rules about the pool area."

As the waiter stared at the check, Bruce walked to the pool. Kiki and Sooze grabbed his jacket and pulled him in beside them.

Later, dressed in robes they had gotten from one of the hotel's shops, their hair still wet, Bruce, Kiki, and Sooze presented themselves at the valet station.

"Bruce?" someone called.

Bruce turned and saw Rachel by the cab stand. She was wearing a cocktail dress, her shoulders bare, and looked stunning.

"Hello, Rachel," Bruce said.

"I heard you were back." Rachel looked at Bruce's robe. "What are you doing?"

"Just . . . swimming. It's good to see you."

"You were gone a long time."

"I know. How are things with you?"

"The same. The job's getting worse."

"You can't change the world on your own."

"No. I guess not. But what choice do I have? You're busy swimming."

Bruce lowered his head and spoke in a near whisper. "Rachel, all this . . . it's not all I am. Inside, I'm different."

An attendant parked the Lamborghini at the curb.

"Come *on*, Brucie," Kiki called, stamping her foot. "We have more hotels for you to buy."

Rachel started to walk away. She stopped, looked back at Bruce, and said, "Deep, *deep down,* you may be the same great little kid you used to be . . . but it's not who you are underneath—it's what you do that defines you."

Bruce got into the Lamborghini and told Kiki and Sooze that maybe they'd better make an early night of it.

Rachel's night was ruined. For just a moment, she thought that maybe there was some hope for Bruce. For just a moment, he was a grown-up version of the earnest child she had known so long ago. Then he reverted to being someone she would cross the street to avoid.

She glanced at her watch. *Whatshisname* . . . her date—was he an investment banker?—something like that . . . He should have been here a half hour ago. She'd give him another five minutes.

At nine the next morning, Dr. Jonathan Crane unfolded his long, lanky body from the front seat of a Lincoln Town Car, got a briefcase from the backseat, and crossed an asphalt lot to the front gate of the Gotham County Jail. The man inside the guardhouse peered at him through the Plexiglas window. Recognizing him, the guard buzzed Crane in. He went past another guardhouse, was buzzed through another door, and was met just inside the main building by the warden.

"Dr. Crane, thank you for coming down," the warden said.

"Not at all. So he cut his wrists?"

"Probably looking for an insanity plea, but if anything happened . . ."

Crane patted the warden's shoulder. "Of course. Better safe than sorry."

She escorted Crane through a series of barred doors to a narrow chamber deep inside the jail.

"Would you like me to stay?" the warden asked.

"That won't be necessary," Crane replied with another reassuring pat. "The therapeutic process is best conducted in private."

She hesitated. "I guess it'll be okay . . . If anything happens, holler. A guard'll be within earshot."

Crane entered the room and sat at a Masonite table across from Carmine Falcone. Falcone held up his bandaged wrists and smiled.

"Oh, poor me, Dr. Crane," he whined. "It's all too much, the walls are closing in, blah blah blah." He laughed and in his normal voice continued. "Couple more days of this food it'll be true."

Crane leaned forward. "What do you want?"

"I wanna know how you're gonna convince me to keep my mouth shut."

"About what? You don't know anything."

"Well, yeah, I do. For instance, I know you wouldn't want the cops taking a closer look at the drugs they seized. I know about your experiments on the inmates at your nuthouse. I don't get into business with someone without finding out their dirty secrets. Those goons you hired . . . listen, I *own* the muscle in this town."

Now it was Falcone who leaned forward, until his eyes were inches from Crane's. "I've been smuggling your stuff in for *months*, so whatever he's got planned, it's big. And I want in."

Crane contemplated Falcone and sighed. "I already know what he'll say. That we should kill you."

"Even he can't touch me in here. Not in my town."

"There's something I'd like you to see."

Crane placed his briefcase on the table between them and pulled from it an odd contraption: a breathing apparatus attached to a piece of burlap with eye-holes cut in it. "I use it in my experiments. Probably not very frightening to a guy like you. But those crazies . . ."

Falcone shifted in his chair and inched away from the table. Crane pulled the mask over his head; he looked like he should be standing in a cornfield somewhere.

Falcone sneered. "When did the nut take over the asylum?"

A puff of smoke rose from Crane's briefcase and wafted into Falcone's face. Falcone coughed.

"They scream and cry," Crane said. "Much as you're doing now."

And Falcone began screaming. He stared wide-eyed at Crane, screaming and crying.

A guard ran in brandishing a club as Crane was putting the mask back into his briefcase. "Dr. Crane, are you all right?"

"Yes, but I'm afraid he isn't." Crane gestured to Falcone, who was curled into a fetal position beneath the table. "It looks like a total psychotic breakdown."

"You think he's faking?"

Crane moved past the guard and said, "No, no faking. Not that one. You'd better put him someplace where he can't hurt himself. I'll talk to a judge, see if I can't get him moved to the secure wing of Arkham. I can't treat him here."

Heat lightning lit the horizon and a cool breeze swept down the alley behind James Gordon's apartment. Gordon, a sack of garbage in his hand, paused to look through the kitchen window at his wife Barbara, who was coaxing their young daughter to eat. Thunder rolled from the sky and lightning flashed again.

"Storm's coming."

Gordon immediately recognized the voice and turned to see Batman crouched on the fire escape.

"The scum's getting jumpy because you stood up to Falcone," Gordon said, lifting the garbage-can lid.

"It's a start," Batman said. "Your partner was at the docks with Falcone."

"He moonlights as a low-level enforcer."

"They were splitting the shipment in two. Only half was going to the dealers."

"Why? What about the other half?"

"Flass knows."

"Maybe. But he won't talk."

"He'll talk to me," Batman said.

"Commissioner Loeb set up a massive task force to catch you. He thinks you're dangerous."

"What do you think?"

Gordon dropped his sack into the can and replaced the lid. "I think you're trying to help . . ."

He was talking to himself. Batman was gone.

". . . But I've been wrong before."

A few minutes later, the rain began to sweep across the docks, where District Attorney Carl Finch was walk-

ing beside a man in beige overalls, checking the tags
of shipping containers with flashlights.

They stopped before a particularly large container
and Finch said, "*This* is the one I'm talking about."

"What's your problem with it?" the dock worker
asked.

"It shouldn't exist. This ship left Singapore with
246 containers and arrived with 247. I'm guessing
there's something I'm not supposed to find in there."

The man in overalls winked at Finch. "Lissen,
Counselor, we know the way things work in this
town. You and me—we don't *wanna* know what's in
Mr. Falcone's crates."

Finch glared at the man. "Things are working differently now. Open it."

The man in overalls shrugged and pulled the container door open. Finch swept the inside with his
flashlight beam and saw what looked like some kind
of industrial machine the size of a small refrigerator.

"What the hell is this thing?" he asked and then was
struck in the back by a bullet. He fell to the ground,
dead.

The man in overalls put a .25-caliber automatic
back in his pocket. He grabbed Finch's ankles and
dragged the body into the container.

By nine, rain was falling throughout Gotham and
the suburbs. Most of the city's street workers had
given up for the night and gone home, or were huddled somewhere hoping the storm would end. But in

the theater district, one food stand had remained open and there, under its canopy, Flass stuffed a falafel into his mouth, half chewed it, and swallowed. Bowing his head, he left the shelter of the canopy and ran into the pelting rain. He turned a corner and continued running down a narrow alleyway.

Suddenly something looped around him and he was no longer standing on the pavement; he was being lifted. He stopped when his face was inches from a black mask. He then realized that the masked man was holding him by the ankle, about forty feet above the concrete.

"Where were the other drugs going?"

"I don't know," Flass gasped.

Batman released Flass and the cop dropped twenty feet. His scream was lost in a crack of thunder. The wire that looped around him halted his fall. Batman pulled him back up.

"I never knew," Flass whispered. "Shipments went to some guy for a couple days before they went to dealers . . ."

"Why?"

"There was something else in the drugs, something hidden."

"What?"

"I don't know . . . I never went to the drop-off. It's in the Narrows . . . cops only go there in force . . ."

Batman released his hold on Flass. Flass dropped quickly and jerked to a sudden stop just inches from the ground. Then Batman gently lowered him to the ground and disappeared, leaving Flass speechless.

* * *

Like everyone else in Gotham City Bruce Wayne knew about the area locals called "the Narrows." But, like most who lived uptown, or in the suburbs, he had never visited the neighborhood, an island in the middle of the Gotham River with an insane asylum at one end and a labyrinth of dilapidated public housing at the other, accessible only by three bridges and a tunnel. Bruce Wayne would have no business in the Narrows. But Batman—that was something else.

It was early evening by the time he got there and the rain had increased to a heavy and constant downpour. He entered the housing project grounds by climbing over a chain-link fence and glided to one of the seven bleak, boxlike structures that were crammed with men, women, and children—families of up to ten surviving in tiny, three-room apartments with leaky pipes, peeling paint, and long, dark, treacherous corridors. Batman caught the bottom rung of a fire-escape ladder and began climbing. He halted at a fourth-floor window and took from a belt compartment a small viewer equipped with a night-vision lens. He lay on his back below the window and angled the periscope to see into the apartment beyond. In the greenish night lens he saw that the place was empty except for a few boxes and a large pile of stuffed rabbits.

From the next apartment, he heard shouts of anger. A little boy opened the window and crept out onto the fire-escape platform. In the ambient light from inside the apartment, Batman could see that the boy, who was about eight, had a smear of grime across his forehead and what looked like a bruise on his cheek. His clothing was torn, his blond hair unruly and falling in a cowlick over his forehead.

A long way from what scrubbed, pampered, adored Bruce Wayne looked like at that age . . .

"You're here to get that guy?" the boy asked.

"I guess I am."

"They already took him. To the hospital."

From inside the boy's apartment came a woman's shrill voice. "Get your ass back in here."

"The other kids won't believe I saw you," the boy said.

Batman handed the viewer to the boy. "It's yours."

Before the boy could thank him, Batman lifted the window to the empty apartment and climbed inside. He took one of the stuffed rabbits from the pile. It had been ripped open. As Batman was examining it, there was a noise at the door. He melted back into the shadows.

The door opened, and in the glow from the hallway, Batman saw Jonathan Crane and two other men enter.

Crane pointed to the pile of stuffed rabbits. "Get rid of all traces."

"Better torch the whole place," one of the men said. He took a bottle of amber liquid from a coat pocket and poured it on the toys. The air was suddenly filled with the pungent odor of gasoline.

Crane had moved to the open window and looked out onto the fire escape.

"Wait a minute," the man with the gasoline said. "I gotta take a leak."

He went into the bathroom, switched on the light, and glanced into the cracked mirror over the washbasin. What he saw made him open his mouth to yell—

Batman smashed him into the mirror and as he was bumping against the basin and falling to the floor, Batman was already moving to the bathroom door. There he met the second man and took him out.

Batman shoved past the falling man to confront Crane, who had donned a burlap mask. Crane raised his hand and a tiny cloud of smoke puffed from his sleeve. Instinctively, Batman turned his head to avoid inhaling it and leaped at Crane. There was a second puff of smoke and this time Batman breathed part of it in and choked . . .

. . . *and the Batman who was Bruce who was a child at the bottom of a well was not looking at a funny man in a funny mask, oh no, not now, not anymore— he was seeing a monster coughed up from hell with flaming eyes and long tentacles spinning, spinning, spinning, spinning . . .*

"Stop the spinning!" Was that his voice, yelling like that?

Batman staggered, shook his head. He had to make the vision go away. Somehow.

Crane smashed a bottle over Batman's head. Amber liquid trickled over his mask and the reek of gasoline stung his nostrils. Batman gasped and coughed.

. . . the gasoline stink congealed into another hell-spawned monster with gaping jaws . . .

The window. Maybe salvation lay outside, in the air, in the rain. If only he could get to the window. The window should be easy to reach. The window was only a few steps away.

. . . but the room was suddenly miles long and the window was receding into the horizon . . .

. . . and bats were exploding from a dark crevice . . .

Crane was holding up a cheap plastic lighter.

"Need a light?" he inquired pleasantly, and flicked the wheel. When a tapered flame sprouted from the top of the lighter, he tossed it at Batman.

Gasoline ignited and Batman was swathed in fire.

The window!

. . . no matter how far away it is, got to reach the window . . .

Batman closed his eyes and flung himself at where he knew the window had to be. He felt something crack and heard glass breaking and knew he was on the fire escape. His momentum carried him forward and he flipped over the railing and, cape trailing flame, he fell. He pressed a stud in his cowl and the cape popped open and became rigid—a wing. No, only *half* a wing; fire had damaged the other side. Still blazing, he spiraled out and down, the damaged part of the wing flapping—

His fall was broken by a car. As his flaming body struck the vehicle, he fell through the roof into the rear of the car. The heavy rain had extinguished the flames. He lay, gasping for breath, mentally scanning his body, seeking broken bones. None: not that he could detect. He worked his way out of the wreckage of the car and struggled to regain his balance.

Two men, hands in pockets, approached.

"Hey, wait up a minute, got something to show you," one called in a singsong voice.

Batman stepped into the light of a streetlamp—a gaunt, black figure with smoke rising from it.

"Never mind," the man said, and he and his companion ran.

Batman limped into an alley and from his utility belt pulled out a tiny phone. He pressed a button, and in a hoarse whisper said, "Alfred?"

Forty minutes later, Batman lay sprawled on the rear seat of Alfred's Bentley as Alfred turned toward the manor. The smell of scorched fabric filled the car.

"We'll be home soon," Alfred said, putting the car into gear.

Batman pulled off his mask. "Blood poisoned," he whispered.

. . . *and the car was filled with bats, screeching, tearing* . . .

He knew they could not be real but also knew, absolutely, that they were.

15

Bruce opened his eyes. He was in Wayne Manor's master bedroom and Alfred was sitting next to the bed.

"How long was I out?" Bruce asked, almost not recognizing the hoarse rasp that was his voice.

"Two days. It's your birthday. We're having a party, remember?"

Bruce sat up, lifted a glass of water from the nightstand, and quickly drained it. "It was some kind of weaponized hallucinogen administered in aerosol form. I've felt something similar before. If I'd breathed in a whole lungful . . ."

"You are definitely hanging out at the wrong clubs," said a familiar voice. Bruce turned; Lucius Fox was sitting near the window, his legs crossed, an amused little smile on his face.

"I called Mr. Fox when your condition worsened after the first day," Alfred explained.

"I analyzed your blood, isolating the receptor compounds and protein-based catalysts," Fox said.

"Am I meant to understand all that?" Bruce asked.

"No, I just want you to know how hard it was. Bottom line, I synthesized an antidote."

"Could you make more?"

"Planning on gassing yourself again?"

"You know how it is, Mr. Fox. You're out on the town, looking for kicks . . . someone's passing around the weaponized hallucinogens . . ."

Fox stood. "I'll bring you what I have, but the antidote should serve as an inoculation for now." He nodded to Alfred. "Alfred, always a pleasure. I'll see myself out."

After Fox left, Alfred drew the curtains and advised Bruce to get more sleep.

Bruce slept for another two hours. Then he arose and showered. His hair was a problem; the stink of burning gasoline that clung to it was stubborn. But after several shampoos, the smell abated. Bruce went into the bedroom and was putting on a dressing gown when he heard the front doorbell ring. He went to the top of the stairs and looked down at the front door. Alfred was speaking to Rachel.

"Are you sure you won't come in?" Alfred was asking. "The other guests should be arriving shortly."

"I have to get back," Rachel said, and extended a small, gift-wrapped package to Alfred. "I just wanted to leave this."

Bruce descended the steps and called Rachel's name. She looked at him and frowned. He knew how he appeared: hair tousled, eyes red, unsteady on his feet.

"Looks like someone's been burning the candle at

both ends," Rachel said. "Must have been quite an occasion."

"Well, it *is* my birthday."

"I know. I was just dropping off your present."

Bruce heard a ringing sound coming from Rachel's shoulder bag.

"Excuse me," she said. She pulled out a cell phone and spoke into it. "Rachel Dawes." A pause. "What? Who authorized that? Get Crane there right now and don't take no for an answer. And call Dr. Lehmann— we'll need our own assessment on the judge's desk by morning."

Rachel stuffed the phone back into her bag. She did not look happy.

"What's wrong?" Bruce asked.

"It's Falcone. Dr. Crane moved him to Arkham Asylum on suicide watch."

"You're going to Arkham now? It's in the Narrows, Rachel."

"You have yourself a great time. Some of us have work to do. Happy birthday, Bruce."

She raced down the walk, got into her small car, and sped away.

Bruce found Alfred in the dining hall near a table heaped high with wrapped gifts. "Can I see what Rachel left?"

"Certainly, sir," Alfred said and handed Bruce a small box wrapped in gold foil.

Bruce removed the wrapping and took the lid off the box and found himself looking at something he had not seen since he was eight years old. An arrow-head lay on a cushion of white cotton across a slip of paper with the words "finder's keepers" handwritten on it.

"I have an errand to run," he said.

"But, Master Bruce, the guests will be arriving shortly."

"Keep them happy until I arrive. Tell them that joke you know."

Bruce strode into the study and to the big grand piano in a corner of the room. He hit four notes and a large, ornate mirror swung forward to reveal a doorway behind it. This second entry to the cave was Alfred's idea and it was a good one. Bruce passed through it and went down a stone staircase. He arrived at a landing and a spiral staircase with a dumb-waiter in its center. He stepped onto the dumbwaiter and tugged a lever. The dumbwaiter plummeted down and, with a rattling of chains, stopped at the bottom of the stairs. Bruce stepped out of it and into the cave. He went to a wardrobe. The Batman costume was inside, a phantom that seemed to be staring at him.

As William Earle hurried down the lowest corridor in Wayne Tower, he was speaking into his cell phone: ". . . Oh, and, Jessica, I've got to attend the Wayne party. I guess I'd better bring a gift. Get something nice. He'd probably like a blond, but make it respectable. Silverware or something. You know—expensive."

Earle passed through the door marked APPLIED SCIENCES and saw Lucius Fox manipulating a box with screens and dials. Fox was absorbed in whatever it was that he was doing and did not hear Earle come in.

Earle cleared his throat. "Having fun?"

Fox swiveled his chair around. "Bill. What's a big shot like you doing in a place like this?"

"Has Wayne been around much?"

"In and out. Nice kid."

"Forget about kissing his ass to get back to the executive suite, Lucius. Despite his name, he's only an employee."

"You came all the way down here to tell me that?"

Earle shifted his weight from his left foot to his right. "Actually, I need information. The Wayne Enterprises forty-seven B1-ME."

Fox scooted his chair close to his desk and began typing at his computer's keyboard. After a minute, he said, "Here it is. A microwave transmitter . . . designed to vaporize an enemy's water supply."

"I know all that. Any other applications?"

Fox rubbed his chin with the back of his hand. "Well, as I recall, rumor was, they tested dispersing water-based chemical agents into the air. But that would be illegal, wouldn't it? And you wouldn't be interested in anything illegal."

"Cut the crap, Fox. I need everything on the project development up to my office right away."

Earle moved toward the door.

"What happened?" Fox asked. "You lose one?"

Earle stopped and turned. "By the way, I'm merging Applied Sciences with Archiving," he said in a monotone and then chuckled. "You're at the top of the list for early retirement. Didn't you get the memo?"

16

Night had fallen by the time Rachel Dawes guided her car off the bridge and onto the island known as the Narrows. She drove slowly, trying to avoid the many potholes that made some Gothamites liken the area to the surface of the moon. Light was virtually non-existent; there were few streetlamps. Those that did exist were never serviced when they broke or burned out. The moon was no more than a dim smudge behind clouds. Rachel stopped in front of the sprawling architectural monstrosity that housed the famous—some said *infamous*—Arkham Asylum: high window-less walls and steep roofs. Rachel shuddered at the thought of entering this nightmare, but parked her car and walked through the front door anyway.

She spoke to a guard at a security desk, and a minute later a white-clad nurse with orange hair escorted her into the patients' wing.

Rachel saw Dr. Crane approaching from the other end of the corridor.

"Ms. Dawes," Crane said, "this is most irregular. I've nothing to add to the report of Mr. Falcone's condition that I filed with the judge."

Rachel met his gaze and said, "Well, I have questions about your report."

"Such as," Crane said in the tone of the unjustly victimized.

"Such as, isn't it convenient for a fifty-two-year-old man with no history of mental illness to have a complete psychotic breakdown just when he's about to be indicted?"

Crane gestured to a wire-reinforced window that looked in on a cell. In it, Carmine Falcone was strapped to a bed, staring at the ceiling, his lips moving.

"You can see for yourself, Ms. Dawes . . . there's nothing delusional about his symptoms."

"What's he saying?" Rachel asked.

"Scarecrow," the orange-haired nurse volunteered.

"What's 'scarecrow?' "

Now Crane adopted the manner of a professor lecturing a particularly dense class. "Patients suffering delusional episodes often focus their paranoia onto an external tormentor, usually one conforming to Jungian archetypes. In this case, a scarecrow."

Rachel looked at Falcone. "He's drugged?"

Crane nodded. "Psychopharmacology is my primary field. I'm a strong advocate. Outside, he was a giant. In here, only the mind can grant you power."

"You enjoy the reversal."

"I respect the mind's power over the body. It's why I do what I do—ultimately, I'm just trying to help."

"I do what I do to put scum like Falcone behind bars, not in therapy," Rachel said, letting anger into her voice. "I want my own psychiatric consultant to have full access to Falcone, including bloodwork to find out exactly what you have him on."

"First thing tomorrow, then."

"Tonight. I've already paged Dr. Lehmann."

"Would you also like to inspect our facilities, Ms. Dawes?"

"It wouldn't hurt."

"Follow me." Crane led Rachel to an elevator door, which he opened with a key. Once inside Rachel felt them descending—three floors, she guessed—and when the doors again opened they exited into a long, dim corridor. Rachel shivered, both because the place was chilly and because it was so creepy—a horror of dripping pipes and grotesque shadows.

. . . *If they scare you, they win* . . .

Crane, with Rachel a step behind, paused at a door marked HYDROTHERAPY and opened it. Rachel blinked to adjust her sight to the brightness of the place, a vast room with dozens of stainless-steel tables on which were scales and aluminum kegs. Workers—asylum inmates?—were busy transferring white powder from the kegs to cloth sacks. Two of the workers were pouring powder from a barrel into a large hole in the floor. One of them stared . . . not *at* Rachel, but *through* her. Rachel was certain she had met him somewhere and then her breath caught as she recognized the murderer Victor Zsasz.

"This is where we make the medicine," Crane said. "Perhaps you should have some. Clear your head."

He was talking to no one.

If they scare you, they win, yes, but sometimes dan-

*ger is real and immediate and the only sensible thing
to do is run.*

In the corridor, Rachel stumbled: *Damn boots . . .*

She continued running toward the elevator. Inside,
she pressed the button marked 2.

Nothing happened. She jabbed at the button again
and again. Nothing. She hit all the other buttons. Still
nothing.

Someone appeared in the open door, wearing a
scarecrow mask.

Crane?

"Let me help you," he said. He reached toward
Rachel and a small puff of gas shot from his sleeve.
The back of Rachel's throat stung and she gasped.
She coughed into her fist and when she looked up—

*. . . worms slithered and fell from the stitching of
the mask . . .*

Rachel stifled a scream.

Two inmates dragged her back to the hydrotherapy
room and pushed her onto one of the tables. Crane
grabbed her face between his thumb and forefinger
and forced her to look at him.

. . . worms crawling . . .

"Who knows you're here?" Was it the scarecrow
talking? *"Who knows?"*

Rachel wrenched her head away.

Suddenly they were in darkness. Someone had killed
the lights.

Crane pulled off his mask and said, in an awed
voice, "He's here."

"Who?" someone asked.

"The Batman."

"What do we do?"

"What does anyone do when a prowler comes around? Call the police."

"You want the cops here?"

"At this point, they can't stop us. But this . . . Batman has a talent for disruption. Force him outside, the police will take him down."

Crane was fumbling around in one of the table's drawers. He located a battery-operated doctor's light used to examine inmates' eyes if they accidentally got powder in them. Turning it on, he swept the thin beam around at the inmates.

"Get them out of here."

"What about her?" one of the others said, gesturing to Rachel.

"She's gone," Crane said with a satisfied smile. "I gave her a concentrated dose. The mind can only take so much."

"What about the Batman? The things they say about him . . . I heard he can disappear."

"We'll find out, won't we? Call the police."

As Bruce Wayne, at the monastery, he had learned to make use of darkness—any *kind* of darkness. He could conceal himself in shadows or, if necessary and conditions were right, hide in plain sight. None of that was necessary here. This ugly monstrosity of a building seemed to radiate its *own* darkness and there were no lights on the grounds to dispel it. And the dim moon was no problem, either. An elephant could have tiptoed inside without being seen. But Batman had played it safe and cut the power lines anyway. He knew, from his earlier research, that no surgery was done this late at night and there were no artificial life-support systems in the asylum, so he was probably not endangering anyone. Probably. He couldn't be certain, not now. Later, he promised himself, he would find ways of being *certain* in situations like this.

He had descended from the roof and was halfway to the ground. He paused, and conjured up a mental picture of the asylum schematic he had memorized before leaving the cave. There was a hydrotherapy room in a sub-basement that seemed to be unused. That might or might not be where Crane and company would take Rachel if they meant to do her harm, but it was as good a place as any to start his search. He dropped to the ground and crouched.

This has to be the right window . . .

Crane had positioned gunmen on either side of the door and the window. They waited, but not for long.

Someone groaned. The sound came from above, in the rafters.

"Shoot!" Crane commanded.

The other gunman fired upward blindly. A blackness quickly descended on him and he was quiet.

There was the sound of a muffled blow from across the room and Crane knew that the third man had been taken down. Then another muffled blow and Crane knew he was alone.

Except for the woman. Maybe Rachel could be his

ace in the hole. Where was she? Still on the table, probably. Give her another whiff of the gas as insurance, then—

Someone grabbed him, spun him around, and ripped off his mask. Crane's arm was pinned between his body and Batman—it *had* to be Batman—his fist against his own chin. He felt a compressed air gun being triggered and realized, a half second before a puff of smoke blew into his face, what was about to happen.

"How about a dose of your own medicine," Batman said. He released Crane and the doctor fell to the ground. Batman hauled him up by his collar and asked, "What have you been doing here? Who are you working for?"

As Crane tried to answer, his breath came in sharp, staccato gasps. Finally, he managed to say, "Rā's . . . Rā's . . . Rā's al Ghūl."

Batman pulled Crane closer. "Rā's al Ghūl is dead, Crane. I'll ask you one more time . . . *Who are you working for?*"

But Crane did not, and apparently could not, reply. For almost a minute, he simply stared, and continued to gasp. Then his breath became normal and he said pleasantly, "Dr. Crane isn't here right now, but if you'd like to make an appointment . . ."

17

Batman gave himself a quick mental inventory to determine if the puff of gas from Crane's sleeve had affected him. Nothing seemed to be wrong; Fox's antidote was proving to be an effective vaccine. He guessed that Crane would not provide any useful information for the foreseeable future. He wondered about what the doctor *had* said.

Rā's al Ghūl ? What an odd lie to tell. And how did Crane even know about Rā's?

Batman released Crane and let him sink to the floor. He took a step toward Rachel, who was lying unconscious on a table.

From his belt, he removed a tiny light and used it to examine the room. There was a large hole in the floor and several empty sacks around it. He shone his flashlight into it and saw the curved top of a large pipe. *A water main . . . has to be.* Other empty sacks, hundreds of them, were tossed into the corners.

Which adds up to what?

A loud *something* came from outside the window and Batman realized that he was hearing someone speak, distorted by a bullhorn and the echoing against the old building. The sound came again and he was able to discern the words:

"BATMAN. PUT DOWN YOUR WEAPONS AND SURRENDER. YOU ARE SURROUNDED."

The speaker did not identify himself as a policeman. He did not have to. Batman picked Rachel up and carried her out of the room.

Outside, the flashing lights of a dozen police cruisers threw grotesque, reddish shadows on the walls of the asylum. Behind the open doors of each car stood a uniformed cop, some aiming sidearms, others with shotguns.

Flass stood next to a man in a captain's uniform, who was holding a bullhorn.

"What are your waiting for?" Flass demanded.

"Backup," the captain said.

"Backup?"

"Listen, Flass, the Batman's in there. SWAT's on the way. But if you want to go in now . . . Hey, I'll be right behind you."

"Well, if SWAT's on the way . . ."

Jim Gordon parked his car at the perimeter of the police cordon, grabbed a flashlight from the glove compartment, and hurried to Flass.

"I heard about it on the radio," he said. "What's going on?"

"Got a call, said it was from inside the nuthouse,"

Flass replied. "Some guy said Batman was loose inside there."

Gordon pushed past Flass and was going through the front entrance of the asylum as a large van screeched to a halt and a half-dozen SWAT officers, carrying rifles with flashlights attached and wearing flak jackets and helmets, spilled onto the sidewalk.

Once inside, Gordon felt his way along the walls. He had seen the arrival of the SWAT team and wanted no part of it. Those guys had their orders: apprehend, subdue, use force if necessary. Gordon's mission was different: find out what the hell was happening and leave the bullets inside the gun.

He heard shouts and heavy footfalls behind him: the SWAT guys, probably spreading out, keeping in contact with lapel radios. Did he have a chance to find the Batman before they did? Well, he'd soon find out.

In the brief bursts of red light from the police cruisers that were coming through the window, he saw an elevator. He pressed the button on the wall next to it. Nothing. No surprise. The radio call he'd intercepted reported that the asylum was without electricity. Okay, he'd do it the hard way. He switched on his flashlight and began to ascend a staircase next to the elevator, slowly—

—and he was grabbed around the waist and pulled off of his feet, rocketing upward. He stopped and was placed on a landing, a gloved hand covering his mouth.

Below, the SWAT guys, rifles and lights aimed ahead of them, shouted and began to climb the steps.

"Okay, we go higher," someone said in Gordon's ear, a low, rasping voice that he recognized immediately.

In the ambient glow from the SWAT lights, Gordon saw Batman aim some kind of gun at the rafters. Batman again circled Gordon's waist with his arm and triggered the gun. There was a faint hiss and again Gordon was shooting upward. Just as quickly, they jolted to a stop.

Somehow, Gordon had managed to hold on to his flashlight during his ascent. He swept its beam around him and saw that he was in some sort of attic. Batman grasped Gordon's wrist and gently pushed it down; Gordon's beam shone on Rachel Dawes, who was curled on the floor, her eyes wide, her lips moving soundlessly.

"What happened to her?" Gordon whispered.

"Crane poisoned her with a psychotropic hallucinogen," Batman said. "A panic-inducing toxin."

"Let me get her down to the medics."

"They can't help her, but I can. I need to get her the antidote before the damage becomes permanent."

"How long does she have?"

"Not long. Get her downstairs and meet me in the alley on the Narrows side."

"How will you get out?"

Batman lifted his heel and pressed it. "I just called for backup."

Batman glided toward a window, hesitated, then turned back to Gordon. "Some things you ought to know in case something happens to me. Crane was at the Narrows. He was up to something before I got here.

"Do you know what's he planning?"

"No."

"Was he working for Falcone?"

"No. Someone else. Maybe someone far worse."

Gordon heard an odd sound coming from beyond the asylum's walls: a *screech* melded with what sounded like wings flapping. "What's that?"

"Backup," Batman said.

The clouds had dissipated and a full moon shone in the sky. That's how Flass first saw them—wiggly shapes crossing the moon. There were only a few at first. Flass and some of the cops noticed them but then ignored them. What were a few bats? You'd expect them in a creepy place like this. But now there were more than a few, a lot more—hundreds, no thousands . . . Maybe even more? They flowed in an unending stream from the north, so many they almost concealed the moon. They flew straight for the building and found entrances and flew inside.

"It's *his* doing," Flass said to the uniformed captain. "Can't be a coincidence, not bats. What kind of thing *is* he?"

Inside the asylum, a black mass, flapping and screeching, flooded into the stairwell, past the SWAT team who ducked and covered their faces with their forearms, and soared upward.

Batman stood in the midst of the swarm. The image of himself at the bottom of a well flitted across his mind for only a second, but the memory had long ago lost its power to frighten him. He had originally doubted that this would really work, this summoning of the bats that lived beneath Wayne Manor. He had planned to test it later, but there was no need for that now. He was surrounded by proof that, yes, the device in his heel performed as expected.

But most of the bats were past the SWAT team and Batman needed them occupied for a minute or two more. He pulled the device loose from his boot and dropped it down the stairwell. Immediately, the bats veered and plummeted downward, following the device, and the SWAT guys scattered. Batman jumped into the middle of the stairwell, almost invisible amid the black swarm, and opened his cloak into its wing configuration. He landed hard, swayed to get his balance, and as he ran toward the inmates' quarters, refolded the cloak.

He was now standing in a corridor with barred doors on either side. He took a mini mine from his belt and threw it at the nearest door lock. A second later there was an explosion and the door fell smoking to the floor. Batman climbed over the door and entered the cell.

He nodded to the two men who, wide-eyed, were cowering in a corner and said, "Excuse me."

He threw a second mine at the barred window and

told the inmates that they'd better cover their faces. There was another explosion and the bars clattered onto the ground outside.

Batman took three running steps, leaped, and dove through the window.

18

Gordon was sitting in the alley behind the asylum, cradling Rachel's head, when Batman emerged from the darkness.

"How is she?" Batman asked.

Before Gordon could answer, a police helicopter flew past the asylum and shone a blindingly bright searchlight on them.

Batman lifted Rachel. "I've got to get her out of here."

"Take my car," Gordon said.

"I brought mine," Batman replied and, still carrying Rachel, loped into the shadows at the end of the alley.

"Yours?" said Gordon.

A few seconds later, a pair of headlights lit the area and Gordon heard the low *thrum* of a powerful engine. The headlights moved and something black and vaguely automotive lurched forward. It picked up speed and passed Gordon, heading for the street. A police cruiser appeared and stopped, blocking the exit to the alley, and Gordon cringed, waiting for disaster because whatever Batman was driving did not slow—no, it moved even faster. An ugly, life-taking collision seemed inevitable.

Two cops scrambled from the car and ran.

Batman's vehicle smashed into the cop car, its huge front wheels crushing the hood and bouncing on toward the street.

One of the cops spoke into a lapel radio. "He's in a vehicle."

The receiver squawked. *"Make and color?"*

"It's a black . . . tank."

"Tank?"

Batman turned onto the street, north, away from the asylum and the army of officers, and accelerated onto the bridge, swerving past a delivery van and a sedan, steel missing steel by inches.

Rachel awakened and, for a minute, shook her head slowly as she strained against her seat belt, arms straight before her, hands braced against the dash.

"You've been poisoned," Batman told her. "Stay calm."

He touched a stud on the steeling wheel and a screen between him and Rachel brightened. It was criss-crossed with lines, some dotted, some solid.

"Global positioning display," Batman said, glancing at it. "Tells me what's ahead."

Rachel's breath was shallow and harsh.

As Batman was turning onto a freeway ramp, two police cruisers appeared in his rearview mirror, sirens howling, red lights blinking. Batman touched another

stud and a strip of tensile plastic studded with metal
spikes dropped from the rear of his vehicle. The first
cruiser's tires hit the spikes and exploded. Sparks shooting from its bare wheel rims, it spun and skidded sideways into the second cruiser. The hoods of both cars
popped open and steam began rising from their engines.

Batman's fingers danced on a row of buttons beneath the screen and the images blinked and changed.

Rachel's breathing continued to be erratic.

"Breathe slowly," Batman said. "Close your eyes."

"That's worse," Rachel gasped.

Batman looked down at the screen, twisted the
steering wheel, and left the freeway. He moved into
an industrial area, deserted at this late hour.

Three cruisers were blocking the intersection ahead
of him.

Batman slewed into a turn and into the entrance of a
multilevel parking garage. His vehicle smashed through
the ticket machine and wooden barrier and roared up
a ramp.

"What are you doing?" Rachel whispered.

"Shortcut."

Batman's vehicle erupted onto the top level, the roof
of the garage. A helicopter, hovering directly overhead,
surrounded it with a circle of light.

Batman braked, and smoke rising from its tires, the
vehicle skidded to a stop.

*　*　*

Gordon had been following the progress of the chase on the police radio. He knew where Batman had gone and went there too, hoping the man in the mask was not trapped, that he could somehow escape. But when he parked his car across from the garage, he could see that it was hopeless. The place was ringed with cops, cruisers blocking every entrance and exit, a chopper hovering overhead, a spotlight on its underbelly glaring down at Batman's vehicle, and armed officers moving into place. There was nothing Batman could do and nothing Gordon could do for him.

"We've got the bastard now," Flass said to the uniformed captain as they trotted toward the garage. He holstered his service automatic and commandeered a shotgun from a uniformed officer. He was remembering being hauled up the side of a building and being so scared he could hardly answer questions. Being dumped into garbage and all that made him feel like a puke and the only way he could *stop* feeling like a puke was to watch the bastard die at his feet. And that was going to happen. Real soon. Because he couldn't go on feeling like a puke.

Rachel was leaning against the passenger-side window, staring at the blurred images around her. "Brace yourself," said Batman. "This might be a little rough."

* * *

Batman had a momentary doubt. What he was about to try *might* work. Maybe *should* work. But would it? Would even this wild fantasy of a muscle car, this *Batmobile*, be able to do what he required of it? *Doubts are pointless and unproductive—I learned that at the monastery.* And he floored the accelerator. And the . . . *Batmobile*—for that's what it was—sped toward the edge of the roof.

"So the bastard's taking the coward's way out," Flass said to the captain. "Gonna off himself."

Gordon was hoping he wouldn't do it, wouldn't drive off the roof and fall six floors and into a crash that he surely would not survive. But that's what he seemed to be doing.

Rachel did not know much because she could not discern the real from the phantasmagoric and she knew that she could not. But she was about to die. Of that she was certain.

Batman pulled a lever next to the gearshift. The Batmobile shifted into its formal driving position. The car lifted off the roof and started a rampless jump.

So far, so good.

The vehicle soared thirty feet to the neighboring roof. It landed with a jolt. But the tires held and Batman sped toward the next roof.

Flass stared, the shotgun forgotten in his hands.

Gordon thought: *Maybe?*

Rachel wondered if she were already dead.

The Batmobile did its leap-and-soar maneuver twice more and finally landed on a steeply pitched, chateau-style roof. Its tires bit into red tiles, crumbling some and sending others flying down into the street, where a few of them pelted the tops of police cruisers that were tracking the Batmobile.

Batman glanced at the global positioning screen—*okay!*—and up through the window at the chopper, which was still in pursuit.

"This last bit might be the roughest," he told Rachel. "But we'll be fine if the roof holds."

It almost did not. The tiles were raining inward and falling, baring cracking timbers, when the Batmobile shot off a gable and dropped onto an elevated free-way twenty-five feet below. Batman's navigational gear told him that the nearest on ramp was almost two miles to the south. By the time a police cruiser could get to it and then get to where Batman was now, the Batmobile would be only a memory. But there was still the chopper. The chopper was a problem. As long as he stayed on the freeway, the chopper could follow him.

"Hold on," Batman said. "Just hold on."

Warning signs seemed to race past them: the freeway was still under construction and the pavement ended in less than a mile. There were no lights; the electrical lines had not been extended this far yet. Batman accelerated. The Batmobile smashed through wooden barriers and down into a clearing below, then veered under the elevated road. Batman killed the exterior lights and the windshield immediately tinted night-vision green. He tapped a control near the screen, which converted it into a television receiver tuned to an infrared camera at the rear of the vehicle, and reverted the engines to stealth mode. They made no sound as the Batmobile sped silently away from Gotham City. The chopper hovered and descended, its searchlight probing the area under the road. It moved forward, in the opposite direction from the Batmobile.

The Batmobile lurched forward and flew off the edge of a lookout, over a river gorge, straight at a waterfall.

The vehicle splashed through the waterfall to the stone floor of a cave. Steel hooks sprang from its rear chassis and engaged a cable. The Batmobile stopped.

"Quite a ride," Batman said, but Rachel did not hear him; she was once again unconscious. The top of the Batmobile hissed open and slid forward, and the seats rose up to allow Batman to exit the vehicle.

Batman lifted Rachel from her seat and carried her into the damp blackness of the caverns. He entered a section that was brightly lit and laid Rachel down on a medical examining table. He ran up steps to his computer station. A small cardboard container lay on the desk next to his monitor. Batman removed from it a vial and a hypodermic needle. He filled the needle with milky fluid from the vial, cleared it of air bubbles, and returned to where Rachel lay, now whimpering quietly. He removed her jacket and rolled up her left sleeve.

"I hope this won't hurt," he said. He jabbed the needle into her biceps, and fed the fluid into her body.

He stepped back and watched. Within a few minutes, she stopped her whimpering and her breathing slowed and became deep and regular.

"I think we're home free," he said.

Rachel's eyes fluttered open and widened. Batman knew she was seeing the bats hanging high above. She closed her eyes again.

"How do you feel?" Batman asked.

"Where are we?" Rachel's voice was hoarse.

Batman was silent.

"All right, then, why did you bring me here?"

"If I hadn't, your mind would now be lost. You were poisoned."

"Am I still?"

"No. Your left arm probably hurts a bit where I injected the antidote. How much do you remember?"

Rachel frowned. "Nightmares. This face, this mask . . . It was *Crane*." She swung her legs around and stood. "I have to tell the police. We've got—"

Her knees buckled. Batman caught her and put her back on the table.

"Relax," he said. "Gordon has Crane."

He stepped back into the shadows.

"Is Sergeant Gordon your friend?" Rachel asked.

"I don't have the luxury of friends."

For a moment, Batman completely vanished. When he again stepped into the light, he was carrying a syringe. "I'm going to give you a sedative. You'll wake up at home." He held up two syringes. "And when you do, get these to Gordon and Gordon alone. Trust no one."

"What are they?"

"The antidote. One for Gordon to inoculate himself, the other to start mass production."

Batman gave Rachel the syringes.

She tucked them into a pocket. "Mass production?"

"Crane was just a pawn. We need to be ready."

Batman gestured with the syringe and Rachel offered her arm. "I guess if you wanted to hurt me, you would have by now."

Batman performed the injection and waited. Rachel put her head down on the table and, a few seconds later, began breathing deeply. Batman put the syringe in a cabinet near the table and returned to where Rachel was sleeping.

He pulled off his mask. He was no longer the Batman; he was Bruce Wayne, gazing at a person he had known all his life. He was motionless except for his eyes, which shifted from Rachel to the mask and back again.

Do I love her?

The answer was almost certainly yes. But to tell her how he felt would be to assume certain obligations—of trust, of fidelity—and to abandon what he had begun to create. That, or subject her to continual danger.

He put the mask on and strode into the darkness.

19

Flass had vanished after the chase at the parking garage, so Gordon had to supervise the investigation at Arkham Asylum alone. He began by summoning crime-scene technicians and a hazardous materials team from headquarters and putting them to work in the hydrotherapy room. For the next two hours, he questioned the staff and those of the inmates who were able to answer him, scribbled a few lines in his notebook, and after sending the staff home, returned to the basement and the hydrotherapy room. Two crime-scene investigators were taking flash photos and a man wearing a hazardous material protection suit was at the edge of the large hole, shining a five-cell flashlight down into it.

"They get any of the toxin into the mains?" Gordon asked.

The hazmat technician nodded inside his plastic helmet. "Oh, yeah."

"Okay. Notify the water board. There's gotta be a way of isolating the area's—"

"You don't understand. They put it *all* in the water

supply. They've been doing this for weeks. Gotham's entire water supply is laced with it."

"Why haven't we felt any effects?"

"Near as we can figure, it must be a compound that has to be absorbed through the lungs."

"I don't know if that's good news or bad," Gordon said. "Keep me posted."

Bruce Wayne's birthday bash was in full swing when Bruce emerged from the hidden door behind the mirror now dressed in a dinner jacket and pants; the top two buttons of his white shirt were open. Hundreds of people were in the big hall, drinking champagne and chattering, and the members of a fourteen-piece orchestra were running through their repertoire of antique dance tunes.

Alfred was waiting. "Have a pleasant drive, Master Bruce? I believe you *did* say that your activities are not about thrill seeking."

"They're not."

Alfred pointed to where a television, sound muted, was tuned to an all-news channel. The Batmobile, barely visible in the dim light, was soaring between two buildings. "Well," Alfred asked, "what do you call *that*?"

"Damn good television?"

"It's a miracle no one was injured."

"I didn't have time to observe the highway code, Alfred."

"You're getting lost in this . . . creation of yours."

"I'm using my *creation* to help people. Like my father did."

"For Thomas Wayne, helping others was never about proving anything to anyone. Including himself."

"It's *Rachel*, Alfred."

"Miss Dawes?"

"She was dying. She's in the cave, sedated. I need you to take her home."

Alfred nodded and went to the hidden door. He looked at his reflection in the mirror, and at the reflection of Bruce standing behind him. "We both care about Rachel, sir. But what you're doing is beyond that. This thing . . . it can't be personal. Or you're just a vigilante."

Maybe he's right. No! I can't afford to entertain doubts . . . not at this point.

"Look, Alfred, we can discuss this later and we will, for as long as you feel is necessary. But now, we've got to send the partiers away."

"Those are Bruce Wayne's guests out there. You have a name to maintain."

"I don't *care* about my name."

"It's not just your name. It's also your father's. And it's all that's left of him. Don't destroy it."

Alfred went through the mirror door and Bruce left the library. He allowed himself to slouch and let the corners of his mouth became slightly slack and his gait became loose and a bit awkward. He completed the disguise by turning those slack lips upward, into a smile that did not reach his eyes, and ambled into the big hall.

"There's the birthday boy himself," someone cried over the sound of the music. There was a smattering of applause. Bruce moved through the throng, shaking hands and grinning his vacant grin. The band abandoned the chorus of "Begin the Beguine" it had been playing and struck up "Happy Birthday."

Bruce stopped in front of William Earle, who wished him a happy birthday.

"Thank you, Mr. Earle. I hope your birthday is happy, too, when you have it. There was something I wanted to ask you . . . what was it? Oh, I know. How well did the stock offering go again?"

"Very well. The price soared."

"Who bought?"

"A variety of funds and brokerages . . . it's all a bit technical. The key thing is, our company's future is secure."

"Hey, that's *great*!" Bruce said. "You have a good time, Mr. Earle."

Bruce shambled on, grinning, shaking hands, trading pleasantries, until he reached where Lucius Fox was leaning against a wall, watching the festivities with the slight smile of a man bored, but amiable.

"Thank you for that . . . special present," Bruce said.

"I'm sure you'll find a use for it."

"I already have. How long would it take to manufacture on a large scale?"

"Weeks. Why?"

"I'm pretty sure someone's planning to disperse its . . . opposite. They plan to use the water supply."

Bruce laughed, and Fox laughed with him. To the partiers, it looked as though they were enjoying a joke.

Fox said, "The water supply isn't going to help you disperse an inhalant, unless . . ."

"What?"

Fox guffawed as though Bruce had just told him a really good one. "Unless you have access to a microwave transmitter powerful enough to vaporize the water in the mains. The kind of transmitter Wayne Enterprises has recently misplaced."

"Misplaced?"

"Earle just fired me for asking too many questions about it."

"I need you to go back to Wayne Enterprises and start making more of the antidote. I think the police are going to need as much as they can get their hands on."

"My security access has been revoked."

"That wouldn't stop a man like you, would it?"

This time, Fox's smile was genuine. "No, it probably wouldn't."

Fox moved himself away from the wall and toward the nearest door. Bruce returned to his shambling and hand-shaking until an elderly woman in a strapless organdy gown and a lot of makeup grabbed his arm.

"Bruce," she gushed. "There's somebody here you simply *must* meet."

"Not just now, Mrs. Delane—"

Mrs. Delane ignored Bruce's protest. She grabbed his shoulders and turned him to face a man whose shaved head was turned away from Bruce.

"Now am I pronouncing it right," Mrs. Delane asked as the man slowly turned around. As Bruce's gaze fell on a blue poppy in the Asian man's button-hole, she completed the question, "Mr. Āll Gool?"

The slackness left Bruce's mouth and his eyes were no longer vacant. "You're not Rā's al Ghūl. I watched him die."

"But is Rā's al Ghūl immortal?" someone whispered in Bruce's ear and even before Bruce turned he knew who the whisperer was.

Ducard, dressed in a black tuxedo and leaning on a polished ebony cane, beamed at Bruce. "Are his methods *supernatural*?"

Bruce replied, "Or are they cheap parlor tricks to conceal your true identity . . . *Rā's.*"

Outside, Alfred was holding the limp form of Rachel Dawes in one arm and, with the other hand, opening the rear door of his Bentley. He shoved a set of golf clubs aside and lowered Rachel onto the seat. A caterer, who had been taking a smoke break, asked if everything was okay.

Alfred smiled at him. "Lady's a little the worse for wear, I'm afraid."

"That'll happen," the caterer said.

20

Jim Gordon could not remember ever having been so weary, not even overseas, in the Army, when he had fought a war, sometimes for days on end. He desperately wanted to go home and crawl into bed next to Barbara, who would be sleeping, and take comfort from her warmth and closeness. But he could not, not yet. There was one more task he had to perform before he could tell himself what he always *had* to tell himself—that he had done everything possible.

He unlocked the cell door, went in, and sat across from Dr. Jonathan Crane, who was handcuffed to a chair.

"What was the plan, Crane?" Gordon asked. "How were you going to put your toxin in the air?"

Crane apparently did not hear the question. He was staring at a spot on the wall behind Gordon's shoulder and murmuring, "Scarecrow . . . scarecrow . . . scarecrow . . ."

Gordon leaned forward. "Who are you working for?"

Crane ignored Gordon. He sat still, only his lips moving, repeating his "scarecrow" litany.

Gordon was aware that Crane might be faking, but he did not think so. He'd seen a few psychos in his day and he'd be happy to bet his next paycheck that Crane was among their number. He rose and moved to the door.

Suddenly Crane said, "It's too late, you know. You can't stop it."

Gordon stared hard at the handcuffed man. Oh, Crane was still a psycho, but Gordon was sure that he was now a psycho who was telling the truth.

Only a few seconds had passed since Bruce had called Ducard by his real name. Nothing had changed: the music was still playing, the partiers were still dancing and eating and drinking.

Rā's bowed his head in acknowledgment of Bruce's conclusion. "Surely, a man who spends his nights scrambling over the rooftops of Gotham City wouldn't begrudge me dual identities?"

"I saved you from the fire."

"And I warned you about compassion, did I not?"

Bruce scanned the room and silently berated himself for not noticing them earlier—these grim men from the League of Shadows who hovered at the edge of the crowd, obviously out of place: hard, dangerous men, some of whom Bruce recognized from the monastery. Bruce looked at his guests: laughing, chattering, some of them tipsy.

"Your quarrel is with me," he said. "Let these people go."

"You're welcome to explain the situation to them," Rā's replied.

Bruce tried to read Rā's's expression. Amusement? Certainly. But something else, too. Contempt? Resolve? Hostility?

He grabbed a drink from a passing waiter and shouted loudly enough to be heard over the music: "Everyone. *Everyone!*"

He raised his glass and swayed a bit. His words were slightly slurred. "I just want to thank you all for . . . drinking my booze."

There was a brief burst of laughter.

"No, seriously," Bruce continued. "The thing about being a Wayne is you're never short of a few freeloaders to fill up your mansion . . . So here's to *you* people."

Bruce downed his drink and slammed the empty glass down on a table near Joe Fredericks, his father's old friend and colleague. Fredericks rose and clasped Bruce's elbow. "That's enough, Bruce."

Bruce pulled his arm away. "I'm not finished." He got another glass from the table and raised it. "To you false friends . . . and pathetic suck-ups who smile through your teeth at me . . . You had your fill, now leave me in peace. Get out. Everybody. *Out!*"

Bruce was surprised to realize that much of what he had said, he believed.

Most of the partiers were already moving toward the doors, snaking their way around tables and chairs, being careful not to look back at Bruce. The vast room was silent except for the sound of their movements.

Bruce could hear automobile engines starting in the driveway outside.

Joe Fredericks planted himself in front of Bruce. "The apple has fallen very far from the tree, Mr. Wayne."

"Sorry you think so, Joe. And for what it's worth, I didn't mean you."

"Like hell!" Fredericks turned on his heel and stalked away.

The musicians finished packing their instruments and sheet music and left.

The room was empty except for a dozen men who stood with their arms hanging loosely at their sides, weight centered in their bellies, and Bruce and Rā's al Ghūl, who faced each other.

"Quite a performance," Rā's said. "Amusing but pointless. None of these people have long to live—your antics at the asylum have forced my hand."

"Crane was working for you?"

"His toxin is derived from the organic compound in our blue poppies. He was able to weaponize it."

"He's a member of the League of Shadows?"

"Of course not. He thought our plan was to hold the city for ransom."

"But you're really going to unleash Crane's poison on the entire population."

"Then watch Gotham tear itself apart through fear."

"You're going to destroy millions of lives."

"Only a fool would call what these people have 'lives,' Bruce."

Rā's walked to the door and motioned for Bruce to join him. The dozen League of Shadows members started to follow, then stopped when Rā's held up a flat hand.

Rā's and Bruce left the big hall and were in a long, dimly lit corridor lined on one side with books and portraits of Bruce's ancestors, and on the other with windows, through which could be seen the silhouettes of hills against the glow of a sky lit by Gotham City's lights. There was no carpeting here and Rā's's cane tapped on the hardwood floor.

Rā's gestured toward the distant city. "The League of Shadows has been a check against human corruption for thousands of years. We sacked Rome. Loaded trade ships with plague rats. Burned London to the ground. Every time a civilization reaches the pinnacle of its decadence, we return to restore the balance."

"Gotham isn't beyond saving. There are good people here—"

"You're defending a city so corrupt we infiltrated every level of its infrastructure. Effortlessly."

Bruce looked at Rā's's profile, limned against the window, and saw what a disguise the Ducard persona had been. Rā's had not changed his clothing or altered any particular thing about his appearance, yet he was a different man—taller, straighter, with eyes that gleamed from beneath a ledge of brow, and an enormous dignity. His words were those of a fanatic, but his manner was not at all fanatical. He seemed grave, and sad.

Is this something I learned from him without know-

ing it? Bruce asked himself. *This way of altering appearances?* The answer had to be yes.

"You have no illusions about the world, Bruce," Rā's said. "When I found you in that jail you were lost. But I believed in you. I took away your fear and showed you a path. You were my greatest student . . . it should be *you* standing at my side, saving the world."

"The world?"

"Of course. Gotham City is only a necessary beginning. The worst parts of us Homo sapiens are now dominant, destroying both what is good in the race itself and the planet that sustains it. For the sake of what can be noble in humanity, the many must be destroyed so that the few can survive to evolve and grow, to fulfill our potential."

"And slaughtering millions . . . no *billions*—that doesn't bother you?"

"Do I look as though it does not bother me?"

He did not. He looked like a man maintaining his bearing under a tremendous weight.

"Stand with me?" he whispered.

"I'm standing right where I belong—between you and the people of Gotham."

"No one can save Gotham. When a forest grows too wild, a purging fire is natural, and inevitable. Tomorrow the world will watch in horror as one of its great cities destroys itself. The movement back to harmony will be unstoppable this time."

"You've tried to attack Gotham before?"

"Yes. Over the ages our weapons have grown more

sophisticated . . . with Gotham we tried a new one . . . economics."

"You created the depression twenty years ago?"

Rā's nodded. "Create enough hunger and everyone becomes a criminal. But we underestimated certain of Gotham's citizens . . . such as your parents."

Bruce felt anger surge through him and he neither could control it nor did he want to. His jaws clenched, his muscles tightened. He knew that Rā's was aware of his reaction and that Rā's was playing him. He remembered how to relax and he did.

"Unfortunate casualties of the fight for justice. Slain by one of the very people they were trying to help. Their deaths galvanized the city into saving itself, and Gotham has limped on ever since. We're back to finish the job."

Rā's looked back at the ballroom and nodded. His men began to emerge into the corridor. Bruce mentally counted and confirmed his earlier estimate: there were indeed a dozen of them.

"Proceed," Rā's said to them and they fanned out and pulled lighters from their pockets. They began to ignite drapes and furniture.

"Is this necessary?" Bruce asked.

"Perhaps not. But its symbolic value pleases me."

The flames lit Rā's's face and danced in his eyes. "This time, no misguided idealists will be allowed to stand in the way. Like your father, you lack the courage to do all that is necessary. If someone stands in the way of true justice, you simply walk up behind him and stab him in the heart."

Bruce was caught by surprise as a ninja descended from the rafters above him. He spun and grabbed the ninja's throat and as he did Rā's slid a long blade from his cane.

The corridor was filled with smoke that stung Bruce's eyes and scratched at the back of his throat. Flames had ascended the walls and were licking across the ancient ceiling beams. He had experienced something like this once before, when he had set the monastery afire. Then, it had been a disadvantage, but now . . . He knew every inch of this house and his opponents did not. If seeing became difficult, or impossible, that could be a help . . .

Bruce struck the ninja on the base of the skull and as the man crumpled Bruce pivoted toward Rā's. Rā's thrust with his blade. Bruce took the point near his abdomen, felt it slice into tissue and hit bone. He remembered something an instructor at the monastery had said: *Fighting with sharp edges, you will be cut. It is inevitable and it will hurt.* True, it *did* hurt, but nothing vital was damaged. Bruce twisted his arm to the right and slapped the blade with his palm and the sword flew from Rā's's grasp.

"Perhaps you taught me too well," Bruce said.

"Or perhaps you will never learn . . ." Rā's struck a supporting column with his cane, as he had once struck the ice beneath Bruce's feet. Bruce raised his eyes in time to see a flaming beam falling toward him, but too late to avoid it.

Rā's's next words were almost lost in the crackle of

the fire. ". . . to mind your surroundings as well as your opponent."

Bruce tried to rise, tried to push the beam off his body. He got his hands under it and strained; it lifted an inch, two . . . and he felt as though his muscles had suddenly emptied. The beam slipped down on top of him. He could not move.

Rā's bent to pick up his sword. He slid it into the cane and regarded Bruce. "Justice is balance. You burned down my house and left me for dead. Consider us even."

But Bruce did not hear Rā's's final words. He had lost consciousness.

Rā's strode to a door and opened it. Followed by a billow of smoke, he stepped outside the house.

A group of his men were awaiting his orders.

"No one comes out," Rā's said. "Make sure."

The men in tuxedos dispersed, each going to a different door of the manor. Most of the windows were glaring redly and a column of smoke rose into the sky. Eventually, someone, a neighbor, would notice and call for help. But the nearest fire department was fifteen minutes away. By the time it arrived, the old building would be gone and anyone inside it would be ashes.

Rā's murmured, "We would have been magnificent together."

He went to a SWAT van parked on the lawn and to the open doors of the trailer hitched to it. He climbed inside. He stood beside a large, industrial-type machine, which he patted, as though it were a cherished pet.

Jonathan Crane felt something drop into his lap. He lifted it and stared at it: his mask. He thought this delightful, and put on the mask, and looked around for someone to thank. Two men in uniforms stood in the open door of his cell.

"Time to play," one of them said.

Crane—or *the Scarecrow,* as he now thought of himself—followed the uniforms out into the corridor. There was a loud *clang* and all the doors of all the cells swung open. Slowly, the inmates stumbled out, wide-eyed, some of them obviously dazed. They stood, some in small groups, some alone, backs pressed against the cell bars. A lot of them were mumbling.

"What are we waiting for?" the Scarecrow asked, and nobody answered him.

The uniformed men left Crane and hurried outside to their van. They got several bags of plastic explosives and detonators and began placing them on the walls surrounding the grounds.

Alfred found the keys to Rachel Dawes's apartment in her purse. It was in a converted brownstone near the theater district, an old dwelling without a doorman, so Alfred had no trouble getting inside and not *much* trouble hauling Rachel up the stairs, into her rooms and onto her bed. Although she occasionally mumbled in her sleep during the drive from the suburbs, she did not awaken. He wondered if he should leave her a note but decided not to. He was not sure what, exactly, had transpired between her and Bruce and so he did not know the appropriate thing to say. In the end, he simply went back to the limousine and began the return to Wayne Manor.

The trip was quick and easy, until the last two miles. At this time of night, traffic was sparse, especially once he was away from midtown. The freeway was deserted for miles at a stretch, and driving was a pleasure. He wondered if there would be any partiers left. Probably. Some of Gotham's elite tended to stay as long as there was a morsel left to eat or a drop to drink.

As he was turning off the down ramp and onto the access road that led to Wayne Manor, Alfred noticed a glow in the sky. A false dawn? No, not this early, and not to the north. Then what?

A fire!

Rachel did not know how long her eyes had been open, how long she had been staring at the pattern made by light from outside her window shining on her bedroom ceiling. She was lying on her bed in her darkened bedroom, fully clothed. She tried to remember how and when she had gotten here and found herself confronting a phantasmagoria of images:

. . . a scarecrow with wormy eyes . . .

. . . a flying automobile . . .

. . . a corridor that had no end . . .

Then she had the most disturbing thought of all: Had she been drugged? That had happened once before, in law school, at a party, when a classmate had slipped an hallucinogenic into her lemonade and for the next fourteen hours she saw things that were not real. And she hated things that were not real, hated the very idea of them.

She stood, on wobbly legs, and snapped on a bed-table lamp and looked at herself in her dressing-table mirror: her clothes were mussed but intact and a few strands of hair had pulled loose from her ponytail and strayed across her face, but there were no visible cuts or bruises. She mentally scanned her body, kicked her legs, waved her arms: nothing broken, no unusual sensations, everything apparently intact.

"So I fell asleep and had the mother of all nightmares," she said aloud and somehow the sound of her voice was reassuring.

She looked at her alarm clock: ten in the evening. So when had she dropped off . . . And then she saw them: two small syringes.

In the nightmare, she had been given two small syringes by the bat man.

No nightmare: in a rush, she remembered everything—the trip across the bridge, the asylum, Crane, the rescue, the chase. Everything.

She sat on the bed and picked up her phone. There

was work to do and Rachel Dawes had always been
at her best when she was at work.

The Arkham inmates stumbled into the exercise
yard, which was lit by mercury-vapor lamps arrayed
on the walls and fences. Some stood numbly, slowly
surveying the area, obviously waiting either for something to happen or someone to tell them what was
going on. Others moved quickly into the shadows or
to the gates.

There was a sudden, deafening explosion and a
chunk of the rear wall spun across the yard and shattered against the building. Debris swept over everyone. Some of the inmates rubbed their eyes with their
fists, trying to clear them of dust and smoke. When
they could see clearly again, they were looking at a gap
in the wall, large enough for six men to pass abreast
through it.

A few of the men, those who had gone to the gate
and into the shadows, ran to the gap and on to the
street outside. The rest followed more slowly, and a
great deal less certainly, to freedom.

Gordon had been in the head nurse's office, which
he had commandeered, sipping cold coffee from a
cracked mug and trying to reach Flass by cell phone,
when he heard the explosion. Through the window
he saw the gap in the wall. Yanking his gun from its
holster, he ran for an exit. By the time he reached the

yard, at least half the inmates had passed through the gap and were dispersing into the city outside. Gordon hesitated: he could shoot a few of the escapees, maybe drop even a dozen or so. But that would be wholesale slaughter and he had no stomach for it. So what else? He grabbed the nearest man and handcuffed him to a drainpipe.

"At least *one* of you is staying put," he said.

Then he got out his cell phone again and speed-dialed headquarters.

Flass and a dozen patrolmen arrived ten minutes later. They examined the hole in the wall, an absolutely useless waste of time in Gordon's opinion, and flashed their lights around the yard, presumably searching for anyone who had not yet fled.

Flass joined Gordon. "They're all gone?"

Gordon nodded yes and both men stared through the gap into the dark street.

"How many were in maximum security?" Flass asked.

"Dozens . . . serial killers, rapists, assorted socio-paths. I called the city works office and asked them to raise the bridges, maybe keep some of the nutcases on the island. I'm still waiting for an answer. By the time I get one, it'll probably be too late."

"Yeah, probably. So we got a whole lot of homi-cidal maniacs running loose in Gotham, that what you're telling me, Gordon?"

"That's what I'm telling you."

* * *

Alfred accelerated. He skidded through the manor's front gate and his worst fears were confirmed . . . No, not his *worst* fears. The house was afire and that was terrible, but his worst fears concerned the location of Bruce.

First things first: get help. He braked and picked up the car phone. No signal, not this far from downtown Gotham. To be expected.

He drove toward the house and saw something that did not belong, a tractor-trailer truck parked on the lawn, on top of a flower bed. There were no cars in the driveway, which meant that the guests had already gone, but in the glow of the fire, he could see strange men standing at intervals around the blaze. Guards? Almost certainly. But they were looking *toward* the house which meant . . . ?

Which meant that their job was to prevent anyone from *leaving* the conflagration!

They would not welcome the Waynes' sixty-something butler, of that Alfred was certain. No, were he to appear, they would do him harm. But their position meant that someone was still in the house and that someone very likely was Master Bruce. He might already be dead but Alfred refused to make such an assumption. Therefore, he must get past the guards. But how? He was not a violent man, nor an especially athletic one. True, he had played cricket effectively as a youngster back in Nottingham, but that

was long ago, in another country, before he had met
Thomas Wayne and his life had really begun.

No matter. As always, he would do what must be
done. He was probably no match for the intruders in
hand-to-hand combat, about which Alfred knew extremely little, and without doubt they were armed. A
weapon was in order. There were a pair of eighteenth-
century dueling pistols in the library, alleged to be
those used by Alexander Hamilton and Aaron Burr in
their fatal encounter, but they were hardly of any use
to Alfred here, assuming they could be made to function. And there were no other firearms on the estate.
But guns were not the only weapons. There were ar-
rows and swords and cudgels . . . *Cudgels?* Now *that*
was a thought! Of course, he had no access to an *actual* cudgel, but perhaps he could employ a substitute.
And he knew just what it would be! He stopped the
car beneath a beech tree and pulled a golf club—a
nine iron—from the bag in the backseat.

He crept forward. The house was now fully aflame,
sending torrents of sparks into the night sky. It was
almost beautiful, yet it was the most horrid thing Alfred had ever seen and his stomach churned. He wanted
nothing more than to lie down and be sick, but he
could not, not until he had ascertained Bruce's fate
and helped, if help was possible.

The truck and another vehicle were at the front of
the house. Therefore, it seemed likely that the greatest
opposition would be encountered there. Perhaps there
would be fewer potential obstacles at the *rear*, near
the greenhouse and the old well. Moving as quickly

as his somewhat arthritic bones allowed, Alfred circled the house, keeping just outside the glow cast by the fire. He paused and squinted. He could see only one man, who was standing, arms akimbo, in the courtyard by the kitchen door.

He approached the guard from the rear and swung the nine iron at the man's back and the metal connected with skin and bone and made a sickening *clunk,* and the man dropped to the grass. Alfred stared. It was justified, what he had just done, and even necessary, but it was also bestially violent and he was deeply shocked that he had been capable of it, had done it without thinking. Perhaps that was the reason he had been able to do it: He had acted without thought.

But had he killed a man?

He knelt, placed two fingers on the man's neck, and—*thank heaven*—felt a pulse.

A bit of flaming debris landed on the grass nearby and smoldered briefly. Well! That reminded Alfred that work had to be done! It wouldn't get any easier, putting it off!

He ran into the house.

It was as though he had run into a wall, so intense was the heat. The air was sucked from his lungs and he stopped dead in his tracks. Then there was a muffled *whumpf* and Alfred was flung backward, out through the door into the garden. He surmised that the cooking gas had just ignited and thus the explosion. Through the door he could see what appeared to be a solid wall of flame. No getting into the manor *that* way, not anymore!

But the greenhouse . . . ?

He went into the glass structure and . . . yes! There were a couple of old blankets, too worn to be used inside, but put here in case some botanical use might be found for them. And he had personally supervised the reinstallation of the plumbing; he knew the water faucets were functioning. And indeed they were! He soaked the blankets until they were saturated, wrapped them around his head, filled his lungs with cool air, and getting a running start, again ventured into the inferno. This time, thanks to the blankets, he was able to penetrate the fiery wall and, choking and coughing, made his way into the long corridor that skirted the ballroom. He tried to call Bruce's name, but his voice was a thin rasp, inaudible in the roar and crackle all around him. Nothing to do but soldier on!

A few yards farther, he saw the young man on the floor, mostly hidden by a heavy oak beam. Alfred knelt by him, and as loudly as he was able, croaked, *"Master Bruce!"*

Bruce's eyelids fluttered and his lips parted. Alfred wrung a bit of moisture from the corner of one of the blankets. The water dropped into Bruce's mouth and his eyes came fully open.

Alfred began: "Sir, I'm afraid—"

"I know, Alfred."

Bruce twisted his body. The beam did not move.

"Can't budge it," Bruce whispered.

Alfred injected a modicum of exasperation into

what was left of his voice. "Sir, whatever is the point of all those push-ups if you can't even—"

"Can it, Alfred," Bruce said, and got his palms under the beam. He bent his knees, exhaled loudly, and pushed.

The beam inched upward, but not far enough. Alfred lay next to Bruce and put his hands on the beam. Together, they strained. The beam moved, not much, but Bruce rolled out from under it. The beam dropped to the floor.

Bruce managed to stand, swayed, then fell.

"Very well," Alfred said. He put one of the blankets around Bruce, grabbed him beneath the armpits, and dragged him to the mirror near the piano. He played the four notes—*Thank the stars that the fire had not yet damaged* this *delicate mechanism!*—and the mirror swung on its hinges. Alfred pulled Bruce into the hidden passageway and onto the elevator. Shrugging off the blanket, now almost completely dry, he pushed a button and heard the generator start somewhere. The lights below flickered on. With a creak, the elevator began to descend into the cave.

The air became cooler and Alfred could again breathe normally. The elevator jolted to a stop and as it did, Alfred heard a deafening crash. Fragments of dirt and stone rained down around him and he realized that the house must have collapsed.

Bruce stirred and, leaning against the side of the elevator, got to his feet. Alfred helped him to the workbench. Bruce looked up at the ceiling. There were tears in his eyes.

"What have I done, Alfred? Everything my family . . . my father built . . ."

Alfred was tugging off Bruce's jacket. The white shirt beneath was stained with blood. Alfred tried to speak, but could not. He coughed, and tried again: "The Wayne legacy is more than bricks and mortar, sir."

Alfred tore Bruce's shirt off and peered at a gash on Bruce's side, sticky with congealing blood.

"I thought I could help Gotham," Bruce said. "But I've failed."

Alfred ripped a long strip from the shirt and began to wind it around the wound. Without looking up from his task, he asked, "And why do we fall, sir?"

Alfred knotted the improvised bandage and answered his own question. "So that we might better learn to pick ourselves up."

"Still haven't given up on me?"

"Never."

21

At first, Rachel had wondered if she was in any condition to drive. She still could not separate what was real from what was imagined about the wild drive and chase through the city, but she had vivid and accurate memories of everything that had preceded it. And she remembered the cavern and the masked man who had saved her: that was clear in her mind. But she *had* been drugged, twice, and maybe she was still suffering aftereffects, not fit to be behind the wheel. No, she *had* been given an antidote and, besides, she felt okay. *Better* than okay; she was rested and her senses were sharp and clear.

And she had to find Gordon.

She needed transportation, desperately, but her car was still parked near the asylum in the Narrows, miles away. But her mother's wasn't. No cabs on the street, not this late, but her mother's condo was only a mile and a half away and Rachel ran in the park as often as her schedule permitted.

She began to jog and, after two blocks, quickened her pace to a run. Eighteen minutes later, she was talking to a graying woman in a nightgown, her mom, who

was at first angry at being awakened and, when she
had finished rubbing her eyes and splashing cold water
on her face, worried. Rachel assured her that, no,
everything was okay, she just needed to borrow a car
for an hour or two. Five minutes after that she was
driving her mom's ancient gas guzzler from a garage
beneath the condo.

It was almost midnight by the time she arrived at
the Narrows. From several blocks away, she saw police flashers clustered around the bridge to the Narrows. As she approached it, a red-faced cop with a
beer belly held up a warning hand. Rachel braked
and rolled down her window.

The cop put a forearm on the car's roof and leaned
toward her. "Look, lady, we're about to raise the
bridges. You won't have time to get back over."

Rachel fumbled in her purse and found her ID,
which she held in front of the cop's face. "Officer, I'm
a Gotham City district attorney with information rele-
vant to this situation, so please let me pass."

"Let me talk to my sergeant," the cop said. "You'll
have to leave your car here."

For an hour, Gordon, Flass, and two uniforms had
been prowling the streets and alleys of the Narrows,
aware that citizens were peering at them from windows and porches. Then Gordon's flashlight beam hit
a man dressed in Arkham Asylum coveralls, cowering
behind a Dumpster. The inmate began to hop away

on one foot and Flass said to Gordon, "Keep your light on him."

Flass brought the inmate down with a tackle.

"Harassment, I see harassment," someone yelled from a backyard.

Flass pointed his gun at the nosy neighbor. "Wanna see excess force?"

Gordon pushed Flass's gun down. "Flass, cool it!"

Gordon stood the inmate on his feet and cuffed him.

The inmate began to whimper.

"Take it easy," Gordon told him.

"Hey, Gordon," one of the uniforms shouted, "somebody to see you."

Gordon flashed his light up the street and saw Rachel Dawes, from the D.A.'s office, coming toward him.

"What are you doing here?" he asked her.

"Our . . . mutual friend sent me with this." She took the two syringes from her purse. "These counteract Crane's toxin. One is for you, and the other is to start mass production in case things get worse."

Gordon accepted the syringes.

"Hopefully you won't need them," Rachel said.

"I won't. Not unless the perps have some way of getting it into the air. Okay, Ms. Dawes, thanks. Now you'd better get off the island before they raise the bridges."

Gordon motioned to the cop, who led Rachel back into the darkness.

* * *

The word had finally come through; finally, the cops had permission to raise the bridges. Sergeant Harry Bilkie, who had been waiting for an hour, hung his walkie-talkie on his belt and went into the cramped iron cabin that housed the bridge controls.

A police van tore up the avenue and squealed to a stop. Harry gave it the once-over: regular cop van.

"You guys gotta get across?" he shouted.

"In a hurry," the driver shouted back.

"Okay, last one," Harry said, and waved the van on.

Harry waited until he saw the van's taillights vanish, then pulled a lever. The bridge split in half and each side began to pivot upward.

Harry spoke into his walkie-talkie. "South side's up."

There was a squawk and three other voices reported that the north and west sides were up, too, and the tunnel was closed. The Narrows was completely cut off from the rest of the city.

Someone had finally seen the fire on the Wayne property and made the necessary call. The engines from the nearest station arrived ninety minutes after the blaze had been started and the engines from the second nearest did not arrive until almost two hours had passed. The firemen went through the motions of pumping some water onto the conflagration, but realistically, they knew there was nothing they could do except, as one of them said, "Break out the marshmallows and call the insurance company."

In the vast, dim cavern underneath the remains of Wayne Manor, Bruce Wayne was transforming himself. He seemed to be in no hurry. He put on the flexible tunic, the tights, the boots, the graphite cowl, and the cape. He thrust his hands into the scalloped gloves and buckled the wide, compartmented belt around his waist.

For a moment, he looked up at the bats, barely visible, fluttering among the stalactites. Then he turned to Alfred, who had been watching him, and said, "This might be the Batman's last ride."

"Then I suggest you make it a good one."

"I'll do my best."

Batman strode to the Batmobile, climbed into the cabin, and started the engine. It roared, and the bats swarmed from their hiding places.

A few seconds later, the vehicle erupted from behind the waterfall and sped into the night.

Rachel followed the cop down the alley, which ended in a square at the base of a monorail tower. She saw a SWAT van parked nearby and several uniformed, vested men deployed in the area, looking up at the monorail track. A little boy, about six, with blond hair falling in a cowlick over his forehead was tugging at the sleeve of one of the SWATs.

"I can't find my mom," the boy said.

The SWAT shoved the boy, who stumbled backward and fought to maintain his balance. Rachel ran to him and put a steadying hand on his shoulder.

"What the hell are you doing?" she snapped at the SWAT.

The SWAT ignored her and as Rachel held the boy's hand she shouted at the SWAT. "Hey, you. Look at me!"

The SWAT turned, drew a pistol from his holster, and aimed it at Rachel.

"Gentlemen!" It was a voice new to Rachel: deep, grave, impressive. She saw a tall man with deep-set, burning eyes under a ledge of brow step from the rear of the van. Behind him, there was a bulky industrial machine of some sort.

"Time to spread the word," he said, "and the word is . . . *panic*."

He pressed a button on the machine and—

Within moments, the reaction spread throughout the Narrows. It was as though cannons were fired simultaneously along every street and alley. Fire hydrants shot their caps into the streets and began gushing. Manhole covers flipped high into the air. Sewer pipes split. Steam pipes burst. Soon there was broken glass and water seeping from foundations and spouting from sprinklers. Avenues were flooded and cars were stalled. Alarms rang and sirens shrieked. Tens of thousands of men, women, and children awakened, blinked, looked first at clocks and then out of windows, and muttered, "What the hell," and ran to their phones to call neighbors and relatives and ask if *any*one had any idea what was going on.

One man in his eighties found his air raid warden helmet, last worn during World War Two, and put it on and told his wife that he *knew* it would come in handy someday, dammit.

Some went to the nearest house of worship and many, many more simply prayed wherever they happened to be.

And others made preparations to begin looting.

Jeff Benedict had thought tonight would be an easy one. He'd pulled the midnight-to-eight shift at his place of employment, the Water Board Control Room, housed downtown in Wayne Tower, and heck, the graveyard shift was usually a snap. Even Gothamites, maybe the world's biggest night owls after New Yorkers, had to sleep sometime and sleepers didn't use water, at least not much. And his boss was Lon Calter, one of the real nice guys, easy to get along with, to talk sports with, to do whatever needed doing with. So some guys bitched about the graveyard, but not Jeff. To Jeff, the graveyard was cake.

He was leaning back in his chair, reading the sports section of the *Trib*, when Lon said, "Looka that," and Jeff saw that the monitors were going crazy.

Jeff and Lon moved to their workstations and began pushing buttons and checking gauges.

Jeff pointed to a dial. "Wouldja look at that pressure? It's *spiking*."

"Can you tell where?" Lon asked.

Jeff swiveled his chair to a computer screen, tapped some keys, and said, "Right there. Southeast sector."

"That's the water main under the Narrows," Lon said. "Something's . . . cripes—something's vaporizing the water."

"That ain't possible," Jeff said.

"No? Take a look at the temperature. Going through the roof."

"Whadda we do?"

"Beats me. Whatever this is, it ain't covered in the manual."

Something had exploded near Rachel, knocking her down, and something else scalded her cheek. The hem of her skirt was ripped and her knee was scraped— that was what she was first aware of. She shook her head and blinked her eyes and began trying to make sense of things. The street was filling with . . . what? Fog? But it couldn't be fog, not when the air was clear a moment ago. So what? *The drugs?* Was she experiencing a drug flashback? No—*steam*. That's what the mist was! She heard a child's whimper and saw the little blond boy lying in the gutter. He was hurt. She began crawling toward him.

* * *

Gordon had been standing near a sewer when the lid shot into the air, taking parts of the street with it, and a cobblestone struck the side of his head. He went down and heard Flass screaming incoherently. He got to his feet and felt warmth and wetness, first on his hands and face and then soaking through his clothing. Steam was rolling in waves over everything. He saw Flass, a dark silhouette, waving his gun and continuing to scream.

Flass fired. At what? Something Gordon couldn't see? Or . . . maybe something that wasn't there.

Flass fired again and this time the flash from the muzzle of his gun elongated and grew tentacles that reached toward Gordon—

He knew he was hallucinating and that he had only a few seconds before the toxin he must have inhaled would fry his mind completely. He fumbled in his pocket and found one of the syringes Rachel Dawes had given him. He got it out, but then he had a problem; his thumbs and fingers had become as thick as sausages and he couldn't make them slide the cardboard sleeve from the needle. He grabbed the sleeve in his teeth and pulled it free of the needle and somehow jabbed the needle into the back of his hand. He pressed the plunger with his chin and felt molten fire sizzle into his vein.

His fingers and thumbs returned to their normal shape and size.

Something sang past his ear. Flass was still waving his gun and shooting; a bullet had missed Gordon by inches.

Now Flass was aiming at a kid, a teenager, who stood trembling on the curb.

"Flass—no!" Gordon shouted. "He's unarmed."

Gordon brought Flass down with a tackle. They locked arms and legs and rolled on the cobblestones. Flass freed his hands and began to choke Gordon. Gordon elbowed Flass in the face again and again, and finally Flass's grip relaxed and he dropped off Gordon's body and lay still. Gordon dragged Flass to a drainpipe and handcuffed him to it.

Gordon stood panting, and he heard it then. It began as a moan and became a howling that increased in volume until it seemed to fill the universe. What kind of beast . . . ? And Gordon realized that he was hearing many voices, thousands of them, wailing in mortal terror.

In the few seconds it took Rachel to crawl to the blond boy, she realized what must have happened. She wasn't drugged, but everyone else was. The toxin was in the steam and the guy in the police van must have caused it with the odd machine.

The boy was sobbing uncontrollably. Heaven only knew what he thought he was seeing.

"It's okay, it's okay," Rachel cooed. "No one's going to hurt you."

"Of course they are," someone said behind Rachel and the boy. She turned and looked up. A dark, massive shape was emerging from the mist: a saddled horse, dragging a dead cop from the stirrup, with Jonathan Crane astride the animal, wearing his burlap mask. Other shapes were gathered behind him: inmates from the asylum.

"Dr. Crane," Rachel said.

"Not *Crane,*" the mounted man screamed. "*Scarecrow.*"

Rachel was a lawyer, not a psychiatrist, but she realized that Crane had gone round the bend in an odd way. He apparently believed he was this "scarecrow."

She picked up the boy and ran into the mist. Crane galloped after her. Rachel stumbled and hit a telephone pole, but blundered blindly on.

She slammed into a wall. Dead end.

Crane reined his horse only a few feet from Rachel and the boy and said, "Let me help you."

The inmates crowded around Crane.

Rachel put the boy down and reached into her shoulder bag.

The horse reared back, front hooves pawing the air.

"Try shock therapy," Rachel said, and pulled her Taser from her bag. She shot it at Crane and the barbs caught in the sacking of his mask. Electrical sparks arced across Crane's face. He went limp, and slid from the saddle. The horse whinnied and galloped back the way he had come, dragging the dead cop from one stirrup and Crane from the other.

The inmates scattered.

Rachel knelt by the boy and put her arms around him.

* * *

Gordon had found an empty patrol car and had driven it to the nearest bridge, now raised and impassable. Police flashers were visible across the river, which meant cops were there, help was there. He keyed the cruiser's radio and identified himself.

The radio squawked. *"We hear you."* Gordon recognized the voice of Commissioner Loeb. *"What the hell's going on over there?"*

"We need reinforcements," Gordon said into the microphone. "Tac teams, SWATs, riot cops—get 'em in masks and—"

"Gordon, all the city's riot police are on the island with you."

"Well, they're completely incapacitated."

"There's nobody left to send in."

Batman had been monitoring the police bands ever since he had rocketed out from behind the waterfall and had heard the exchange between Gordon and Loeb. He was not surprised at the helplessness of the authorities in this emergency. He remembered dinnertable conversations between his father and guests about how the city was woefully unprepared for anything out of the ordinary, from an earthquake to a serious civil uprising, and how sooner or later the odds would catch up with it, with a disastrous aftermath. Joe Chill had killed Thomas Wayne before he could force the lethargic city planning commission to at least study the situation: another casualty of Rā's al Ghūl's economic marauding.

He saw the red lights of police flashers glancing off walls before he actually saw the cluster of vehicles and the men standing around them. Just beyond the police group was the bridge, its halves pointing toward the sky, forming a vee with a forty-foot gap at its apex.

Okay, here we go.

Batman shifted and floored the accelerator. The Batmobile leaped forward, crashed through the wooden sawhorses blocking the entry to the bridge, and tilted upward, gaining speed. It left the roadway and was flying in a high arc across the river.

Gordon reached through the open window of the cruiser and dropped the microphone on the seat. Now what? No help coming, and as far as he could tell, he was the only sane man left on the island. No way to get back to the mainland, either. So what's the plan? Hide until things cool down, if they ever do?

Two circles of light appeared on the pavement in front of him. He looked up and over his shoulder and saw headlights coming toward him—from above—and heard the roar of a powerful engine.

He ducked. A large vehicle landed a dozen feet away, bounced once on its oversize tires, and stopped. Its top slid forward and a seat rose. Batman stepped out.

"Nice landing," Gordon said.

Batman moved near and spoke in that raspy growl: "Anything I should know about?"

"Rachel Dawes is in there somewhere. The Narrows is tearing itself to pieces."

"This is just the beginning. They intend to destroy the entire city."

"They've incapacitated all the riot police here on the island."

"If they hit the whole city with the toxin, there'll be no way to stop Gotham from tearing itself apart in mass panic."

Gordon looked at the raised bridge. "How could they do that? There's no way to get that machine off the island. Except—"

"The monorail follows the water mains right into the central hub beneath Wayne Tower. If they drive their machine into Wayne Station, it'll cause a chain reaction that'll vaporize the entire city's water supply."

"Covering Gotham with a fog of fear toxin."

Batman tilted his head up and for almost a minute gazed at the monorail tracks overhead. Finally, he said, "I'm going to stop them loading that train."

"And if you can't?"

Again, Batman was silent for long seconds. Then: "Can you drive a stick shift?"

Batman tossed an ignition key to Gordon.

The blond-haired little boy was trembling, but Rachel managed to hang on to him as she inched her way through the mist. If she could just get him inside somewhere, if they could only survive till daybreak . . .

Shadows appeared in front of her, black shapes in

the undulating white—a lot of them, twenty at least. One of them stepped into a splash of light from a nearby window and she saw that he was wearing inmate's coveralls. She recognized him immediately: Victor Zsasz.

Rachel darted to the side of a building and tried to lift the boy onto the bottom rung of a fire-escape ladder. But she was not tall enough.

She hugged the boy to her and stepped sideways. She stumbled over something, teetered, regained her balance, and looked down at the dead body of a uniformed cop.

The inmates drew closer. One of them was giggling.

Rachel left the boy next to the wall and knelt by the body. She pulled the cop's sidearm from its holster . . .

How do these damn things work . . . ?

She remembered, and pulled back and released the slide, and thumbed off the safety.

Zsasz stepped back into the light.

"Go away, Victor," Rachel said. "I'm warning you . . ."

Victor and the others kept coming.

Rachel took a deep breath and aimed the gun. Her finger tightened on the trigger. She couldn't stop all of them, but she could do her best . . .

A rasping command came from above her: "Grab the boy."

Something dark dropped between Rachel and Zsasz. Zsasz grunted and fell.

Rachel grabbed the boy, and Batman grabbed Rachel. He took something from under his cape, pointed it upward, and then they were shooting past the brick wall, over a parapet, and onto a roof.

Rachel shrugged off her jacket and put it around the boy. She took his hand and they went to where Batman was standing, looking over the city.

Mist still roiled in the streets, punctuated here and there with fire. Occasionally, they heard a scream or a moan. Rachel thought that the moans were worse.

Batman stepped onto the parapet.

Rachel grabbed his cape. "Wait! You could die."

Batman nodded.

Once more, Rachel was certain that, somehow, she *knew* this man. "At least tell me your name."

Batman turned, hesitated, turned back to Rachel. He spoke in a normal voice, a pleasant baritone: "It's not who I am underneath . . ." He touched his chest. "But what I do that defines me."

Of course. It had to be him. "Bruce."

He leaped to the top of the parapet and stepped off it into darkness.

He wanted to consider what had just happened, how it almost certainly changed everything in his life. But there were tasks to be accomplished and they required him to focus. He slid his hands into the activating pockets of his cape and immediately the cloak became a rigid wing, smashing into the wind, halting his downward plunge. His fall became a glide, controlled by his arms. He flew into the labyrinth that was the Narrows. Buildings and streetlamps flashed past, fires seemed to burst out of the fog. He glanced at the sky. Through a gap in the mist, he glimpsed stars and oriented himself:

Need to go east . . .

He tilted his body and swerved in midair. The tip of his cape hit the top branch of a tree and he spun madly, out of control, for a second, helpless. Then he flattened his body and was again flying smoothly. A man and a woman cowering in a doorway looked up and saw him and screamed in unison.

Ahead, a huge cloud of steam billowed into the air. *Probably from a broken water main . . .* Batman glided into it, felt himself lifted by an updraft, and for a moment, experienced a great calm.

When I emerge from this whiteness, I will be engaged in a conflict, perhaps the last one of my life. Failure is unthinkable and yet I fear what success might do to me. But for now, for this moment, I am peaceful . . .

And suddenly the cloud was behind him and he was swooping over a rooftop and nosing downward. Just ahead, the roof of a blocky concrete monorail support loomed, its edges softened by the mist. Batman dropped his legs so he was in a vertical position and used the cape wings as air brakes. He lost speed. When his boots touched the roof, he ran a few steps and stopped. He thrust his hands into the cape pockets and the wings seemed to melt until they were only black fabric, hanging from his shoulders.

He looked around. To his back, there was a street, and to his front, a steep drop down to buildings arrayed along a narrow avenue that wound down to the edge of the river. On a rooftop to his left, two ninjas were putting a bulky machine—the microwave transmitter—into a train.

That's the devil's toy. That's what I have to destroy . . .

Rā's al Ghūl stood a few yards away, mist swirling around him.

"It ends here," Batman said.

Rā's raised his eyebrows. "You're not dead? You should be dead."

"But I'm not."

"I have to admire your persistence. But the costume . . . you took my advice about theatricality a bit literally, don't you think?"

Two ninjas came around the corner of the monorail support and positioned themselves in front of Rā's.

"They won't save you," Batman said. "Give it up. Or meet me man to man."

"I doubt that you would be able to do me serious harm because I doubt that you would be able to look upon yet another father figure lying dead before you. But no matter. I decline your invitation to combat. I've done you the honor of killing you once today and I can't save the world by killing one man at a time."

"You think I can't beat your pawns?"

Four more ninjas rappeled down from the rail above them.

Batman tackled the man nearest him, and locked together, they both went over the side of the monorail support. In midair, Batman twisted, and a half second later hit the rooftop below with the ninja under him, cushioning his fall. As he was getting to his feet, two more ninjas landed nearby and crouched into combat stances. Batman reached under his cloak and, in a single smooth motion, brought out a Batarang and spun it at one of the ninjas while he kicked another off the roof and onto a fire-escape landing.

How many more . . . ? Can't afford to fight them all. I've got to smash the microwave transmitter . . .

Batman lifted his grappling gun from his belt, but before he could aim it, a length of narrow chain wrapped around his wrist and jerked. The gun left his hand and, as it vanished into the fog, fired, sending the monofilament and hook hissing into the darkness. Batman grabbed the chain in his other hand and pulled. The ninja who had thrown it, and was still holding the far end, stumbled forward into Batman's fist.

Something landed at Batman's feet and exploded with a blinding flash and a puff of acrid gas. Reflexively, Batman turned his head, closed his eyes, and held his breath as he leaped in the direction from which the explosive had come. A ninja was in the act of throwing a second small bomb when Batman smashed into him. They went over a parapet and down onto a sheet of corrugated metal that served as a canopy over a parking area. A beam under the iron snapped and Batman and the ninja slid onto the pavement as an iron sheet clanged beside them. Batman elbowed the ninja's chin, knocking him unconscious, and levered himself to his feet.

He mentally scanned his body. There was plenty of pain, but that was irrelevant. Was anything broken? Was he incapacitated in any way? Apparently not. The armor in his costume had done its job.

How to get back up to Rā's . . . What happened to the grappling gun?

He saw it then, in the ambient glow of the monorail lights. Across the street: his gun, in the hands of a bald, mustached man in a business suit, who was turning it over and over in his hands as though it were a fascinating new toy he could not quite understand.

The man would be no problem. But he was surrounded by other men and women and even a few children, staring and shuffling out of the mist toward him.

"Monster," someone screamed, and the mob ran toward him.

Batman dodged the first few to reach him, but his back was to a wall and he had no possible escape route.

I can't harm them. They're drugged . . . they don't know what they're doing . . .

Fingers clutched his ankles and his arms and tugged at him until Batman fell. As bodies swarmed over him, he heard the grinding and hissing of brakes from the monorail and the sound of steel wheels turning.

It had taken several minutes to get the microwave transmitter loaded onto the train, and another minute for Rā's to be certain he understood the train's controls. When he was satisfied, he pushed a red lever forward. The train jerked, rattled, and began moving.

A minute after Batman had vanished, Rachel found a trapdoor in the roof and managed to get it open. Inside, there was a steep flight of steps. She urged the blond-haired boy onto them and together they entered the building, an ancient tenement that smelled of cooking odors and other, less pleasant smells. Several doors along the dimly lit hallway were open and one had been torn from its hinges. The apartments behind them were deserted—in two, television sets were still on. But the occupants might return, and would be crazy when they did. So Rachel and the boy descended farther, all the way to the basement. The floor was wet, but Rachel found a platform that once supported a futon leaning on its end against a back wall. Straining under the weight, she lowered it and then she and the boy climbed on top of it.

The boy had stopped trembling, but his eyes were wide and occasionally he gasped. Rachel put her arms around him.

If only we can get through the night . . . If only those lunatics don't find us . . .

Once, Rachel had dreamed of doing grand deeds, of making the world a better place and gaining renown in the process. Now, all she wanted was to save one small child.

*   *   *

The bald man tugged the ends of his mustache, as though that would make his brain work better, and continued to stare down at the grappling gun. He squeezed the trigger. Suddenly the wire that trailed from its muzzle retracted, hauling a three-pronged hook from the fog. It snapped against the gun barrel with such force that the man stumbled backward. He yelped, spread his fingers, pulled his hands wide. The gun clattered to the cobblestones and the man kicked it away.

Batman saw it land through a forest of legs. The members of the mob were moaning, clawing at one another more than at him. Batman hunched his shoulders, thrust out his arms between the nearest pair of calves, and separated them. The kid who owned the calves toppled into several other people and for an instant there was a clear area between Batman and the gun. He scuttled forward, flattened, closed his fist. He had the gun. He rolled onto his back, lifted and aimed, and shot.

The grappling hook soared over the top of the monorail, reached its apogee, dropped, and caught on the air vent of the train's last car.

The monofilament went taut as the train moved and yanked Batman to his feet.

Two of the ninjas grabbed him.

The train's speed increased.

Batman was pulled from the grasp of the ninjas and left the ground.

*   *   *

How the hell does this thing open? Gordon stood beside Batman's car, or whatever it was, trying to get inside. He had a key, sure, but there was no keyhole. His thumb tightened on the key and the roof of the vehicle slid forward.

Oh. That's how it works. Some kind of microwave transmission.

Gordon climbed in and the roof slid closed above him. He put his hands on the wheel, tried the pedals with his feet, scanned the dashboard. He had no idea what most of these buttons, levers, and dials were for, but the basic operation of the . . . *car?*—that seemed conventional enough.

There was a keyhole on the steering column, just like on the car his wife drove. Okay, good. Put the key in the keyhole, give it a twist—

The engine rumbled to life.

Gordon depressed the clutch and ran the stick through its various positions. Six forward gears and reverse. Pretty fancy, but not too exotic. Okay, time to go. He shifted into first, released the clutch—

The enormous rear tires began to spin and smoke, but the vehicle did not move, which seemed to indicate that the front wheels were locked, somehow. There had to be a brake release handle. Gordon groped under the dashboard and found something. He tugged and pushed and—

He was at the other end of the block, heading straight for a wall. How long had it taken? Two seconds? Three? He stomped what he hoped was the brake pedal and jerked the wheel. The vehicle skidded around a corner and immediately accelerated again.

Cripes! This baby would take some getting used to . . .

Steering awkwardly with one hand, he got out his walkie-talkie with the other and keyed it.

"This is Gordon," he said. "Lower the south bridge. I'll be there in a minute or two."

Rā's insured that the train was running properly and would continue to do so without any further attention from him. He moved away from the controls to the microwave transmitter and activated it. The machine hummed.

Commissioner Loeb relayed Gordon's request and watched the two halves of the bridge's roadway descend and meet. For whatever good that would do.

He pulled back the sleeve of his uniform coat and squinted at the luminous dial of his watch. Almost two-thirty in the A.M. He'd been standing on this godforsaken bridge since . . . what? Since midnight. Standing here with a bunch of uniforms and a couple of plainclothes guys and waiting for something to happen. But nothing was going on, either here or, as far as he could see, at the other end of the raised roadway, in the Narrows. Maybe nothing *would* happen. Maybe he was wasting his time when he could be at home getting his eight hours. 'Cause he *needed* his eight hours. He didn't get his eight hours, the next day he wasn't worth a thing. And where was Gordon? It'd been . . . what?—fifteen minutes, at least, since he'd heard from the sergeant.

He felt something through the soles of his shoes. Some kind of shaking. And he heard a rumbling.

"Commissioner, look!" one of the uniforms said, and Loeb looked in the direction the cop's finger was pointing: the monorail, which ran above the bridge and *way* above the river. The mist was getting brighter and that was because . . . The headlamp of a train was shining through it. Which meant the train was moving. Coming this way.

Loeb got a pair of binoculars from the nearest patrol car and put them to his eyes and twisted the focus wheel until the monorail and the train were sharp in the lenses. Yeah, the train was coming, all right, picking up speed, too. But what was that behind it?

A man?

The first few seconds had been bad. The first few seconds had nearly killed him. He clutched the gun and was pulled upward toward the rim of the track bed that overhung the street, his face scraping along a rivet-studded beam. He estimated that he was already moving at twenty miles an hour. If he hit the rim at this speed, it would either take off his head or knock him to the cobblestones below. Either way, he would be dead.

He managed to put both his feet against the steel

beam and push. His body flew outward and he missed the track bed by maybe two inches.

One hurdle passed.

He was being dragged behind the rear of the train, bumping along the tracks. His costume was some protection—ordinary clothing would have been shredded by now—but it would not last indefinitely. And sooner or later, one of these bumps would snap a bone.

The train was over the bridge. Batman could see lights gleaming on the river underneath it.

He squeezed the trigger of the grappling gun and the line began to retract, pulling him toward the train.

The train's speed increased and Batman's body left the tracks and, for a couple of seconds, trailed the train like some kind of bizarre streamer. Then the line finished retracting and Batman was clutching the rounded end of the car, looking through a window at rows of empty seats and empty cardboard cups rolling on the filthy floor.

Batman reached up and curled his gloved fingers around the tiny metal lip running around the top of the car. Not much to hang on to. But maybe enough.

As the train passed overhead, Loeb drew his gun. Then he realized that he had absolutely no use for it and reholstered it. And then the fire hydrant next to him exploded and a hard gush of water knocked him flat on his back. He rolled over onto his hands and knees and saw a manhole cover flipping end over end and sprinklets of water arcing up from cracks in the pavement. Across the street, another hydrant exploded.

Jeff Benedict and Lon Calter were busy again. For a while, after the ruckus at the Narrows, things had quieted down. Lon had called the bosses, all of them, and they'd all promised to be right down, but that was forty minutes ago and none had shown yet. No surprise. Most of them lived in the northern suburbs— long drive.

Jeff asked Lon if he had any idea what had caused the ruckus and Lon said that he'd seen nothing like it in his thirty years with the Water Department. But in the morning, the engineers would get it figured out, and anyway, the worst seemed to be over. Course, there'd be a lot of people in the Narrows without water, but that was life in Gotham City . . .

Then it started again. The control board lit up and the emergency alarm clanged. Jeff and Lon ran to their monitors.

"What's that?" Jeff asked.

"The pressure's moving along the mains . . . blowing all the pipes," Lon said. "Some kind of chain reaction."

"Coming toward us."

Batman jumped, and that gave him enough altitude to get his palms onto the top of the train car, and he straightened his arms and slid on his chest until his entire body was on the silvery roof.

The train was still accelerating. He saw a geyser of water shoot up alongside the track bed and knew pipes and hydrants were exploding below.

The train rounded a bend and canted sharply to the left. Batman recentered his weight and regained his balance.

Rā's would be in the first car, so that's where he had to go. And fast. With each passing second, more toxic spray was releasing into the air, to be breathed in by innocent men, women, and children—to drive them insane.

Lon swiveled his chair away from the control board and stared at Jeff. His eyes were wide, his mouth slack, his entire expression one of helpless panic.

"What?" Jeff demanded.

"Pressure's building underneath us. We gotta . . . hell, I don't know. We gotta evacuate the building."

"Why?"

" 'Cause Wayne Tower sits right on the central hub. If that pressure reaches us, the water supply across the whole city will blow."

Jeff glanced at the nearest pressure gauge. The needle was already in the red zone and moving higher.

"Let's get outta here," Lon said, standing and grabbing his jacket from where it hung on the back of a chair. "We're sitting on the hub—and she's gonna blow big."

* * *

Gordon struggled to keep control of Batman's vehicle. Rounding a corner, he misjudged the speed-distance ratio and sideswiped a parked SUV.

"Sorry," he muttered.

He swerved onto the South Bridge, grateful that Loeb had managed to get it lowered, and in a couple of seconds, sped off it and onto the street on the other side. He passed Loeb and a cluster of cops, all of whom were milling around their cars aimlessly, all of whom were wet. So they'd undoubtedly breathed in the toxin and in a minute, maybe they'd be howling lunatics. Well, he couldn't worry about them. He had to follow the damn train, which was no great feat, because from here, there was only one place it could go. To the center of the city. To Wayne Tower.

The train sped over a major intersection, and at the periphery of his vision, Batman saw a manhole cover flipping end over end. Wind howled in his ears, the sound mingling with the screech and clatter of steel wheels on steel rails, and the car swayed under his feet. Ahead, he could see the silhouette of the familiar Gotham City skyline, black against the moonlit blue of the sky, with Wayne Tower dwarfing the other skyscrapers. At this speed, the train would pull into the Tower station in a minute or two. Bruce Wayne was no engineer, and so neither was Batman, but he was familiar enough with the city's infrastructure to realize that Rā's al Ghūl's machine would blow every main within a twenty-mile radius if it got close to the complex of tunnels under the Tower.

There would be an unimaginable epidemic of insanity. The cost in human lives and human suffering would be incalculable.

He ran, jumped to another car, ran and jumped . . .

There was a tunnel directly ahead.

Batman flattened himself on the car as it tore beneath a concrete arch.

He stood, swayed, continued running and jumping.

In the Wayne guesthouse, Alfred sat hunched, a cold cup of Earl Grey tea between his palms, wearing his favorite garment, a velvet bathrobe given to him as a Christmas present by Martha Wayne decades ago. It was worn and frayed now, and its rich scarlet color had faded to a bland pink, but it was still his favorite. He was staring at a television tuned to the local all-news channel and on the kitchen table beside him were two radios, a short-wave tuned to the police bands and an ordinary receiver tuned to a news station. He had pieced together some of what was happening. He knew that Master Bruce had eluded the police and that something hellish was occurring at the Narrows. But the reports were maddeningly incomplete. He felt, in his bones, that Bruce Wayne was still alive, but he was by no means certain.

*   *   *

Batman reached the lead car, swayed for a moment as he considered his options, and decided that he could not afford to waste time strategizing. He had to operate in the moment, letting instinct guide him.

He might have only seconds left.

He sat on the edge of the car and swung his legs backward. His boots struck a shatterproof window and knocked it from its frame. As it dropped to one of the seats, Batman was already sliding and twisting through the empty frame and landing inside the car. He landed in a crouch on the floor facing the front of the train.

The microwave transmitter blocked the aisle, humming and vibrating slightly. Behind it stood Rā's al Ghūl.

"You're still not dead," Rā's said.

"Obviously not. We can end this now, Rā's. There's no need for further bloodshed."

"Oh, you are wrong, Bruce. There's an enormous need."

"I'll stop you."

"No. You won't. Because to stop me you would have to kill me and you will not do that."

"You're sure?"

"Yes. You could not stand to see another father die." Rā's edged around the machine and slid his sword from the cane. "But I have seen many of my children die. Another one won't make much difference to me."

Rā's advanced, the sword in one hand, the cane in the other. He feinted with the sword and swung the cane at Batman's head. Batman trapped it in one of his scallops, twisted, and the cane went spinning over his shoulder.

Rā's thrust the sword point at Batman's chest. Batman pivoted and the steel slipped past his chest, grazing his costume. Rā's kicked. Batman sidestepped and Rā's kicked again, striking Batman's hip. As Batman stumbled, trying to regain his footing, Rā's arced the blade downward toward Batman's head, but Batman crossed his wrists and trapped the steel in the scallops of both gauntlets.

"Familiar," Rā's said. "Don't you have anything new?"

"How about this?" Batman yanked his arms in opposite directions and the blade snapped in two. Then Batman drove the palm of his right hand into Rā's's chest, and as Rā's stumbled backward, Batman jumped onto a seat and past Rā's to the train's controls.

He looked out the front window and saw Wayne Tower looming ahead. He grabbed the brake lever but before he could pull it back, Rā's's cane was thrust into the mechanism, jamming it. Before Batman could free it, Rā's swung his clenched fist at the back of Batman's head, bouncing it off the windshield. Rā's struck again and Batman fell and rolled onto his back and Rā's was straddling him, his hands clenched around Batman's neck, his thumbs pressing into Batman's throat.

"Don't be afraid, Bruce . . . you hate this city as much as I do, but you're just an ordinary man in a cape. That's why you can't fight injustice and that's why you can't stop this train."

"Who said anything about stopping it?"

At four in the morning, it hadn't made any difference that Gordon had run every red light between the Narrows and downtown Gotham. Eight minutes later, he was racing along beneath the monorail. He passed the speeding train and pulled ahead of it. The Wayne Tower station was just two blocks ahead, so whatever he was going to do he had to do now. If he'd understood Batman's instructions correctly and if everything worked as Batman had predicted, Gordon was about to break the law, big time.

He was scared, but so what? Being scared was nothing new.

Gordon tried to remember what the Batman had told him about the weapons on board the vehicle. He looked for the buttons that indicated where the guns were and eventually found them. He pushed a button and squeezed a trigger. Two missiles shot past the monorail support and exploded inside a parking garage. Gordon cursed himself for not aiming first and steered the Batmobile closer to the monorail support.

Aiming as best he could, he depressed the trigger again and fired. This time the missiles hit their target. Gordon exhaled and leaned back in his seat.

As he watched, the support crumbled and the monorail tracks smashed into the street.

* * *

The train car shook and Rā's's grasp relaxed for an instant. He looked through the windshield at the track, twisted and smoking.

"You'll never learn to mind your surroundings," Batman said, "as much as your opponent." He slammed his right gauntlet into Rā's's face. Rā's toppled sideways and Batman scrambled to his feet. He grabbed Rā's's hair with his left hand and pulled a Batarang from under his cloak with his right. He raised the weapon over his head; a single downward swing would bury it in Rā's's skull.

Rā's smiled. "Ah. You have finally learned to do what is necessary."

Batman flung the weapon at the windshield. The glass cracked and then broke. "I won't kill you . . ."

Batman pulled a small mine from his belt and threw it at the back door of the car. There was an explosion and the door was gone.

"But I don't have to save you."

Batman moved to the other side of the microwave transmitter and thrust his hands into the pockets of his cape. It stiffened and became a wing.

There were no cameras, no news crews. But there were three eyewitnesses: Jeff Benedict, Lon Calter, and James Gordon. Jeff and Lon had just left the Tower and were racing toward where Lon's minivan was parked when the monorail support disintegrated, scattering debris in all directions. Not knowing what else to do, utterly bewildered, they simply stopped in their tracks and waited for whatever would happen next.

Gordon couldn't believe what he was seeing. The explosion that took out the monorail also took out one of the two streetlamps in the area, leaving most of the block in heavy shadow, with most of the illumination coming from the moon.

This is what Gordon thought he saw:

The back door of the train shooting out and hitting the front of the car behind it just as the windows on either side of it disintegrated into a hundred fragments and sprayed outward. The uncoupling of the front cars from the rest of the train—caused by the explosion?—and then a man flying out of the twisted door frame, a giant wing on his back lifting him high into the air as the two front cars derailed and careened off the rail bed and dipped down into the plaza, shattering concrete and marble, raising clouds of white dust.

Then the car exploded.

Gordon, trembling with shock and excitement, was too stunned to react. He simply watched.

The three of them—Jeff, Lon, and Gordon—were momentarily blinded by the flames that followed the final explosion. But Jeff and Lon were pretty sure, and Gordon was certain, that they witnessed one final, bizarre thing: a giant bat, soaring above the rooftops, plainly visible against the moon, but only for a moment.

Batman had caught a thermal that lifted him a couple of hundred feet into the air. He looked down. There was a fire gouting up the wall of the Tower and in it he could see the silhouette of the monorail car. To the south, he saw the flashing red lights of fire engines and he heard the distant wail of sirens, mingled with the sighing of the wind.

He shifted his center of gravity and began his long, slow descent. If he calculated correctly, and could maintain the shallow angle of his glide, he would land on the access road north of the freeway, a short distance from Wayne Manor.

The sky was beginning to lighten in the east. False dawn, but the real item would appear very soon.

He touched a button on his belt, activating a transmitter in his cowl, and told Alfred where he expected to be in ten minutes.

Then he relaxed and allowed himself to enjoy the early morning air, the gentle motion of his flight.

He remembered instruction given at the monastery: *Know your emotional state at all times in order that it not deceive your intellect.*

So what *was* he feeling? Exhaustion, sure. But *emotionally?* He couldn't find any distinct emotion within him. Maybe later?

The earth was rising up to embrace him, and that was enough, for now.

* * *

Gordon stood next to the Batmobile. The gutter nearest to him was full of rushing water, as though the city were in the middle of a major storm. But the sky was clear. So the water was coming from burst pipes, hundreds of burst pipes.

What was left of the fallen monorail cars was burning with a hard, blinding, blue-white flame. Gordon had no reason to continue looking at it, so he went to look for help.

During the short ride to the Wayne property, Batman used the car phone to call Lucius Fox and, in his ordinary voice, issue some instructions. Although it was almost five in the morning, Fox sounded fully alert, and when Bruce had finished the call, Fox had sounded truly delighted.

Alfred parked the limo next to the guesthouse and Batman allowed his old friend to help him inside.

First, Alfred made tea, a cup of Earl Grey for both of them. Next came the ordeal of removing the costume. Together, they managed to get it off and Alfred surveyed the bruises on Bruce's flesh.

"Stimulating night?" he asked.

"It had its moments."

Bruce moved his arms, legs, touched his toes, and rolled his head around on his neck; nothing seemed to be broken. But, under Alfred's prompting, Bruce admitted to being in pain. Alfred was pretty sure that he could persuade Dr. Harkins to prescribe a sedative. Perhaps that young Wayne wastrel had tumbled from a polo pony?

"No drugs," Bruce said, and that closed the discussion.

William Earle arrived at Wayne Tower at his usual time, seven-thirty. He stepped from his limo and paused to survey the damage caused by the monorail accident. Or whatever the hell it was. The politicos he'd talked to didn't seem to know their asses from Christmas . . . yeah, *that* was different—and the reporters and cops weren't being helpful, either. But it was bad. The remains of the cars had been hauled away, but there sure as hell was damage. This whole side of the building might have to be redone, at least up to the fifteenth story; what wasn't cracked and falling apart was blackened by fire. The sidewalks would have to be replaced, but maybe the city would handle that, and the monorail was a total loss too, but maybe it could stay broken . . . who rode the damn thing anymore, anyway?

He entered the building, which stank of smoke, ignoring the "Good mornings" he got from various employees, rode his private elevator to the forty-ninth floor, strode to the boardroom, ignoring more greetings, and tossed his coat to Jessica, who stood by the reception desk.

"Mr. Earle, the meeting's already started," Jessica said.

"*What?*"

Without waiting for an answer, Earle flung open the boardroom door. Lucius Fox was standing in Earle's place at the head of the table, a sheaf of papers in his hand. His bow tie, today, was bright green.

"Fox, what are you doing here?" Earle snapped. "I seem to remember firing you."

"You did," Fox drawled. "But I found a new job." Fox inspected his papers for a few seconds before adding, "Yours. Didn't you get the memo?"

Earle's mouth became a straight line and his eyes narrowed. "By whose authority?"

Fox leaned over an intercom and said, "Jessica, put Mr. Wayne on the line, please."

There was the scratch of static and then a tinny version of Bruce's voice: "Yes?"

"What on earth makes you think you have the authority to decide who runs this company, Bruce?"

"The fact that I'm the owner?"

"What are you talking about? Wayne Enterprises went public weeks ago."

"And I bought most of the shares. Through various charitable foundations, trusts, and so forth. Look, it's all a bit technical, but the important thing is, my company's future is secure. Right, Mr. Fox?"

"Right you are, Mr. Wayne," Lucius drawled. He looked at Earle, and grinned.

In the back of a brand-new limo, Bruce switched off the phone. Alfred, driving, asked, "Have you seen the morning papers? Batman may have made the front page, but Bruce Wayne got pushed to page eight . . ."

Bruce opened a copy of the morning edition of the *Gotham Times*. As Alfred had said, a story about Bruce was on page eight, headlined: DRUNKEN BILLIONAIRE BURNS DOWN HOUSE.

" 'Drunken' seems a bit strong. 'Woozy,' maybe. 'Tipsy,' even. But 'drunken'? Remind me to send an outraged letter to the editor."

"Should I really?"

"No."

"You *are* becoming a bit of a figure of fun, Master Bruce. 'Billionaire klutz' is one of the sobriquets being applied to you."

"Good."

Alfred turned into the Wayne driveway and stopped at the guesthouse.

"Let's go on up to the manor," Bruce said. "Or what's left of it."

The remains of the once-imposing home were even uglier in the morning sunlight than they had been in the semidarkness of early dawn, when the last of the firemen had splashed water on the final smoldering embers and gone away. Nothing was left of the superstructure except a few blackened timbers and stone walls on two sides. Most of the foundation was still intact, buried under tons of ash.

Rachel's little car was parked around the back, at the kitchen garden. Bruce left the limo and went to where Rachel was staring at the remnants of the green-house, mostly bent metal framework. Broken glass crunched under Bruce's shoes and Rachel turned to greet him.

"Good to see you—again," she said.

"And you."

They walked past the greenhouse to the well.

"Remember the day I fell?" Bruce asked.

"Of course. I was so scared for you. I've spent a lot of time being scared for you."

"Rachel, I'm . . ."

"Bruce, I'm sorry. The day Chill died, I said terrible things."

"True things. Justice is about more than revenge."

"I never stopped thinking about you . . . about us . . . when I heard you were back, I started to hope . . ."

Rachel stood on her toes and kissed Bruce on the lips. Then, abruptly, she pulled away. "That was be-fore I found out about the mask."

"Batman's just a symbol, Rachel."

Rachel brushed her fingertips across Bruce's cheek. "*This* is your mask. Your real face is the one criminals now fear. The man I loved—the man who vanished—he never came back at all."

Bruce took both her hands in his and stood silently looking into her eyes.

"But maybe he's still out there, somewhere," Rachel said. "Maybe one day, when Gotham no longer needs Batman, I'll see him again."

Bruce released her hands and turned toward the

ruins of the house. "As I lay there, fire and smoke all around me, I *knew* . . . I could sense it."

"What?"

"That even if I survived, things would never be the same."

"Well, you proved me wrong."

"About what?"

"Your father would be proud of you. Just like I am."

Rachel moved slowly toward her car. Bruce started to follow her, but stopped when his foot hit something buried in rubble. He picked it up: his father's stethoscope.

Rachel opened the door to her car, pointed to the ruins, and called to Bruce: "What will you do?"

"I've just this minute decided. I'm going to rebuild it just the way it was. Brick for brick."

Rachel waved, got into her car, and drove away.

Alfred was standing at Bruce's shoulder. "*Just* the way it was, Master Bruce?"

"Yes. Why?"

"I thought we might take the opportunity to make some *improvements* to the foundation."

"In the southeast corner?"

"Precisely, sir."

Gordon stepped from the patrol car, turned to thank the cop who had given him a lift from headquarters, and watched the cruiser's taillights dwindle and vanish.

He trudged up the short walk to his front porch, bone-weary. It had been a long day—weren't they all? But at least he felt he was accomplishing something. In the week since the monorail incident and the massive disruption of the city's infrastrucure, Gordon and his cops had restored order and the public works guys had completed the most necessary repairs to the water system. Pretty soon, everyone who wanted one would have an injection of the serum Rachel Dawes had given him and the nutso stuff Crane and Rā's al Ghūl had put into the air wouldn't ever again be a threat. Every drug lab in the state was helping turn out batches of the serum and most of the severely damaged citizens had already been injected and were returning to their sane selves. Those who had been under the influence of Crane's hallucinogen the longest would need years of therapy, but there were only small numbers of those. There were also a couple of hundred people dead, but nothing could be done about them except to mourn. Even the Narrows area was returning to normal, or at least as "normal" as the Narrows ever got. Gordon had never exactly been a Mr. Sunshine, but he felt cautiously optimistic. Maybe things *were* looking up.

A shadow detached itself from the darkness at the side of the house and said, "Hello."

"I was wondering when I'd see you again . . . *Batman*—is that what you really want to be called?"

"If you have to call me anything."

"It's just that I feel silly saying it, but okay, *Batman* . . . what's on your mind?"

"Has your forensics team finished examining the monorail car?"

"Yeah, they're done. I got the report this afternoon."

"And?"

"Well, everything's inconclusive. They still aren't sure what made it burn so hot. Something in the machine that guy . . . *Rā's al Ghūl*, is it?"

"Yes."

"Anyway, there was something in the machine that caused the extreme heat. Most everything was melted to slag."

"Human remains?"

"No body, not even any bones. But like I say, nothing's conclusive . . ."

Gordon stopped talking when he realized that he was talking to himself.

Batman perched on a Wayne Tower ledge and surveyed the city below him; its geometric regularity and the steep walls and narrow streets for which Gotham was famous, the butt of a thousand jokes on television talk shows and a perverse source of pride to locals. There were only a few lights, this late, but in Gotham somebody was always going somewhere, doing something.

He liked to come up here and lurk, unseen, and think. Someday, he might figure out why.

Tonight, he was thinking about the conversation he'd had with James Gordon an hour earlier. No surprises. He'd seen that blue-white fire—he knew it must have destroyed anything inside the monorail car.

But he was not satisfied.

Almost certainly, Rā's had perished in the fire.

Almost.

But if he hadn't?

The body of Carl Finch, the district attorney, had been found at the docks, and to everyone's surprise, Rachel Dawes was appointed to replace him. She was, at thirty, the youngest D.A. in the city's history.

For almost a month, Batman had been an empty costume hanging in a cave below the blackened ruins of a once-grand house. Bruce Wayne stayed away from both the cave and the suit, and also from Gotham City. He kept to the guesthouse he shared with Alfred and passed the weeks reading books recommended by Sandra Flanders.

Finally, one night just before midnight, Bruce left the guesthouse and, by the light of a gibbous moon and an electric lantern he carried, picked his way through the remains of Wayne Manor until he came to the secret entrance to the cavern.

From an upstairs window, Alfred watched Bruce cross the lawn and, after some hesitation, followed him.

When Alfred came to the bottom of the winding

staircase, he found Bruce staring at the Batman costume, which was illuminated by the lantern.

"Have you decided?" Alfred asked.

"About what?" Bruce gestured to the costume. "Him? Bring him back to life or let him join the urban legends? No, I haven't. He could be useful, and maybe he's the only way *I* can be useful."

"Hardly, Master Bruce. Your philanthropies, your efforts on behalf of education . . ."

"All good things. But not enough. Not enough for me. I need something more and Batman just may be it. Any thoughts?"

"The course you contemplate is dangerous, but you know that. Indeed, danger is part of the attraction. What's interesting about it is, it provides an outlet for your creativity."

"Afraid not, Alfred. We Waynes aren't artsy types—"

"On the contrary. In her youth, your mother played classical piano."

"Come to think of it, she mentioned that once—"

"And your father's ardent support of the arts indicated a love of them. Your creative impulse has been submerged, but it has always existed, waiting for the proper opportunity."

"And Batman was it, huh?"

"I believe so. What you have created is akin to architecture. It has a practical aspect, but also an aesthetic one. And I imagine it gives you great satisfaction—"

"Oh, come on!"

"You described the excitement you felt running over the rooftops after your burglary and I *saw* you when you returned here with Ms. Dawes. You were a man exhilarated."

"Okay, I guess I was. So I should put on the costume again?"

"I'm certain you will, regardless of what I may advise. I ask only this, that you be aware of the dangers."

"Any dangers in particular, other than the obvious ones?"

Alfred stared down at the floor while answering. "The greatest danger, I think, is that you may not be able to relinquish your creation when you should. You're young now, but you won't always be. You will reach an age when you'll be a bit slower, not quite as agile, nor as strong. Then, you will either have to give up Batman and pursue your goals by more quiet means or . . ."

"Or what, Alfred? *Die?*"

"Or be grievously injured, or humiliated . . . there are a number of melancholy possibilities."

"Thank you," Bruce said, and took the costume from its hanger.

Winter came early to Gotham City that year. By Thanksgiving, the days were dark and the nights unremittingly cold. There had been no heavy snowfall, not yet, but flurries were common and the frequent rain was usually mixed with sleet.

Everyone anticipated a white Christmas.

At eleven-thirty, on the night of December first,

James Gordon stood on the roof of Central Police Headquarters, sipping coffee from a cardboard cup next to a giant spotlight with a metal stencil of a bat bolted across its lens. Its beam was directed toward the roiling gray clouds and the fuzzy bat shape was intermittently visible on them.

Gordon heard a fluttering and then Batman was on the other side of the light. He reached out with a gloved forefinger and tapped the stencil.

"Nice," he growled.

"Couldn't find any mob bosses to strap to the light."

Gordon switched off the light.

"Well, Sergeant?" Batman asked.

"It's *lieutenant* now. Loeb had to promote me. And he finally officially disbanded the task force hunting you. Amazing what saving a city can do for your image." Gordon crushed his empty cup and tossed it into a trash barrel. "You've started something. Bent cops running scared, hope on the streets . . ."

Gordon stopped speaking.

"There's a 'but' coming, isn't there?" Batman asked.

"*But* . . . there's a lot of weirdness out there right now . . . The Narrows is lost. We still haven't picked up Crane and some of the Arkham inmates he freed."

"You will. Gotham will return to normal."

"Will it? What about the escalation?"

"Escalation?"

"We start carrying semiautomatics, *they* buy automatics. We start wearing Kevlar, *they* buy armor-piercing rounds."

"And?"

"*And* . . . you're wearing a mask and jumping off rooftops." Gordon fished in his breast pocket and pulled out a clear plastic evidence bag. "Take this guy . . . armed robbery, double homicide . . ."

Batman took the bag. In it, he could see a playing card, a Joker.

"Leaves a calling card," Gordon said. "Got a taste for theatrics, just like you."

"I'll look into it."

"I never said thank you, by the way."

"And you'll never have to."

It had been a hectic fall. Bruce and Alfred had to do the work of sealing off the cave themselves; no hired workman could be trusted not to be too curious about the vast cavern underneath the green lawns of the Wayne property. Alfred had made a study of the art of masonry and what he was not able to do in terms of physical labor he more than compensated for with meticulous planning and execution. When, after a month, the work was done, Bruce called in architects and contractors and began the task of building an exact replica of the mansion that had been destroyed by fire.

The builders had gotten the foundation laid and part of the framing up when work was halted by the worst snowfall in ten years. Everyone agreed that winter was not the time for building and the job should be resumed in early March.

Bruce Wayne drove his Lamborghini into the city several times a month, often managing to put a dent in one of the fenders, and was seen filling the car's shotgun seat with an assortment of models and actresses. None rode in the Lamborghini for more than a single evening, but all received lavish gifts soon after leaving it.

Alfred flew to England to spend Christmas with his niece and returned New Year's Eve, just ahead of what Kassie Cane told her viewers was "Mama Nature dumping record amounts of the white stuff on poor old Gotham."

By noon on New Year's Day the snowfall had finally stopped. Bruce trudged to the skeleton of his home-to-be, plowing through waist-deep snow, carrying a sledgehammer. He smashed through one of the masonry seals he and Alfred had placed over the smallest access to the cave and, shining a penlight ahead of him, descended the winding staircase. He found what he was looking for and carried it up the steps and out, beyond the kitchen yard and the greenhouse.

From his room in the guesthouse, Alfred watched Bruce get a pickax and shovel left in the greenhouse by the builders and begin clearing snow from an area next to his father's grave. Then he used the pick to break through the frozen dirt and began digging a hole.

Alfred put on his outdoor clothing and walked in

Bruce's footsteps to the gravesite. He arrived just as Bruce was putting a ragged garment in the hole.

"You're burying the outfit you wore back from Kathmandu, Master Bruce?"

"I'm actually burying the bloodstain. It's all that's left of Rā's al Ghūl."

"And you're putting these remains next to your father?"

"They both gave me my life. It seems fitting that they be buried together."

"And do you mourn them together?"

"Yes. I do."

It began to snow again as Bruce finished his task. He and Alfred stood over the three graves with bowed heads until the sky darkened.